The Battle for Big School

An award-winning broadcaster and journalist, Sarah Tucker was a presenter on the BBC1 *Holiday* programme and, more recently, anchored *I Want That House Revisited* on ITV1. She regularly contributes to women's magazines, *The Sunday Times* Travel Magazine and *The Guardian*. Sarah Tucker is the author of *The Playground Mafia* and three romantic comedies published by Harlequin.

Praise for Sarah Tucker

'Scandal, backstabbing, illicit affairs . . . a fab, girlie read!' *New Woman*

'Mums will be able to see the truth behind this fun novel' *In The Know*

'A real laugh-out-loud tale' *OK! Magazine*

Also available by Sarah Tucker

Fiction
The Playground Mafia
The Last Year of Being Single
The Last Year of Being Married
The Younger Man

Non-fiction
Have Baby, Will Travel
Have Toddler, Will Travel

The Battle for Big School

Sarah Tucker

arrow books

Published by Arrow Books 2007

6 8 10 9 7 5

www.randomhouse.co.uk

Addresses for companies within The Random House Group Limited can be found at: www.randomhouse.co.uk/offices.htm

The Random House Group Limited Reg. No. 954009

A CIP catalogue record for this book is available from the British Library

ISBN 9780099498469

The Random House Group Limited makes every effort to ensure that the papers used in its books are made from trees that have been legally sourced from well-managed and credibly certified forests. Our paper procurement policy can be found at: www.randomhouse.co.uk/paper.htm

Mixed Sources
Product group from well-managed forests and other controlled sources
www.fsc.org Cert no. TT-COC-2139
© 1996 Forest Stewardship Council

FSC

Typeset in New Baskerville by Palimpsest Book Production Limited, Grangemouth, Stirlingshire
Printed and bound in Great Britain by CPI Cox & Wyman, Reading RG1 8EX

For Tom.

And to William, his great-granddad.

Acknowledgements

A huge 'thank you' goes to the following: to Nikola Scott, for her incredible support and wisdom; to Jacqs, for all her brilliant guidance; to Diana, for her exacting eye for detail; to the brilliant marketing and sales team at Arrow, for all their hard work on *The Playground Mafia*; to Louise, for all her excellent advice; and to Glenn, for the brilliant cover. It says it all.

And lastly, here's to the lovely Kim, Caroline, Amanda, Claire, Nim, Coline, Helen, Linda, Dodie, Hazel, and the ski and summer crowd, who know who they are, and the Fredericks crowd, who do too. You're all wonderful people. Thank you also, Jeremy. I write about nice men these days . . .

Chapter 1
Head Start

'The head will see you now, Mr and Mrs Dearl.'

An elegant, somewhat vampiric-looking woman with blood-red lips, dressed top to toe in tweed, ushers us into the headmaster's office, closing the door firmly behind us.

Mike and I are here to meet, or rather be interviewed by, a certain Dr Henderson Totham, venerable and esteemed headmaster of The Oaks. The Oaks is a grammar school – no, *the* grammar school – in the area, with an excellent overall reputation but particularly strong in sports and the arts. The Oaks has some of the best football and cricket coaches in the country, and it regularly turns out artists and graphic and interior designers who receive national acclaim. It's no surprise, then, that it's fiercely coveted in the area, the only public alternative being a smattering of church schools and the awful Readmere Comp, an absolute hellhole of a school if you ask me, that seems to gobble up hordes of unruly kids each morning and spews them back out at the end of the school day, leaving them free to roam the streets of Letchbury. A gross generalisation, I know, I know, but there's more than a shred of truth in it and, regardless, it's simply no match for The Oaks. Which means, sadly, that every year everyone flocks to The Oaks in droves. People say that competition is fierce and I've seen mums get quite anxious when enrolment time approaches, but I've tried to stay out of that and just hope that Tim won't have too much of a problem getting in. I don't know where he gets the brains from (not me, that's for certain), but he's been top in his class for the last three years, and the much-fêted captain of the rugby team as well. And I'm not just saying that in my role as doting mother of three – Ms Townsend, head teacher at Somerset School, only recently sent home a report card saying that 'Tim is a credit to himself and the school. Wherever he goes he will prove to be the cherry on the icing on the cake,' which I thought was quite charming and rather quirky, a bit like Ms Townsend and Somerset School itself really. Tim gets his patience and calm nature from his dad, and Mike says he gets his tenacity and good looks – almost five two at the age of ten, dark blond hair, striking green eyes – from me. Well, I don't know about that. He is far more considerate and thoughtful than I am even today and as I sit here waiting to be interviewed by one of the top state schools in the county, I think that The Oaks will be lucky to have him.

Now, Mike squeezes my hand and, looking back cautiously at the door and the vampire typing behind it, we tiptoe over to the big floor-to-ceiling picture window.

It's a bitterly cold wintry day outside, bursting with brittle blue winter sunshine that creates a rainbow on the walls, making the heavily panelled room less severe, magical almost.

I take this as a good omen, because we really, really want Tim to get into this school. It's crazy, and I'm sure I'm losing perspective, but I'm actually feeling quite nervous now. Tim might be a dead cert but why the hell are *we* here? I look at Mike to reassure myself and he gives me a slightly strained smile.

'I'm sure it'll be fine, sweetheart.' Well, we'll see.

Through the window we can see all over Letchbury and I point out the café where Jane Anderson, the highly competent PTA chair at Somerset, hurries every Monday at nine fifteen prompt, just after drop-off, for her half-hour casual coffee mornings with the movers and shakers of the school and local community. And there's the slightly fancier coffee bar (further from the school, which is often a blessing) where I meet Julie and Karen, my two best friends, for the occasional afternoon treat before we each collect our respective broods, to discuss how we've shaken our butts at the local gym that week. Mike thinks our house is just behind those big trees, although I personally think he's pointing to Giorgiano's, our local bakers, which makes wonderful ciabatta and where Tim had a Saturday job until football training took over recently.

Letchbury is more urban than suburban thanks to the regular rail links in and out of London. The constituency is just outside London, and our local MP, Mr Wallace T. Heavie, is good at getting his own way, so whatever he wants Letchbury to have, Letchbury gets, regardless of whether Letchbury actually wants it or not. Consequently, our town has an ice rink instead of a multi-storey car park, a swimming pool instead of a block of flats, and rows of tree-lined avenues. Perhaps because of the heady combination of beauty and convenience, our town is also an expensive place to live and somewhere people visit rather than stay. They come here to work or to walk their dogs in the manicured parks and gardens at weekends. They pour in to have Sunday lunch by the river in one of the many overpriced gastro pubs, and wander down the narrow cobbled lanes, exploring the delightful little shops full of exquisite nonsense.

The view exhausted, we tiptoe back to our seats. How annoying to be kept waiting like this. Well, admittedly we *were* half an hour early.

I eye up the large lacquered-oak gilt-edged noticeboards, listing the names of past pupils and their achievements, and recognise some of the parents' names picked out in gold leaf. Some of the pupils have won so many awards they've had to make the wording smaller and the leaf has smudged into one great golden blob of praise.

Interestingly, most of the pupils seem to come with quite a good pedigree. Fisher Bolden, the property tycoon; Tyler Villier, the mobile-phone maverick; and Lynda Dunworthy, the famous Royal Ballet ballerina. I think I met her once in Tatiana, the boutique owned by my exotic, beautiful and rather flighty neighbour.

Which reminds me, I wonder how Jenny is doing in her ballet exam? At six, my daughter is more Tomboy than ballet dancer – a real tree climber – but I'm desperately trying to instil a modicum of femininity and grace into the girl. I'm sorry I can't be there with her today – one of the mums at school kindly volunteered to take her along – but we couldn't get another appointment. And I hope Henry hasn't terrorised the babysitter yet. At three he's already a bit of a vandal, although he hides it well by just being extremely curious about how things work, which, according to my mum, is a sign of brilliance. At the moment, Henry's latest peccadillo is to put things in the washing machine – light bulbs, breakfast cereals, Power Ranger toys, Jenny's schoolbooks, and once a tortoise which has never completely recovered from his 'great sea adventure', as Henry called it. Even on slow spin, poor Herman was seriously concussed, but managed to survive.

'Look, there are Dennis Resnaur and Francesca Frederic,' Mike interrupts my idle musings.

Dennis Resnaur is a marketing director of Delaylo Interiors, the designers favoured by footballers' wives (although I'm not sure that's much of a selling point). Then Francesca Frederic, who is the MD of NDW Bank or DNW Bank – can't be sure which, but I know she's been in the papers recently as she allegedly had an affair with celebrity chef Randy Hasbro.

We look at each other, slightly intimidated at the prospect of mixing with such illustrious company at parents' evenings. I will need to dust down some of my work clothes from my fashion-editor days at *De Rigueur* magazine. For a while I tried to keep my hand in doing some freelance stuff and the occasional feature but when Henry came I just had too much on. So there isn't much call for rows of funky suits and shoes these days. I think I'll do right by Tim today, though. I looked in the mirror so much before I left the house that Mike finally threatened to leave without me, but I wanted the right amount of style without going over the top. So I'm wearing a Paul Smith skirt and top and cardigan, which are sensible and stylish at the same time. Mike, bless him, would look good in a dustbin liner. As he is wearing a black Paul Smith suit, we look like a brand ad, but he carries it well. He has broad shoulders and has managed to keep his belly at bay by playing tennis, squash, cricket, football and every ball game known to man for the past six years, recently mostly with Tim, for the sake of keeping up not only his son's game, but his own. At forty-five he looks, well, he looks forty-five. But he's a sexy forty-five. Mike says I look ten years younger than I am which would make me thirty-two, hooray, and him the lucky one.

I'm just about to give up on Totham when the sinister-looking assistant finally emerges again and beckons us in with a long-taloned wave. Dr Totham's office is a large, square room, with the same floor-to-ceiling windows as outside, this time overlooking the playing field on one side and the playground on the other. More oak panelling, a large and striking mahogany desk, and a book case covering both walls to the right and left. A black phone – one of those modern ones that looks a little like a boomerang – sits on Totham's desk, as well as a file and a tall, silver spotlight. With the exception of these three items, his desk is clear. I edited *De Rigueur*'s home-improvement pages before moving on to fashion and since then I have found it difficult to walk into a room without taking in every detail. You learn more about people that way than from talking to them, I think. Mike thinks I'm paranoid that everyone has something to hide, but hey, they usually do. There's a sofa, a coffee table and two chairs adjacent to the desk, and it's here that the tight-lipped Ms Dailey asks us to be seated.

We obey and Ms Dailey turns and leaves as swiftly as she entered, without offer of tea or a biscuit. I'd have quite liked a little pick-me-up, or at least something to occupy my hands when talking to Totham, but perhaps that would be asking too much. Strangely, this is starting to feel like an inquisition, maybe because the waiting seems to foster all sorts of forebodings, and my earlier anxiety returns in full force. God, I hope he doesn't ask us to do long division or obscure stuff like the derivation of Mocha, or any of the things Tim brings home these days. Helping with homework has become a new challenge every day.

Mike leans over and takes my hand again, presumably to stop me from fidgeting. I smile back, suddenly leaning over and kissing him quickly on the lips.

'Ah, Mr and Mrs Dearl, good to meet you both,' comes a booming voice from behind. Dr Totham has timed his entrance perfectly.

We scramble to our feet, awkwardly offering our hands.

'So sorry to keep you waiting,' he says, shaking Mike's hand, then mine and smiling warmly which immediately puts me at ease. This is going to be absolutely fine. Tim belongs here. Just one look at the grounds crammed with rugby pitches, tennis courts and football fields, plus the two enormous libraries – it's almost as though the school was made for him.

Mid-fifties, dark haired and wearing thinly rimmed glasses, Totham has been headmaster of The Oaks for over ten years. I Googled him before we came over and found out he's an old Etonian and loves sports – everything from rugby to golf. There was a profile on him in the *Education Gazette* several years ago, lauding him for keeping up The Oaks's standards by making excellent decisions about how the school is run and integrating it closely with the local community.

'Would you like to be seated again?' Totham has a

round face and dark close-set eyes. I've always been suspicious of people with close-set eyes, not just because *De Rigueur*'s women's pages always advised never to trust them – Gordon Brown, Tony Blair and President Bush being cases in point.

I quickly dismiss the eyes and focus on Totham's smile. He opens the red file on his desk and, while reading the first line, picks up a pen.

'So, Lily and Michael – may I call you Lily and Michael?' Totham asks, still smiling. Is this is a test question? To find out if we're a bit too touchy-feely, too liberal for The Oaks? But Mike speaks before I can pursue any of those theories.

'Yes, that's fine,' he replies calmly.

'Now, please tell me a bit about yourselves. What should I know about you both?' he says, pen poised over paper as if ready to note down our every word.

Wow, what a question. Talk about giving you enough rope to hang yourself. I take the safe option and answer a question with a question.

'I don't know if we've got that kind of time, Dr Totham,' I smile. God, stop the lame jokes, Lily. 'What are you interested in in particular?' This may not have come out quite right, but I'm honestly just trying to be helpful.

'Ah, yes, I can tell you're a journalist, or rather,' he looks down at the file, luckily unfazed by my response, 'you used to be a journalist. You are looking after three now, yes?'

'Yes, that's right. I was fashion editor of a women's

consumer magazine, and I still do some freelance writing,' I reply, feeling as though I'm on trial in a courtroom. This meeting is much more interrogation than interview.

'Ah, very interesting. And Michael, you are an advertising director. Excellent. We have a lot of parents who work in media in our school PTA and amongst the parent governors. You'll feel quite at home here.'

I may have got a cross for my answer, but I think Mike just got a tick. So far so good.

Totham then proceeds to ask us how long we've been married, whether it's the first marriage for both of us (it is), how we met (at a cocktail work party neither of us wanted to attend but are pleased we did), where we live, what our house is like (large, sprawling, noisy). Totham runs through the questions one by one, apparently knowing the list by heart now, but I'm completely taken aback by the intimacy of the questions. I thought we were meant to talk about what we bring to the school and, of course, about Tim? No, Totham asks about our favourite country and why (Italy, because of the food, wine and irreverence of the Italians, although I nervously stumble and say 'irrelevance of the Italians' at first, which makes Mike smile but unfortunately not Totham). I feel I'm letting the side down here.

He even asks us our favourite colours (yellow and red) and smells (spring and autumn). I'm starting to think I've come straight into a psychometric test when the questioning suddenly stops. Perhaps we've given too many wrong answers? Perhaps we're the wrong types of parent for the school? Oh, fuck. What's the good of raising the game with our children if we can't keep up ourselves?

As if Totham has been reading my mind, he closes his file, smiles warmly and says, 'Right, well, thank you for answering my questions so thoroughly. I know they may seem irrelevant to you, but they give us a good first impression of the parents. And it's important that we know the children have the back-up they need at home. We are here to teach, nurture and nourish during the day, and parents can either enhance or undo the work we achieve at The Oaks. But we have standards to maintain, and our parents play a crucial role in maintaining those standards.'

I relax, slump my shoulders and exhale. This sounds OK, doesn't it? I think we've done our best.

'One final question,' he says, looking pointedly at me. 'We are very keen on parents who are community-spirited. How are you contributing to the local community?'

Knew it. Just knew it. Every time I think we're home free something comes flying out of left field. Like some karmic force thinks I've become far too smug and need to be taught a lesson. Well, to be frank, we do nothing for the local community, really. I open my mouth and –

'Well, Dr Totham,' Mike cuts in smoothly, wanting to nip any emerging untruths quickly in the bud, 'the truth is that both of us lead very busy lives. I work full-time and Lily has three children to look after, plus a part-time career. Our focus is on our family, on helping our children grow and learn, and this leaves little time for anything else.'

Dr Totham looks disappointed. Shit, double shit. It's true: I'm not one for joining the PTA or working for some local charity. I just don't like the environment and even less do I like the petty power politics of the PTA. I could no more work with Jane Anderson than bake cakes. I'm the queen of the play-date and I always chat to the mums in the playground at pick-up time, but I'm not part of the group that gets involved with the fêtes, dances and lotteries. I've only ever attended one PTA meeting, six years ago when Tim first started school, and it scared me off for life. Jane Anderson wasn't chair at the time, Veronica Walsh was, Veronica who took no crap from anyone. But there was one mum at the meeting, Linda Black, who is still at the school (and only slightly taller than ten-year-old Tim, if you want to be mean). She had a habit of clicking her biro every time she spoke, and the more incensed she became about how much money we should spend on computers or books, the more vigorously she clicked her pen. She clicked it so hard at one point that the ruddy thing flew across the assembly hall and hit the deputy chair in the eye. An ambulance and police were involved and now pens are no longer allowed in the meetings. Since then, I've kept myself out of the line of fire by keeping my head down. Jane Anderson seems to take everything in her stride now, treating with equal civility the 'corporate mums', who like to diarise everything months in advance, and the full-time mums, who tend to wing everything.

I half-listen to Totham drone on about the importance of 'giving back' as I desperately try to remember if I've given anything back recently. I wonder if there is some sort of points system, official or unofficial, that credits parents for their efforts. It's a bit ridiculous, really, as none of this has anything to do with me or Mike – nor should it. This is about Tim, who does a lot for the local community. He's completed his silver Duke of Edinburgh award, he's helped out in the local shops, and he represents Somerset against other schools from other regions and brings home the prizes. Surely Dr Totham can see this? Surely he knows Tim is more than the sum of his parents put together? But as I look at Totham's expectant face, I don't really see any of that there. His smile has become a touch bland, businesslike, and he starts shuffling together his papers, probably to indicate that the meeting is reaching its conclusion.

'And of course, as well as working, I'm always playing golf with my clients,' I suddenly hear Mike break the silence. That stops me short. To my knowledge, Mike Dearl has never so much as held a golf club in his life. I'm not sure he even likes the game. But his throwaway comment seems to do something to Totham's polite mask of civility because he immediately smiles broadly. 'Oh, I do enjoy the game myself. Are you a member of the local club, Michael?' he asks, lowering his chin slightly, as though encouraging Mike to nod in response.

'I have been intending to join for quite some time. It's a very sociable game and I like the people,' Mike replies. Liar liar, pants on fire, but you do have to admire his straight face. And then I spot something that Mike obviously has noticed before me. Perhaps I'm not as keen-eyed as I thought. In the corner behind Totham's desk is a set of golf clubs, silver, worn and shiny, each with a black woollen tea cosy on top, neatly tucked into a black-and-maroon leather golf bag propped up against the wall. I silently congratulate Mike for thinking on his feet. A white lie, well, a greyish lie, but if it gets Tim into The Oaks, it's worth it.

Dr Totham stands and offers his hand. Obviously the interview has at last come to an end.

'Well, I hope to see you at the Letchbury. Perhaps we could have a game one day,' says Totham, looking at Mike who, thankfully, realises that the Letchbury is the golf club he's just lied about wanting to join.

In the car on the way home, Mike and I hold a post-mortem.

'Well, that was a bit of a disaster, wasn't it? I hadn't realised we would count so much. He didn't even say anything about Tim.' I'm still incensed at the interrogation and the implication that we weren't doing our bit.

'I don't think we did too badly, Lily,' says Mike, trying to sound encouraging.

'Well, good idea about the golf club, Mike. It seemed

to distract him from our lacking community spirit, although I still don't see how that counts against us.'

'Everything seems to count these days,' says Mike, indicating out of The Oaks school gates. 'I know you and I think it's all based on merit, Tim's merit, but it does seem that grammar schools have become even more choosy than public schools. It wouldn't surprise me if they checked up on criminal records and credit scores, and interviewed the neighbours.' God, I hope he's joking. 'Sometimes I wonder if The Oaks is the right school for Tim, especially when you've got someone like Totham at the head.' Mike pauses, then says emphatically, 'I really didn't warm to him.'

'No, he wasn't the nicest spirit I've ever met,' I agree, putting the car mirror down and checking to see if my lipstick's bled or my eyeliner's smudged. 'But perhaps that was part of the test as well. I don't think we've done too badly after all, and Tim would have wowed him during the interview, so hopefully he made up for any of his parents' shortfalls,' I add, squeezing Mike's knee.

'Don't be too smug, Lily,' Mike replies, rolling his eyes but smiling as he stops at the lights. 'Our interview went OK, but it looks like it's nowhere near guaranteed that he'll get a place, so we need to be realistic. Maybe think of a back-up plan. Perhaps it wouldn't hurt Tim's chances if I joined the Letchbury golf club, and you should probably think about all that giving-back stuff. It may be too late, but we can still try.'

I sigh. Mike's right. I'll mention it to Karen and see

what her view is. Now that I really think about it, there has been more than the usual share of rumblings about all this school stuff. I'd always dismissed the rumours flying around – people moving house or shifting their front gate a foot to the side to fall within the good catchment areas; parents lying about postcodes, selling body parts to pay for private school, tutoring their children into nervous breakdowns – all that seemed so over the top, belonging to the realm of those over-perfect, over-zealous parents who have a ten-year plan for their five-year-olds. I always thought Mike and I were more hands on than that, wanting the best for our son, but just trying to play it straight. And we've been lucky with Tim – he's the perfect candidate, and once he's in, so will Jenny and Henry be. But apparently I need to be a bit more active, play the game a bit more the way everyone else does. I shudder at the thought, but then I suddenly remember Paul Wilton (my other man as Mike always calls him, only because he's the token house-husband at the school gates and friends with Julie, Karen and me), saying that his wife Jessica has been on at him to double-check the Para Hills catchment area to see if they need to move. He really doesn't want to subject his daughters to the upheaval, even for the best girls' school in the area, but Jessica being the high-powered, strong-minded businesswoman that she is, won't take no for an answer.

'What are you doing this afternoon?' Mike asks as he turns in to the station and parks behind the taxi rank.

'Oh, a kick-box class with Karen. I definitely need to kick someone's ass after this morning,' I say, leaning over to kiss him goodbye as he climbs out of the car to catch his train to work.

'Well, we've certainly done enough *kissing* ass this morning,' he smiles. 'But don't worry too much, Lily. We'll think of something.'

Chapter 2

On Your Marks

'Upper cut, upper cut, jab, jab, punch. Right hook, left hook, shuffle, shuffle, hurrrr. Punch, punch, jab, skip, punch, hurrrr. Punch, punch, jab, skip, punch, hurrr. Elbow, elbow, upper cut, jab. Elbow, elbow, upper cut, jab. Knee jerk, knee jerk, side kick, punch. Upper cut, upper cut, back kick, hook, hook, turn. Hurrr! Yeah!'

Daisy Warte, body-combat instructor, twenty-something five-foot-nothing powerhouse, is built like a tank and booming instructions through a microphone as the mirrored studio steams up with the heat from over twenty bodies punching, kicking and grunting very loudly to Robbie Williams's 'Rock DJ'. It's one of the few things squeezed into my busy schedule during the week that's just for me and I love it. Daisy looks unassuming enough outside the studio, always in jeans, sweatshirt and cap, but inside when this little woman booms, eighteen women and two token males stand to attention, kicking the imaginary arses of bosses, lovers, wives, ex-wives, husbands, ex-husbands, bank managers, estate agents, politicians, mother-in-laws, parking attendants and anyone else they utterly detest.

I've been coming to her class at the Letchbury gym for two years now, in a desperate, last-ditch attempt to get my figure back after three kids. In my darker hours, I grumble to Mike that maybe I should just have had a tummy tuck, like the Chelsea mothers do, but I thought housework, gym, three kids and walking everywhere would eventually do the trick. Obviously not. Daisy might be a bit of a cow, but being a bitch in the studio does work wonders for my thighs.

My gym is full of career women, with and without children. Men are only seen early in the morning and late in the evening. My personal trainer, Rasa – Polish, tall, blonde and beautiful – told me I should try to work out early in the morning as there is some 'real talent' as she puts it. Well, I'm not really a morning-gym person, plus Mike and I are happy. She laughed, saying I must be one of the few around here. When Rasa met and married one of the 'real talents', who happened to be unhappily married at the time, and moved in with him in his converted schoolhouse in Wiltshire, she recommended Daisy.

So here I am, punching, hurrring, kicking, upper-cutting and hooking every imaginary horrible person I know, which at the moment is the parking attendants, but it could be Dr Totham if he doesn't let Tim into The Oaks.

I'm here with my best friend Karen Field. Forty-two, slim with green eyes and long brown hair, mother of Claire, ten, and Simon, seven. We struck up a friendship at NCT classes, since neither of us took them very seriously – yes, we will have every painkiller going; no, we won't use washable nappies; yes, we will give the water birth a miss; no, we aren't in denial just because we want to keep working as long as we possibly can during pregnancy because otherwise we will both go nuts – and have been close ever since. Karen has managed to keep working full-time as a columnist and reporter throughout, partly because as a journalist she can be quite flexible about her hours but mainly because she has a full-time nanny, Carlotta. Karen is more assertive than me, but perhaps that's because she's still working, while I've gone a bit soft having been out of the market for so long, and am now talking Teletubbie rather than local politics. I call her Ms Action List because she never leaves home without a list and seems to achieve more in a day than I can in a week. To her credit, she still tries to be there to either pick up or drop off the kids from school at least twice a week.

'Upper cut, upper cut, punch, punch, jab. Kick, punch, kick, punch. Punch, punch, kick. Upper cut, hook, upper cut, jab. Kick to the front, hurrrr. Kick to the back, hurrrr. And run on the spot *NOWWWWWWWW*!' Daisy booms as we all run as fast as we can on the spot, fists by our sides, teeth grinding, eyes closed, jaws tight, running from everyone we've just kicked the shit out of.

'Aaaaand breathe,' she says softly, as though we've been holding our breath for the past forty minutes. I want to collapse.

'I think Daisy's had a shit week,' says Karen, trying to mop the sweat out of her eyes so she can see. 'She worked us hard today, even by her standards.'

'Well, that's good. I need it,' I say, trying to unstick my necklace from my bra and realising I should have taken it off. The leather cord is now so sodden with sweat it'll break any moment.

'Why, what's the matter?' Karen asks, flicking her hair back from her red face and tightening her pony-tail.

'Oh, Mike and I had our interview at The Oaks today. All very formal,' I say, trying to sound more casual than I feel.

'God, it's ridiculous these days. They interview the parents as much as they do the child. What sort of stuff were they interested in?' she asks as we collect our towels.

'Oh, everything from our favourite colour to the sports we played. Can you believe it? I was half expecting him to ask if we had clean underwear on.'

'Did you?' Karen asks, grinning.

I ignore her and continue. 'You know, all this time I thought it was just about getting Tim into The Oaks, and, to be honest, I thought it would be relatively easy. Tim's so good at sports.'

Karen nods. Tim's prowess on the rugby field is legendary among all the ten-year-olds. 'And his grades are just as strong. I hadn't quite realised that this whole school-selection thing is a different ball game altogether.' Bad pun, Lily, but probably sums it up just about right. 'The way Totham was going on about it, he could have been talking about electing the new cabinet or something. And he wanted to know what we did in the local community. God, not much, really. It's just never really been *me*.'

'Oh, I know, I know,' sighs Karen, opening the studio door for me and waving at Daisy who's chatting up, I mean offering advice to, one of the token men in the class.

'Can you believe it? To get Claire into St Cecile, it seems not only do Jamie and I have to be suitable members of the congregation and Claire's got to pass the entrance exams, but I've got to regularly attend mass!'

'Have you *ever* attended mass?' I ask incredulously. Karen is strong-minded, but not really the religious type.

'Of course I did. Well, I've been christened and I remember going, or rather being dragged kicking and screaming, to mass when I was a little girl. My parents were always looking for 666 on my head because I fought so hard not to go to church. It was so boring, Lily, mostly old people, of course, because they're so scared of dying. Bloody miserable. The Catholics may have the best schools but they've got the crappiest churches. I thought churches were supposed to make you feel inspired, contemplative, still in body and mind and all that. How should I achieve that surrounded by murals of hell and people dying and burning in fires all over the place every Sunday after breakfast?'

I laugh at my friend. 'So you really enjoyed going to church, then?'

Karen giggles. 'Well, there was one good bit. You know, in the service, when you shake hands and say, "Peace be with you." One time I sat next to my brother and when he shook my hand, he nearly tore my arm off. I got my own back by frazzling him with an electric buzzer in my hand the next time. He screamed the church down, of course, and I was told off by Mum and Dad, and had to say millions of Hail Marys. But it was so worth it.' She smiles at the memory.

'I can't believe you want to subject Claire to any of this,' I say, shivering slightly now that we are outside the hot gym.

'St Cecile's is a good school and it's not over the top on Bible bashing. But attending mass regularly is a bit of a cheek. They'll be ordering me to believe in God next,' Karen says indignantly as we walk down the narrow over-air-conditioned corridor, past a neat line of chatting Sweaty Betty-clad women ready for the next Daisy kick-box hardcore hour of fun.

'I would have thought believing in God was mandatory if you wanted to go to a Catholic school,' I say, wondering how they can tell whether parents are lying about their beliefs or not and whether lie-detector tests are in the realm of possibilities? Get a grip, Dearl, I chide myself for the second time today. This school stuff seems to suddenly push the last shreds of my sanity over the edge.

'Well, I guess a little prayer here and there might help our chances,' replies Karen, shrugging her shoulders. 'Do you fancy a coffee?' she says, noticing that I'm looking over at the ladies drinking lattes.

'No, I'm fine. I've got to collect the kids, and my mind's already buzzing. The last thing I need is a coffee.'

'Come on, a tea, then, or something herbal,' Karen insists, leading the way into the sports café and searching out a quiet table. 'I'll pay. What do you want?'

'Oh, anything. Erm, no, I'll have a nettle tea. No, a detox tea if they've got one of them.'

'Fine, one detox for you, one double latte with extra chocolate for me,' she says, grinning like a naughty schoolgirl.

As I wait, watching Karen push her way to the front of the queue without the other women noticing, I idly listen in to some of the other conversations around me, contemplating, not for the first time, the fact that this place is full of obsessive compulsives. There are the jogging bores, who talk about how many beats per minute they went up to in the first five minutes and how high they stayed, and if it's good to stay high for an hour at a time, and has anyone ever measured the gradient of Letchbury Hill? Then there are the tennis bores, the kick-boxing bores, the baby bores, the golfing bores – although in light of Dr Totham's comments about the local golf club, perhaps I should start taking note of the golf bores – and the designer-label bores. As I listen to bits and pieces of the conversations floating around me, it appears that all of these have recently been overshadowed by the school-selection bores. Of which, it seems, I am in danger of rapidly becoming one myself after today. A few tables away I hear the words 'Dr Totham' and 'The Oaks', combined with names of lots of other schools. I try not to look too obvious as I shuffle my chair closer towards them. Maybe I can glean a little information on how to butter up old Totham.

'Oh, my God, Lottie, the trouble I'm having with Harry at the moment with all the entrance exams. He's having a complete strop. The last one he did was for The Oaks, and you know what they're like with getting the right grades.'

'Well, you are getting him to do eight entrance exams, Hetty. That's rather a lot by anyone's standards.'

'Nonsense, nonsense, I hear some parents are putting their kids through fifteen, which sounds ridiculous. Eight doesn't seem too excessive.'

'When you're ten it does.'

'Right, tea for you,' Karen plops a large cup of tea down in front of me, breaking my concentrated eaves-dropping. 'They didn't have detox, so I got you peppermint.'

'Thank you,' I say, picking up my cup and scalding my lips as I strain to hear the rest of Hetty and Lottie's conversation, especially if they've got any more information on Dr Totham.

'What the hell are you doing, Lily?' Karen asks, looking over to my new friends Hetty and Lottie, who pointedly huddle closer to each other. I give up.

'Oh, just school stuff.'

'Not you too. I'm not joking, this school thing is ridiculous. All the women in the queue were talking about who's going to what school, who's doing what exams and bitching about other mothers. You'd think they'd all pull together as they're in the same boat, but instead they're picking holes in each other's children.'

'I know. I haven't really thought about it until today, but Totham's got me all worried now. And Readmere doesn't bear thinking about.'

Karen nods vigorously. 'Yes, indeed,' she sighs.

Suddenly a large figure looms over our table. Charlotte, one of the bracing, jolly-hockey-sticks mums from Tim's class.

'Karen. Lily. So nice to see you here! Were you just in with Daisy? What a frenzy, huh?' She chuckles jovially. I quite like Charlotte, she's always up for getting the kids together and she's good to call upon in an emergency. One of those competent people, who always knows a doctor's name or has an idea for a gift. She's already parked her bum on one of the free chairs next to us.

'Have you heard the latest?' she whispers conspiratorially. Obediently, Karen and I shake our heads.

'You know Andrew Black, Charlie's dad?'

'Vaguely,' we both say evasively.

'Well, he's selling a kidney to get his son into St Thomas's.'

'Don't be so ridiculous,' Karen says impatiently. 'Anyway, I don't think you get much for a kidney these days. They're going to need a lot more body parts before he can afford that place. I hear their fees are over thirty K a year.'

'And you know Jane Anderson, the PTA chairman?' She lowers her voice. 'She is putting her Ella in for sixteen entrance exams this year.'

'Yes, I think those two women behind us were just talking about it,' I say thoughtfully. 'I feel sorry for the kids. Poor things doing all those exams. I remember how I felt with the eleven-plus.'

'Some of the parents in the class are selling up and moving to The Oaks catchment area to increase their chances,' Charlotte continues importantly, 'but the prices have gone up around us loads since a local estate agent realised what was going on and decided to milk the situation. I heard Freddie and Daniella Frost – you know, the couple who look a bit like Kylie Minogue and Jason Donovan – have walked round every house in the street next to us, knocking on doors and asking if they want to sell their house.'

'Never,' says Karen, looking genuinely shocked. Charlotte laughs slightly too loudly, just as I wonder whether the whole world has decided to conspire against me today and fill my head with all this school stuff. Hold on to your sanity, Dearl, it's probably only going to get worse.

'Totally. They eventually made an offer on a three-bedroom mid-terrace villa with a sixty-foot garden when they were living in a four-bedroom detached house with half an acre and a garage. Now they don't even have a parking space. And there's no guarantee John Frost will get into The Oaks anyway. And do you know Christine Hawes?'

'Yes,' I say, unintentionally eyeing up a tennis player who's just entering the men's changing room.

'Her daughter's in Claire's class, isn't she?' Karen says, smiling as she's just seen the same man.

'Yes, well,' Charlotte lowers her voice again. 'I've been told she's in counselling at the moment because all this school-selection business has put such a strain on their marriage.'

She delivers this last bit with a flourish, almost relishing the gossip. I catch Karen's eye and we quickly get up and excuse ourselves. As we walk away, I can see Charlotte moving her chair closer to Hetty and Lottie. We take our empties to the counter before we leave for the changing rooms, and then push our way through several oversized women trying to get into tracksuits two sizes too small for them.

'So ridiculous,' Karen says loudly, only narrowly avoiding being trodden on by one of the women. 'This is all getting so absurd. People having sleepless nights, selling kidneys, downsizing to get into the right school and now marriages falling apart. It's nuts.'

'I know,' I say. 'It's kind of crazy. Suddenly, everywhere I go people are talking about it. Probably the only ones not talking about it are the children.'

'Them and the nannies. They don't care and they're

bored of it,' says Karen, digging into her purse to find her locker key. 'My two are oblivious in any case, although I think they would quite like to stay together with your lot, if truth be told.'

'They probably would, but Tim loved The Oaks. His face just beamed when he saw the playing fields.'

As we undress, we tune in and out of the surrounding buzz about entrance exams, interviews, the cost of tutoring, who's managed to get whom and are they any good, and get our towels ready to shower.

'Let's change the subject,' Karen says impatiently. 'Talking incessantly doesn't solve anything and only stresses me out. I'm far too busy at the moment to worry about anything other than work. What with Claire's hockey, gym and swimming club, Carlotta being on a two-week break and working for an editor who likes everything yesterday, I've got enough on my plate.'

'What are you working on at the moment?' I ask as we walk into neighbouring shower cubicles. Karen's a reporter, and a good one because she's an opportunist, tenacious, nosy and, to be blunt, totally ruthless. She's good at sniffing out a story, cutting through the façade, and identifying the issue rather than what the company or their PR department wants to sell her. One of her hilarious work stories would be welcome right about now.

But, 'Oh, the usual stuff,' she says vaguely.

It's fair to say that Karen is generally an open book, talking about everything and anything with a degree of frankness that's quite often a tad too intimate for my liking and, especially where Jamie and her are concerned, makes my imagination run riot. At the same time, she always seems to be working on something covert and I see her byline cropping up quite regularly these days in the papers with revelations about MPs and local celebrities. I always thought it must be hell for her to keep any of that under wraps for longer than an hour.

'How are things with you? Apart from Totham, that is,' Karen asks now.

'Oh, fine. Just fine. Tim told his dad that his latest ambition is to trek the Amazon in his gap year. He's already written to *Blue Peter* to ask if he can do a report for them. We'll see. Apparently he's written to the producer, as the presenters are only puppets and don't make the decisions.'

Karen laughs. 'God, and he's a ten-year-old?'

'I know. Mike and I can't watch TV without one of those Under-ten-going-on-a-hundred comments. I heard Jenny telling her friend she thought Keira Knightley was insipid last week and that her performance in *Pirates of the Caribbean* was wooden.'

'Oh, that's nothing. Claire regularly tells me I've got to look after myself because if I don't, no one else will.'

'Ms Treadwell called me in about a story Henry told the class about a bearded clam,' I giggle.

Karen snorts. 'Too much *Animal Planet.*'

'I know. Talks non-stop, asking me questions like, how does a snail move? And why is a rabbit called a rabbit? And why don't mummies have pouches like kangaroos?'

'All important things to know at three,' Karen replies as we wrap ourselves in towels and walk past the growing queue of women, some of whom scowl at us. We've obviously taken a little too long but Karen doesn't seem to notice or care.

'How's the photography course going?' she asks.

'Oh, brilliant. I'm really enjoying it. It's only an introductory course to digital photography, but it's fun. I don't feel like I'm just pointing the camera, I'm starting to compose each shot now,' I say, trying to sound vaguely as though I know what I'm talking about.

'Your husband gives nice Christmas presents,' she says as we again navigate the naked bodies to get back to our lockers.

'It's something just for me, nothing to do with the family. Know what I mean?'

'Of course,' she smiles at me. 'You're good at it too. I love your pictures.' She's nothing if not a loyal friend.

'Well, the Picture Desk at *De Rigueur* always used to get tetchy when I suggested an idea. Now I feel like I've got some knowledge if I ever decide to go back into the rat race.'

'Do you think you will?' Her smile has turned a little incredulous and I reply, almost defensively.

'Oh, of course I will, when Henry's of a decent age, but not for a few years yet. It's OK to keep my hand in with freelance stuff so I don't completely lose touch with who the players are in the industry, but my family still have a lot of growing up to do and I'm busy enough now.' I don't tell her that I always get a secret twinge of regret when she regales us with office antics and tales of high-flyers and boozy lunches, every time wondering where I would be if I had continued working at *De Rigueur*.

We stop talking while we get dressed, occasionally looking at the other naked and semi-naked bodies in the changing room. There are a few women with cellulite-free bodies but not many, which makes me feel OK about my slightly careworn shape.

Karen breaks my train of thought by whispering, 'Don't some women ever shave properly? It's a bloody forest around here.'

Trust her to notice. I look around the room and point out a petite woman whose nether regions seem to belie Karen's word. She's got diamonds just below her bikini line in the shape of two hearts.

'Have you seen anything like that?' I nudge Karen.

'Oh yes, you can get hearts, bunnies, flowers, anything you want.'

'Have you ever had it done?

'No, but I'm thinking of surprising Jamie when he next comes back from New York. Maybe a heart shape or a Hollywood.'

'Really? Wow! Do you think it will perk up your sex life?'

'What sex life?' she says, brushing herself down and picking up her gym kit. I smile, not really believing her. Jamie, forty-four, six foot three, dark hair, wide-set brown eyes, is fun, funny and gorgeous. They're totally in love.

'Well, we haven't seen much of each other and it's the usual: we're both tired, both have stressful jobs, both want to spend time with the children, and by the time we get to bed, it's a cuddle, kiss and we're out like lights,' Karen says, shrugging half-amused, half-resigned.

I try to remember the last time I had sex with Mike. I think it was my birthday, but it could have been his. Probably both. We must have done it since November? It's February now. We must have done it at Christmas. Bloody hell, no, we didn't. 'I haven't had sex for over two months,' I admit shamefacedly.

'You beat me by a month then, girl. I had it at Christmas, under the mistletoe, but that's only because I dressed up as a foxy fairy complete with Brazilian, stockings and suspenders, and pinned him to the fireplace. He said it was the best Christmas he'd ever had, the sweetie. Perhaps you should try that one. It worked well with Jamie.'

I laugh. 'Knowing my luck, Mike would probably go up in flames.'

'That's the point,' replies Karen.

'Well, I'm going to try and arrange a romantic evening in a couple of weeks' time. Several months and no sex, that's bad, Karen, isn't it?'

'Well, it's not good, Lily, but it's probably more common than you think.'

'I know, I've tried everything: lingerie, sexy music, sex toys.'

'Blow-up dolls?' Karen interrupts cheekily.

'No, I haven't gone that far, but I'm thinking about

it,' I say, seriously considering it as an option. 'I've tried to talk to him about it a few times but he shrugs things off and says everything's fine. I read this survey somewhere that oily fish, fruit and vegetables and a lot of exercise cause the libido to rise, so I've been cooking meals with loads of salmon and sardines and mackerel, but it hasn't done the trick; it's just made his breath smell. I'm not the only one suffering from lack of sex, though. You know Paul's wife, Jessica, is always away a lot on business? Well, he complains he doesn't get much either.'

'You two should have an affair,' Karen says, I think jokingly.

'Oh, don't be silly. Too complicated. Where would I find the time and, more importantly, he's married and so am I.'

'Anyway,' Karen continues, ignoring my last comment, 'a lot of couples now have busy lives apart from each other. Oh, did I tell you? Jamie's just got a membership for us both at the Letchbury golf club. He's angling for a partnership and needs to socialise with all the right people, so I thought I might make some useful contacts myself. And maybe I can pin Jamie down in the men's changing rooms and have my wicked way with him.'

I tune Karen out as she continues musing about seducing her husband while I lead the way out of the gym, passing the women in the café, still talking about schools. Charlotte is nowhere to be seen.

'Oh, Lottie, but The Pulpit, that's a lovely school. I believe it has a wonderful reputation and facilities and a better sort

of parent sends their child there. You really should go for that one.'

Karen stops her monologue as we head past the women and out into the gym car park, then turns to say, 'You know Julie is trying to get Dominic into The Pulpit?'

'No, I didn't know that,' I reply, looking back briefly at the women, who seem the sort Julie would loathe on sight, 'but it's good to know "a better sort of parent" sends their children there these days.'

Chapter 3
Could Do Better

'Who's stolen my Maltesers?' It's seven forty-five in the morning and Jenny is shouting at the top of her voice at the top of the stairs, loud enough for any passing stranger in Myalin Avenue to know there's a chocolate thief in the house.

'I bet it was Tim!' she yells, accusing her older brother.

'I haven't taken your stupid Maltesers, Jen. I don't even like Maltesers, you know that,' Tim shouts back, gathering his schoolbooks from the kitchen table where he finished off his homework last night. I remind myself to fetch the desk for his room this week. It's been at the Letchbury toy shop for two weeks now and I still haven't collected it.

Unperturbed, Jenny continues to look for the culprit. 'Well, then it must have been Henry. Henrrrry!' she yells, storming off to find her three-year-old brother, who I'm balancing precariously on one hip while trying to get toast out for breakfast and pour warm milk on three bowls of Malted Shreddies without dropping anything.

'Henry hasn't eaten your sweets, Jenny,' I shout upstairs. 'Get dressed and come down and have breakfast. When we're round the table we can work out who ate your chocolates and the culprit will be severely punished, OK?' I say, vainly trying to sound as though I'm in control.

Jenny has a very strong sense of discipline for one so young. Despite being only six, she's already executed several of her dolls for behaving badly. She beheaded three Barbies and threw one of her Action Men over Letchbury Bridge because he wasn't where she thought she had left him. Tim and Henry always keep their toys locked away in case she decides to punish them as well. I don't know where she gets it from, and it's one of the reasons we don't have a pet: I dread to think what she'd do to an unfortunate cat or dog in our midst. Fortunately she's never taken offence to Herman the tortoise.

'OK', says Jenny, walking briskly into the kitchen and sitting at the table as Tim hurriedly puts the last of his books into his bag and out of harm's way. 'But I want the thief to be severely beaten until they bleed, OK? Or at least not be fed for a whole month.'

'OK, Jenny. Now, right, everyone sit down and eat breakfast,' I say, plopping Henry into his chair and squeezing him in so he can't get out.

'Now, Tim, have you got your football kit?'

'Yes, Mum. Are you collecting me from the ground or is Dad?'

'No, I am,' I say, reaching for my diary on the countertop and checking times and dates. Tuesday. Tuesday, Tim has football after school, Jenny has karate and Henry is on a play-date with William Morrison. Not a particularly pleasant prospect as I don't really like Will's mum, Suzanne. She's a real busybody and a total energy zapper. I don't think she means to be, but she's so depressing to listen to. She's got one of those slow monotonous voices and I have to bite my lip because I'm aching to finish her sentence. And then she always goes on about how her eldest, Charlie, is doing at school, and asks how well Jenny is doing as they're both in the same class. Jenny thinks Charlie is a drip, and I agree with her, but Terence at least has got some fire in him. And he and Henry get on well. Mind you, they're only three so it could all change with a single tantrum over who gets which Power Ranger. But for the moment, it's fine. I'll try to avoid the coffee-and-cake offer and make an excuse. I know, I'll tell Suzanne I've got to go and can't stay because I'm collecting Tim's desk. That will give me enough time to get Jenny after karate, en route to Tim after football, then by the time I get Henry I'll have to dash, because it'll be tea, bath and bedtime for all of them. Great.

'Have you got your karate gear, Jenny?' I ask, only just stopping Henry from sticking a Shreddie up his nose.

'Yes, Mum. You know I've got my orange belt next month, don't you?'

'Yes, Jenny,' I say, making sure I've got that in the diary as well.

'And I've got the game against Highton School next week, Mum. You've got to take me, and we've got some practice matches, but Mia's dad said he could take me as he's helping with the coaching.' Tim is already starting to get up.

'That's nice of Paul,' I say, making a mental note to thank him for offering.

'Where's Daddy?' asks Henry now, his mouth still full of brown mush.

'He's gone for a run this morning. He's got an important meeting this afternoon so he wanted to brush the cobwebs away,' I say, realising as I do that I'm about to get a barrage of questions about spiders, why Daddy has cobwebs, do we have spiders in our house, is that a good thing, are spiders good, did I know spiders ate flies, if not why not, why do they have eight legs and not nine, can we go to see one at the zoo, and am I scared of spiders?

Jenny diverts the conversation back to the chocolate thief.

'So who do you think did it? I left my Maltesers in the fridge and they're not there this morning. Someone ate them last night or this morning. Mummy, did you eat my chocolates?' Jenny says, lowering her head and raising her eyebrows at me, which makes me want to laugh because she's only six, but can be truly terrifying.

'No, darling, I didn't, I promise. Cross my heart.'

'Post,' Mike calls from the front door.

'Did you have a good run?' I ask, kissing him on the lips as Jenny scowls and says, 'Er, disgusting.'

Hot and sweaty, grey T-shirt clinging to him slightly, tracksuit bottoms dishevelled, my husband looks like a bouncing puppy that's just been for its morning run.

'What's disgusting about kissing Mummy,' Mike grins, kissing me again, this time on the cheek.

'It's too early in the morning,' says Tim. 'It might put us off our breakfast.'

I smile at Tim. He's only ten, but sometimes he comes out with the most sophisticated stuff. Mad that it seems like only yesterday that I had Tim on my hip rather than Henry.

'Brilliant run,' Mike puffs. 'I went round the green several times and up the hill. I feel much better.'

Looking at him, I make a mental note to schedule that romantic evening – though it's a bit sad when you need to put sex on a 'to do' list.

'Did you catch any spiders, Daddy?' Henry asks innocently.

'What, darling?' says Mike, looking a little confused.

'Oh, don't worry about it, honey,' I start explaining as Jenny intersects with an indignant, 'Daddy, someone ate my Maltesers and they won't own up.'

Mike looks a little shamefaced and I realise Jenny has just found the culprit.

'Oh, were they yours, darling? I'm so sorry, Jenny.'

'You ate my Maltesers!' she says accusingly. 'Mummy says you're going to be beaten and she won't feed you for a month. Didn't you say that, Mummy?'

Jenny crosses her arms in mock anger, but I know Mike can do no wrong in her eyes. He is her hero – Superman, Spider-Man, Batman and Action Man all rolled into one. Jenny, despite being a mini-version of me in temperament and looks, is a daddy's girl, so she forgives him. If I had pinched the sweets, she wouldn't have spoken to me for a week.

'Don't worry about it, but if you could replace them as quickly as possible please,' says the little madam.

The hero smiles, kisses Jenny and plops the pile of post in front of me.

'Can I turn on the TV for the news, honey? See if there's anything I should know about for small talk with these guys I'm meeting today before we start business. It always helps,' he says, turning on the small TV we have in the kitchen, which my mum gave me last Christmas. She says you need to keep on top of things at all times. My dad died five years ago, a stroke that was unexpected but quick, and since then she's been determined to live life and to see her cup as half full all the time. My mum is great at balancing stuff, always has five things on the go when one would be sufficient and unlike me, she manages to get everything done.

The TV goes on but blaring some story about a dog having kittens or something so Mike disappears upstairs as I start to sift through the post. Bill, bill, another bill, postcard from Mum in Costa Rica addressed to the children. What is she doing there? I look at the post date, which is only four days ago. I thought she was going to Madeira. I read the card to the family:

Dear Tim, Jenny and Henry, I am having a fabulous time in a place called Costa Rica, where I've seen lots of volcanoes and sea turtles. One of the volcanoes is live, so I'm hoping it doesn't explode while I am here. I am staying in a reserve tonight and looking out for some wonderful birds. I hope you are all working hard and being good for Mummy and Daddy. Give them a big hug from me. Big kiss to all of you,
  Love Grandma.

Henry starts on the where's Costa Rica, what's a reserve, will Granny die if she gets killed by the volcano, if it's alive does it have legs, how can the volcano kill her, what is a volcano? while Tim asks slightly more pertinent questions, such as why has Grandma gone to a place where volcanoes are still active? Jenny just thinks it's amazingly, brilliantly exciting.

Showered, shaved and dressed in his nicest pinstripe suit, Mike bounds down the stairs. I look him up and down and nod.

'Important clients, then?' I smile.

'Do I look OK?' he asks, preening like a peacock.

'Not as good as Mummy,' Henry says loyally.

'*Mummy.*' Another voice in the room startles me until

I realise that it's coming from the TV. A pretty woman in her late thirties, smart and suited, is talking to the presenter. I turn up the volume as Tim starts collecting the cereal dishes.

'Yes, it's tough being a mummy these days. You're expected to be all things to all people. A successful career woman, a wonderful wife and a great mother, but the point is, it's impossible unless you have help. What I'm trying to do is encourage mothers to manage their lives more effectively, to be able to be more productive as a person, a woman, a wife, a lover, a mother and in her career, as well as allow that little extra time for her. That "me" time every mother so desperately wants.'

'*Hence your book* Putting the Yummy Back into Mummy?' asks the presenter, holding up the front cover of a book to the screen.

Tim starts putting dishes in the dishwasher and drowns out the rest of what sounds like a fairly sanctimonious speech about what mothers do or don't achieve. I swear, talking about mums is all the rage these days. And I bet this woman isn't even a mother herself, or if she is, I'm sure she's got an Imelda or Carlotta in the background.

I'm pleased to note that the presenter seems to agree with me. '*Don't you think women are under enough pressure already without being lectured to by another specialist?*' she asks rather pointedly.

'*Of course not,*' the author responds dismissively. '*Time management is crucial, it's the answer to everything.*'

I sigh and start clearing the rest of the table. I could use a bit of time management myself. Just as I'm about to run upstairs, I hear the presenter mention schools. I stop and turn. '*Yes, it's that time of year again, ladies and gentlemen, when all around the country parents are starting to get nervous about their offspring's continuing education.*'

No kidding, woman, I think savagely, but do you have to remind us of it before eight in the morning? The author vigorously nods, her shiny, red bob flying. She reminds me of a cocker spaniel, as eager as if each question was a bone. How does school selection tie in with time management? Well, apparently Miss Bob is an authority on everything. Sure enough, she launches into another one of her speeches. I squint to catch her name but am too far away to read the writing on the screen.

'*There is incredible competition for schools, as you well know, and as education standards are challenged and the battle for big school grows ever more intense, it's not just the children who are under scrutiny but the parents. Ordinary, decent parents are turned into grasping, twisted monsters by the worry and hope of a school desk. I know a mother who is seriously considering pretending to be Roman Catholic to get into a faith school, another mother who has pushed her daughter through hours of extra work every night and has no social life in order to get her a place at grammar school. These are not overzealous parents per se, they simply want to give their child a decent local education.*'

Well, she's got a point, I grudgingly give her that.

'*This is where I come in. This book will help mothers fulfil their potential.*'

'What's potential, Mummy?' asks Henry, walking up to the screen and taking a closer look at the woman, who's now reading a bit from her book. 'I think she's very pretty,' he says as he looks closer. 'You've got more wrinkles than her, Mummy.'

'That's because she's wearing lots of make-up,' says Jenny, uncharacteristically backing up her mum.

'She has a point about this battle for big school, though,' Mike says, putting on his coat. 'Totham must have suddenly made me susceptible to this whole hysteria, but I'm not joking, I even hear it on the train. You know the Jeremiahs who have Daniel in Tim's year? Well, Andrew Black' – he's the one with the kidney that Charlotte was talking about – 'he told me yesterday that they're using their cousins' address to get into one catchment area. And apparently the Days are moving in with her mother to do a similar thing.'

'Are we going to move?' asks Henry anxiously.

'No, we won't have to move, don't worry,' I say absent-mindedly, looking back at the screen. The woman now seems to be reciting a poem from her book.

> *'If you're a slacker*
> *You need a backer*
> *and a spirit to make you win*
> *to fit in what you couldn't fit in*
> *so box your stuff*
> *and you'll have enough*
> *time to do everything –'*

Enough is enough. Honestly. Mike turns off the TV and I run upstairs to get ready for the day.

The time management reminds me – 'What do you say we organise a lunch in a couple of weeks' time with Karen and Jamie, Paul and Jessica and Julie?' I say when I come back down the stairs. 'Providing Jamie and Jessica will be in the country, of course, and that Jamie and Karen aren't playing golf.'

'If you're a slacker, you need a backer,' mimics Jenny, dancing around the room.

Mike looks confused and I explain that the Fields have just joined the golf club, then smile meaningfully, hoping he'll join in the joke.

'Actually, I've been thinking about a corporate membership,' he says, a lot more seriously than I'd expected. 'Remind me about that, won't you, Lily? The lunch thing sounds great. Pity Julie hasn't met anyone yet,' he says, starting the round of kissing the children goodbye.

'I think she's quite happy by herself at the moment,' I say, scribbling 'Golf membership' on a Post-it note in my diary. 'Which reminds me,' I whisper in his ear as he goes to kiss me on the cheek, 'If I can get the children to bed early, do you fancy a quiet evening in?' I try to sound suggestive without the children hearing.

Mike doesn't pick up on it, though: 'I've got to work late tonight, hon. Sorry about that. I'm sure Henry will keep you company, won't you, Henry?' he says, tweaking Henry's cheek.

So much for trying to fit a little romance into my life.

*

Mike waves goodbye as Tim and Jenny collect their coats and hats. Henry has nursery in the mornings, so I'll have a chance to clean, iron, food shop, contact football, rugby and hockey coaches to ensure they know Tim and Jenny are playing in this month's tournaments, pre-prepare casseroles, organise play-dates, maybe even collect Tim's desk and ensure I've done my photography homework: photographs of the children walking. As mine prefer to run, it's been a more difficult assignment than I'd initially thought. But I've got some wonderful shots of all three of them walking away from me, and then towards me with arms and legs interlocked, singing Monkees style.

Tim and Jenny run on ahead as I tug along with Henry. Having two older siblings, he was the quickest to walk, determined not to be trodden on in the rush for food, cuddles or presents, but he still walks quite slowly, and with a grim look of determination on his face that speaks volumes of his desire to keep up with his siblings.

My three get on very well considering their age-differences, or perhaps because of it. The morning conversations are always full of joke-telling, questions or debates on who's friends with whom in the playground.

'What's brown and sticky, Henry?' asks Tim now, grinning at his little brother.

'I don't know, what's brown and sticky?' asks Henry, looking back at him intently.

'A stick,' answers Tim. 'Want to hear another one?'

Henry finds this joke so hysterically funny he gives

himself violent hiccups and nearly chokes. Oblivious, Jenny argues with Tim about sticks not being sticky so it isn't a proper joke.

As I turn the corner into Rosedale Avenue, the four of us all stop abruptly. The avenue, with its straight and organised beech trees and large four-bedroom terraced houses set well back from the road with their carefully manicured gardens, is usually quite empty and peaceful on school mornings. It's a nice short cut to school, a sort of cul-de-sac with an entrance at the end which you can walk but not drive through. It's usually quite quiet, but this morning, there's a real throng of people milling about in the cul-de-sac end, about twenty women and lots of children. Some I recognise from school, like Competent Charlotte; others are unfamiliar. They all seem to be following a rather stern-looking suited man with what looks like one of the toys I bought Henry only last year, except it doesn't play 'Jingle Bells' when you push it around. Henry notices it too.

'Mummy, he's got a wheelie stick,' he says, clapping excitedly. The man seems completely absorbed in what he is doing and oblivious to the women following him like some suburban pied piper, and he continues to push the little wheel on the stick, occasionally stopping to take notes. The women chatter among themselves, their voices rising and falling urgently in the morning air.

'What are they doing, Mummy?' asks Tim. 'Putting yellow lines on the road so people can't park there?'

'I don't think so,' I say, slightly confused by the unusual tableau on my morning school run.

'I'll ask,' says Jennifer quickly, assertively starting to stride forward, but I manage to catch her hand.

'No, darling,' I say, holding her hand tightly, 'I'll ask.'

I walk up to Charlotte, ushering my lot to do the same. She's towards the back of the line, craning her neck to see what the man is doing while her son John, seemingly resigned to his mother's odd behaviour, is waving at Tim.

'Hi, Charlotte, what's happening?' I ask, falling in step alongside her, much to the annoyance of the women behind her, who tut as though I've barged into the bank or supermarket queue without asking.

'Oh, hi, Lily,' she says, smiling at me briefly but continuing to scrutinise the suit furtively. 'Word's got out that the council are measuring for the catchment areas. One of the mums works in the local council office and mentioned it to Christine, you know, Christine Hawes? We don't really know exactly what school catchment areas are affected. Then Daniella Frost noticed this guy this morning, lurking down Churchill Crescent with his measuring stick, and put two and two together. Now we're trying to find out which schools he's checking for.'

'Are you really sure he's checking for catchment areas?' I say. 'He could be from the water board or traffic or something.' And quite bemused by all the groupie attention, I'm sure.

'Well, no, to be honest, no one's actually confirmed what he's doing quite yet, and some of us have been following him for over ten minutes. But we all suspect it's to do with it,' she says. Tim is pulling at my sleeve, whispering sensibly that we are going to be late for school if we wait around here for too long.

'Well, I'll ask and see what he says,' I say, astonished that none of the scarier mothers has taken the initiative yet. I stride past the other mums.

'Hello there,' I say to the wheelie-stick man, trying to sound as natural as possible. The suit looks up at me abruptly. A grey-haired man of about five foot nine, fifty-something but could be younger, with silver-grey hair, long eyelashes and a thickset jaw. He looks as though he could have been handsome once, but now just seems very tired, like an old cocker spaniel with large soulful eyes. He says nothing, just stares at me, slightly annoyed by my presence, still totally oblivious to the twenty or so women behind him.

'I'm sorry to bother you,' I start.

'You're *not*,' he snaps abruptly, suddenly looking more like a Rottweiler than a spaniel. 'You're not sorry to bother me at all. I took this job because the doctor suggested I do something more relaxing than the tax office and all its abusive punters; I wanted to have less contact with the public so they moved me and *this* is what I get. People following me around and bothering me. So will you please –'

Charlotte, who has sidled up next to me, suddenly lunges and, in an unprecedented move that will go down in the annals of school-selection hysteria, rips the man's notes right out of his hands and disappears down the road at full tilt. You can literally hear the jaws drop open around us, though I can see admiration rather than shock in many of the eyes around us. John just clutches Tim's hand in a slightly bewildered fashion. Wheelie-stick man, however, is staring at his own hands, turning them around with a look of utter shock and fury, then switches his attention to me as though I'm the culprit and have planned this as a diversion all along.

With a baleful glare in my direction, the man seems to come to his senses and drops his measuring stick, then legs it down the road to chase Charlotte, who's now stopped several hundred yards from us and is leafing furiously through the notes, most likely trying to decipher names of schools or roads. When the suit sees that some of the other women in the queue have broken range and are running alongside him, he shouts hoarsely, without slowing his stride, 'That is council property. I can have you arrested for that. Give it back immediately!' Everyone ignores him, the first fast women closing in on Charlotte, who continues to read completely unperturbed. He's almost there, shouting, 'I will call the police, madam!' when Charlotte breaks into a gentle trot, curving away from him around the cul-de-sac, still trying to leaf through the papers as she runs. Her serenity is a little frightening and the other mothers seem to agree as no one bothers to chase her further.

Tim, Jenny and John are transfixed by the scene; Henry has surreptitiously crept towards the wheelie stick and I restrain him just in time. Council property is nothing to joke about.

I cannot help but start laughing, looking at Charlotte, kitted for tennis as she usually is at the gym, running along the pavement, giving the angry, red-faced suit the slip over and over again, followed by a small knot of other women, some with buggies, who have picked up the scent again. Doubling back, she starts to run towards me again and I hesitantly decide to make her see sense. She could be in serious trouble if she doesn't give the man back his notes and he calls the police.

'Charlotte, stop,' I shout, louder than the suit who's still issuing threats in between puffs of laboured breathing. 'It's not worth being arrested for this. Think of your children.'

'I'm doing this *for* my children,' Charlotte says indignantly, but slowing down nonetheless. She finally stops, gains her breath and holds out the notes to the wheelie-stick man.

'Thank you very much, ma'am,' he snatches the sheaf of papers out of her hands with an angry scowl at Charlotte, and then, of course, at me again as though I'm the accomplice. I've done nothing here!

'I am going to ask for police protection next time I do this. This is not worth the money they pay me.' A few people snigger, which seems to enrage him further. 'In fact, I am calling the police right now.' And with that, he starts angrily punching at his mobile.

Seeing that he is actually only punching in three numbers, the women scuttle in all directions like frightened spiders. Jenny is tugging at my arm. 'We should make a run for it, Mummy,' she says excitedly, but Tim picks up the measuring stick and hands it back to the man who takes it without saying thank you. That's my boy.

I nod politely at the suit, who is still flushed with anger and scowling at Charlotte, but I pull her along in the direction of Somerset School before he can do anything more serious to her. Charlotte walks with us, still quite unfazed by the whole thing, I have to give it to her. John and Tim talk about football and Jenny is trying to scare Henry into thinking the police may come round and arrest me, but I give her a stern look.

'So, did you see anything, Charlotte?' I can't help asking. Apparently not, after all this.

'I only really saw all the numbers and there were lots of road names and names of schools, but I couldn't work out what related to what. All I know is that every single school in the area was mentioned, including Readmere and Somerset, so perhaps they're changing the feeder schools for the infant and primary as well as the secondary schools?' She ponders this for a moment, betraying an in-depth knowledge of all this that I'm obviously sadly lacking. I don't think I've ever said the words 'feeder school' in casual conversation.

'So what does that mean?' I ask, worriedly.

'Not sure. Apparently, they are quite literally changing the goalposts, so we don't even know if we're in the right catchment area any more or at the right feeder school. Anyway, I'll see you at the club, that's if I don't get a visit from the local constabulary before then,' she adds, smiling wryly.

'Well, if they arrest you, they've got to arrest us all,' I say reassuringly. 'But the last thing the local council wants is a load of bad publicity or having to explain what they were doing.'

I wave goodbye to Charlotte as we enter the school gates which are teeming with mothers as usual. Four-wheel drives, Minis and Golf GTIs avoid mums on bikes who are cycling in tandem with some of the older children. I notice Paul in his blue Beamer as he waves to me, ushering Mia and Cara out of the car. Mia is clutching her Little Pony backpack. According to Paul, she wants to be a horse vet when she grows up. Cara is in Jenny's class and Jenny tells me she wants to be an actress and that she misses her mummy as she works away a lot. Good source of information, my daughter. Why do sons never pick up on stuff like that?

There's a gaggle of women who've brought their dogs ready for a walk around the park. I recognise a few of them. There's Jane Anderson in her navy skirt and white blouse – she always looks as though she's going in to an office but as far as I know she doesn't work; Ella Fritz, who's as thin as a rake; Suzanne Morrison with her golden retriever – must remember to confirm the play-date with Henry and Terence this afternoon as she's picking them both up from nursery; and Sally Day, the woman Mike mentioned this morning, who has moved in with her mum to get her Freddie into the right school. I squeeze past Linda Black, a PTA member with a nasty habit of blocking any ideas that aren't her own, and wife to the man whose kidney is currently making the rounds at local hospitals to fund their son's education. I don't know much about Linda, but Karen always makes me laugh when she mimics the way she screws up her mouth when you say something she doesn't like, which, according to Karen and Julie, is all the time though I have yet to have the pleasure of seeing it for myself. I head towards Paul, trying to put some distance between me and that crowd. I bet they're all talking school selection and I just can't quite face it after this morning's cul-de-sac showdown.

I stick with Tim and Jenny who are having far more adult conversations about who's going to play in the football team and who's worthy of being in the hockey team and whether they think Ms Harrison, who teaches PE, is really a man. Tim breaks away from his little sister to greet Freddie Day and Charlie Black, both looking rather anxious, and I can hear Charlie saying, 'I didn't get to bed till ten o'clock last night, revising for an exam.' Both look miserable and I feel sorry for them. I don't see how all this study will improve their chances, it just seems to be making them miserable. But perhaps I'm being way too sanguine about all of this. Tim only sat one entrance exam and that was for The Oaks because no other school we visited really worked for us. The Pulpit is out of our catchment area, Para Hills is just for girls, we're neither Catholic nor prepared to get God so St Cecile's is out, and we didn't like any of the others.

I sigh and turn away, hoping to catch Paul some-where, when I see Julie emerging from her yellow VW Beetle. Five foot ten and dressed in purple and green, my friend looks stunning on this chill, grey morning and at least ten years younger than her forty-four years. She's a single mum with two boys, Dominic and Alexander, who are aged ten and seven respectively. I met her at NCT classes the same time as Karen and we bonded immediately. She holds her temper better than Karen, but I think she could be just as ruthless if she wanted to be. She worked in fashion PR, and some of the stories she's told me about the designers are hilar-ious. I'm amazed I never met her directly when I was working at *De Rigueur*; our paths just never crossed until we were comparing bumps at antenatal classes. We've been friends ever since. She gets on well with her ex, Eddie, whom she sees about once a week when he picks up the kids from school and takes them to their various clubs, gives them a pizza and drops them back home. But Julie never talks much about her time with him, so I don't ask.

Julie and Karen have become close friends through our mutual friendships. Well, close-ish, I should say. It's nothing I can really pinpoint but they are always a touch wary around each other. We meet up and go for drinks, we have spa days and chat about anything and every-thing from sex life to jobs, just like other girlfriends, but, at the end of the day, I think I'm better friends with each of them individually than they are with each other.

As I greet Julie and Paul pokes his head around a group of people to join us, I notice that both of them look rather unhappy.

'What's the matter?' I ask, giving Julie a quick hug.

'Mia hasn't got into Para Hills,' Paul replies, shrugging his shoulders. 'Apparently they've just changed the catchment area.' Oh, no. Here we go. The wheelie-stick man has been busy already. 'It seems we're no longer inside it. I had no idea they could even do that. Jessica is furious and wants to sell the house, but we love it here, so I'm trying to dissuade her.'

'God, not you, too,' says Julie, sounding dispirited. 'I just decided yesterday not to send Dominic to The Pulpit in the end, as the Ofsted report was so poor this year and I've been hearing horror story after horror story. And all the decent teachers seem to be leaving in droves, so I'm having a complete rethink about the whole thing.'

I can't help smiling a little as I remember Hetty and Lottie's pompous words. Judging by their attitude, Julie has probably made the right decision.

'God, that's too bad,' I say, ushering the kids towards their classrooms and keeping a firm hold on Henry's hand against the moving throng of mothers who are now exiting the playground en masse. 'What are you going to do now?' I sneak a sideways look at them, hoping against hope they won't say The Oaks. Catching myself at the thought I mentally give myself a good, hard slap on the wrist. Enough, Lily. These are your friends.

'I think I'll have to go for The Oaks,' Paul mutters,

'although it's too competitive. I hope I've even got a chance to get Mia in there.'

'How did your interview go, by the way?' asks Julie, interested.

'OK,' I say, as we follow the crowd out of the playground. 'Although they seem to judge entries not only on your child's ability, but also on who you are as a parent. You wouldn't believe the names we saw on his wall. And he kept going on and on about community spirit.' I sigh. It's all getting quite hard work, this school stuff.

'Oh well, that means I'm out already. I do bugger all for the local community,' says Julie matter-of-factly. 'Perhaps I should offer my services to Tatiana's boutique to get them more publicity. Do you think that will count?'

I laugh. 'Good one, but no, I don't think so, and don't forget, she's *my* neighbour, so if anyone's going to help out there it will be me,' I say, jokingly. Half-jokingly. There really is almost a sense of rivalry here and it dawns on me that if they both go for The Oaks, which they're bound to seeing that there are not that many alternatives, then my friends and I will inevitably be in direct competition for places. I know Julie is especially ruthless about getting what she wants, so perhaps I should play things close to m; chest. I don't like this at all.

As I wave goodbye to Julie and Paul at the school gates, Julie narrowly avoiding getting a parking ticket and Paul arguing with a parking attendant because he's got one, I'm suddenly worried that I'm becoming one of those competitive mums that woman on the TV was talking about, the ones who take things too far. But this is important and I've already been far too complacent about it.

My phone rings. Karen. The theme tune of *The Great Escape* plays when she rings. That's her favourite film and because I always imagine her as the female equivalent of Steve McQueen, daring and unorthodox. I've given Julie AC/DC's 'Highway to Hell', an embarrassing choice when I'm somewhere quiet and I hear some of the expletives booming from my mobile. Mike's tune is 'You Can Leave Your Hat On', because it's such a sexy song and when Mike and I first started going out I used to do my own version of Kim Basinger's *9½ Weeks* striptease for him at least once a week. The tune has always cheered me up, but now it almost makes me feel a little sad. For some reason, I've given Paul the James Bond theme, I think because I could imagine Paul as a spy – charismatic, unassuming, enquiring – plus his dream car is an Aston Martin.

'Hi, hon, how are you?' Karen asks, sounding as though she's rushing somewhere.

'I'm fine, where are you?' I ask, putting my finger to my other ear, cradling the phone against my shoulder so I've still got one hand holding on to Henry's.

'At a train station. I've got to go up to Scotland for a few days.'

'Why Scotland, for goodness' sake?' I ask. 'Who's looking after the kids? Isn't Carlotta away?'

'Yes, but Jamie's back, so he's playing house-husband for a few days, which will be good for him. How are you?' she asks, sounding distracted.

I decide to come straight to the point.

'Paul and Julie have changed their minds about schools. They're thinking of putting their kids down for The Oaks.'

'Well, that's great, isn't it? They all get on well,' she says, sounding unconcerned.

'It means we'll be in competition, Karen. I can already feel this horrible competitive streak coming out in me,' I say, trying not to sound too ungracious.

'Lily, there's room enough for all of you. If anything, it's the other mums who should be worried, not you, darling. Oh, got to go, take care, byeee.'

I hover indecisively in front of Henry's nursery, jostled by the crowds of women walking past, chatting to one another, mainly about schools again, although a few are talking about the weather and extensions and which celebrity is divorcing whom and whether they think the rumours are true. Henry is happily skipping on the spot, totally oblivious to all the fuss.

'You OK, darling?' I say, grinning down at his little face.

'I'm fine, Mummy. Let's go to nursery. I've got a lot to do today.'

Chapter 4
Fingers on Lips

'Point before you shoot, Lily, point before you shoot.'
Gilbert Edwards is a handsome fifty-two, with silver-grey
hair and a twinkle in his eye. He is a retired celebrity
photographer and full-time lecturer at St Michael's
College, Letchbury, and he's always telling me I need
to consider my shots more carefully.

'It's good to be spontaneous, Lily,' he says, sounding
just a tad patronising, 'but a little patience doesn't
go amiss either, even when you're up against a tight
deadline or have a very brief window of opportunity.'

It's nine o'clock and I've just dropped Tim and
Jenny off at school and Henry at nursery, leaving him
talking non-stop about how he wants to learn chess

like his brother and will I teach him how to play, preferably now? My son is even more impatient than I am.

Now it's time for three hours of study with six other aspiring photographers. The photography class, or as Gilbert likes to call it, the 'Photo-Imaging Course', is an introduction to the foundation skills of using a digital camera. It's a bit like going back to school but having all your favourite lessons in one day and, at the end of the three months, everyone gets a certificate, having produced a portfolio of prints, a workbook and photographs of each other, our children, our other halves, and anyone and anything else we think of as creative and unusual. As well as buying me the course for Christmas, Mike also got me a Canon Digital IXUS 55. Compared to some of the cameras owned by the other students, mine looks a little small, but Gilbert assures me it'll do the trick just fine.

St Michael's College is a large, red-brick Victorian building with huge picture windows, and endless corridors that smell of bleach and are punctuated on either side by oak doors. The heavily panelled front door opens into an impressively ornate reception, where a receptionist mans the high desk and sometimes lets pupils use the fax machine and allows them to post their letters if asked nicely. Walking down the corridors makes me regret the fact that I didn't go to university. By the time I finished my A levels I was sick of studying. I wanted to get out into the world and make money – and, more importantly, spend it. I remember when I studied art A level later on at evening class, the teacher, an appropriately named man called Mr Painter, sighed and said after one particularly long philosophical discussion on life and art, 'It's a pity you didn't go to university, Lily. It would have made a woman of you.' Perhaps he just meant I would have been shagged silly, but it's a comment that's haunted me ever since.

Our classroom is a large studio, and we spend a lot of time learning the technical side of our cameras, dissecting them like laboratory rats. Gilbert treats them as though they're living breathing things and we need to, too, because then and only then will they perform. He has set phrases that he often uses: 'Treat the camera as an extension of your arm.' 'Patience is not a virtue with taking good shots, it's a necessity.' 'Use the space.' Patience has never been my strong point, obviously, but I am getting better with the space and extension.

The other students in my class are of all ages and backgrounds. When we first arrived, we were given the task of choosing a partner, finding out about them in five minutes and then telling the rest of the class what we had learned. I must have chosen the most honest person I think I've ever met:

'My name is Tamara Charles Hunt. I'm thirty-six, size eight, even at that time of the month. Prada handbag, Manolo shoes, silver Porsche Targa, as driven by hairdressers, gangsters and bankers.'

I laugh slightly incredulously, but she continues blithely.

'Highlights at De Vere in Kensington; Botox on the forehead and corner of the eyes; favourite colour turquoise except on eye shadow; Leo, Scorpio rising, Mars in Taurus.'

She's had her astrological chart done and it's *so* accurate, she tells me.

'Three-bedroom penthouse apartment overlooking Letchbury Church, which has been in *Homes and Gardens* several times; no children as Terence is on his third marriage and has enough already. I am a bored house-wife, Lily, married to a fifty-something rich, boring corporate lawyer, but I look good, I make him look good and I sleep at night.'

Tamara left me speechless.

We had five minutes; she talked for ten and didn't ask anything about me. Over the past four years, she's taken courses in interior design, upholstery, cordon bleu cooking, holistic massage, aromatherapy, nutrition and then decided that photography would be fun. Terence bought her a Nikon D200 digital (which cost over a grand, she tells me), with a wide-angle zoom lens which must have cost another grand. She did all the other courses because she wanted to pursue them professionally – be an interior designer, an upholsterer, a chef and a masseur. Now she wants to open her own gallery and charge her friends lots of money for taking atmospheric black-and-white photographs of families, looking lovingly at each other and as if they always laugh like that, despite the fact that most of them can't wait to send the little dears off to boarding school. Her words, not mine.

Despite Tamara's world being totally different from anything I've ever experienced, I can't help but find her amusing. We talk fashion a lot because we know the same designers – she wears the labels and I've met some of the creative people behind them. Despite myself, I like her.

There's a ginger-haired IT consultant called Leon Marks, who's gay and very Jewish and lives with his mother as he's in the process of an acrimonious divorce from his boyfriend. He is very friendly but quite intense and currently on sabbatical from his company to try something more creative. He always looks you directly in the eye, which can be a bit disconcerting, especially first thing in the morning.

Then there's Tiffany Jefferies, a pretty brunette, helium-voiced with flat vowels. She lives in Essex and is friendly with Tamara because they have holistic massage in common – Tiffany used to be a beauty masseuse – and are always talking to each other about soleus muscles and neck strain.

When I enrolled, I half-expected to see some mums from Somerset School here, and there actually are two: Ella Fritz, a super-thin thirty-something who doesn't seem to eat solids – well, not when I'm watching anyway – and can always be counted on to pipe up asking if she looks fat in the photographs; and, equally thin if not thinner, Christine Hawes, the one whose marriage is allegedly under pressure because of school selection.

Finally, there's Tony Herald, who's in his mid-thirties and is one of the friendliest people I've met in a while, and ambitious, but not in an overbearing sort of way. He reminds me of a young Gabriel Byrne – well-proportioned and with large light-blue eyes, an open face and an easy manner, more at home outside than in the office. When he smiles, his face lights up, and he has a habit of making me feel like I'm the only person in the room when we're talking. He has his own restaurant in Hartford, not far from Letchbury, which specialises in modern English cuisine (whatever that is). Having got to know him well over the past few weeks, chatting about his various hobbies and travels, I somehow keep thinking of Julie. I'm sure he'd like her. He doesn't have any affectations and doesn't appear to have a dark side (or at least keeps it remarkably well hidden). I haven't talked about sex, drugs, religion or politics yet, but he's a good cook, is fit, sexy, single, and never married. You couldn't ask for more.

I'm just about to see if Tony would like to come to my lunch party on Sunday – I've finally pinned everyone down – when Christine saunters over. She must be in her late thirties and has exceptionally long brown hair which she always ties in a loose pony-tail, wafting behind her as she walks. She's softly spoken but has quite a high-pitched voice, which reminds me of the noise a phone makes when it's been left off

the hook for too long. I can only take so much conversation with her. I met her on Tim's first day of school
and my only thought was, God, you're thin, and it's
been my first thought every single time I've seen her
since. She reminds me of a whippet: lean, sleek, alert
and very highly strung.

'How are you, Lily? Everything going well?' she
enquires, swooping down on me and pretending to be
interested.

I don't want to talk about schools, but I know she's
going to ask about Tim and whether I've heard
anything from The Oaks. Honestly, it seems as though
half our year is now applying for that damn school.
That, or she'll talk about the state of her marriage
and all the counselling she's been going through. I've
listened to her going on about her marriage through
so many tea breaks I've lost count. I know she hasn't
had sex for over a year, which makes me feel immensely
uncomfortable, if slightly better about me and Mike,
and I must remember to tell Karen as well – it's the
kind of gossipy titbit she relishes. Christine is in
obvious need of a good sounding board in general,
but, to be honest, I don't really want to be it when
I'm meant to be enjoying my 'me' time at college.
And, sadly, I'm not thick-skinned enough not to be
affected by what she says. I did the photography course
to get away from the playground politics and mummy
mafia. So I smile off-puttingly blandly and just say,
'I'm fine, and you?'

'OK.' She sighs, then pauses, expecting me to fill

the gap, but I don't do her the favour and just pat her reassuringly, turning to Tony, who's just about to walk away.

'Can I have a quick word?' I ask, nudging him towards the door, trying desperately not to look furtive. The last thing I need is Christine spreading a vindictive rumour that I'm having a fling with him.

'Of course,' he says, sidling out, leaving Christine to find another victim who will pursue the source of her angst.

We stop just by the door and chat for a moment, idly looking around at people cleaning their lenses, ready for the outdoor shots. Tamara is chatting to Tiffany, Ella to Gilbert (who seems to be reassuring her again that she doesn't look fat today), and Adam is musing over his camera, asking Christine, who's stopped sulking, for help on some switch or other. We've done the technical stuff this morning and the classroom white-board lecturing, so we're all a bit saddle- and eye-sore. We each had to take photographs of our gardens and put the results on the walls, so there's a splash of green, brown and stark blue everywhere. Everyone else took views of the garden in estate-agent fashion, making it look larger than it actually is, except for Tony, who did his at grass level, as though he were an insect looking up at an oak in the middle of his lawn. Gilbert thought it was very creative. Slightly out of focus if you ask me. For my attempt, I lay on the ground, looked up at the sky, the branches of our cherry trees framing the shot, and took a photograph of the blue sky and the clouds.

I was quite proud of my angle, but to be honest, it's come out too grey to really stand out. I've got some way to go.

'How can I help you?' says Tony now, arms folded as though I'm about to give him a challenge he's looking forward to.

'Would you like to come to lunch on Sunday? I'm having a few friends over and would love you to join us. I'm cooking, and I promise my cooking is decidedly better than my photography,' I say, trying to sound casual. The last thing I want is for him to suspect I'm trying to play matchmaker.

'That would be great. I think I'm free. Is there anything I can prepare?'

'Oh no, all is in hand. Mind you, it won't be fancy or anything. If your speciality is fresh spider-crab saffron ravioli, this won't be anything like that.'

'God, I hope not, that takes most of the day to prepare and it's ridiculously fussy. It would be really good to meet your family. Are you sure I can't bring anything?'

'No, just bring yourself. I've got friends and their families coming over. You do like children, don't you?' I ask, slightly concerned as there will be seven of them. And unless there's a miracle and we get spring-like temperature, in February, they'll all be indoors on top of us.

'Oh yes, I'm fine. Children for lunch, lovely.'

'Right, everyone,' Gilbert calls from the front of the classroom, with a pile of papers in his hand, 'if you'd all like to come here, I'll give you next week's assignment, then you can go.'

Each week Gilbert gives us some themed homework. Before the gardens, the theme was 'empty spaces', which produced some interesting offerings from the class. Tiffany brought in a photo of her boyfriend, as she claims he's one big empty space, with very little between his ears and a vacant expression on his face. Leon took a photograph of a toilet with the lid open and nothing in it, Christine a rather poignant one of an empty bed, and Ella one of the room in which her mother stays when she visits. Apparently it is kept exclusively for her use, so everything is left untouched when she's absent. Tamara took a photograph of an empty garage, using it, she explains, to hint strongly to Terence that she wants a new car, and she wants it now. I was a bit at a loss, so in the end I took a photograph of the empty studio where Daisy teaches kick-boxing. The mirrors were still fogged up with sweat but there was something quite peaceful about the room; you could almost sense that a lot of noise and movement had been going on, but now it was completely still, like the calm after the storm. Gilbert praised them all and commented that they said more about us than we probably realised at the time.

'With these assignments,' he says as he passes out sheets, 'I'm interested in *why* as much as *how* you've chosen to shoot it,' sounding a little like a Zen master. 'This week I am asking you to focus on your interpretation of "the dark side"; so that's anything from Darth Vader to the shape of a shadow created under a tree, an ill-lit dark alley, or whatever else you feel has or creates a dark side. It's an exercise in how to use light and space appropriately,' he adds.

'Can it be a person we know?' asks Leon, as everyone smiles at him knowingly.

'Do you need a lift?' asks Tony as we make our way out the door.

I look at my watch. I am running late, having spent too much time clearing up, and my car is at the garage.

'Could you? That would be great. But I've got to pick up the kids. If it's not out of your way, would you drop me off at the school gates?' I ask, sounding slightly desperate.

'Sure, it'll be nice to meet your kids,' he says helpfully. He's such a nice guy.

'Great.'

Ignoring the glances from Christine and Ella, I head towards the car park with Tony, waving goodbye to Tamara and Tiffany. Leon is on his mobile, speaking to his divorce lawyer, or rather shouting random things like 'He said what?' and 'No! A blatant lie.' He constantly has to leave the classroom because he's burst into tears for some reason.

Tony's Mini Cooper S is lovely. It has a CD player and electric sun-roof, and is amazingly clean. I've never seen a car this clean. He and Karen would love each other. I hope he isn't one of those obsessive-compulsive people who have an urge to keep their food tins all in the same direction and order.

'Love your car,' I say jealously, eyeing up the dashboard and CD player. What I wouldn't give to zip around town in a car like this, but it's much too small for my family.

'Yes, it is nice. I've just had it valeted. It's not usually this tidy, I'm afraid.' At least he isn't anal. Julie and he will make a great match, I decide with some satisfaction. 'Now where is this school of yours?'

We arrive just as all the mothers gather at the gates. Parking is always a nightmare and I point out the parking attendants hiding furtively behind the bushes in neighbouring back gardens.

'They really are the lowest of the low, aren't they,' he says, shaking his head.

'Totally. Plus, if you don't have a booster seat in the car they snitch on you and you can get fined hundreds of pounds. But you don't have to worry about that, I'm just going to walk from here, our house isn't far. Thanks so much for the ride.'

'Are you sure? I could wait too, if you need a ride home?' he says, stopping briefly on a yellow line, aware of two parking attendants about to pounce.

'Oh, don't worry, it's not far from here. Thanks, though. And see you Sunday, right?'

'Yes, see you Sunday,' he calls as I quickly jump out.

I collect Henry from nursery, where he's had a

wonderful day and wants to tell me about the paintings and the fact that he saw a worm in the nursery garden and Jack cut it in two because he was told it would still be alive and it was and wasn't that clever and did I know that, and wasn't I clever? When Henry has exhausted the worm story and found a Scottie dog to stroke, I pace around by the school gates, absentmindedly listening to the usual heady conversations around me while my head is buzzing with photos, Sunday's lunch and how to break it to Julie that there's a single man coming – a handsome, charming one at that. Linda Black, in her usual blanket of colour, looking a bit like a green broad bean, is talking intently to tall and elegant but sadly quite boring Suzanne Morrison just next to me and although I've kept my distance from Linda since hearing about the pen-flicking incident at the PTA meeting, I still nod and smile when I see her now.

'It's important to be at the appropriate place at this age, Suzanne. You're doing the right thing by moving out of the area to get Charlie into the best school,' Linda says decidedly, stepping aside to avoid passing bicycles and a dog trying to sniff out a good place to mark his territory.

'I know, Linda, but it's such a hassle. Still, better to meet the right people early on. My friend's daughter married a dyslexic halfwit and my friend is forever moaning about not having pushed her to be more focused.' She sighs with sanctimonious sincerity, but I'm a bit confused. What does moving have to do with dyslexic halfwits? She must be mad, I decide. More of a reason to keep my distance.

'I know, Suzanne, I know. And it's not as if the system is completely comprehensive any more. The cream gets taken by the private sector these days, so all the comprehensives are left with are the scum,' Linda nods quite unselfconsciously.

I can't listen to them any more, so I move on, propping myself up against one of the benches, hoping that Tim or Jenny will make an appearance soon. But there's no sign of them and Henry is starting to get fractious.

'When are we going, Mummy? When?' he asks.

'When Tim and Jenny come out that door, so you just watch and wait and tell me when they're here, OK?'

'OK,' he says, turning to the door and glaring at it intently for the first sign of movement.

Sally Day is standing a little ahead of me, talking to Jane Anderson.

'How's it going with your mum, Sally?' Jane asks.

'Oh, fine. OK. Well, not brilliant, really. She's kind of driving me nuts, always hovering around and trying to be helpful with her stupid articles about the education system and how it's all going down the drain and how exam results are far more lenient now than they were in her day. I don't think I can take it much longer.'

Sounds pretty grim. I love my mum dearly, but if I had to move in with her, I'd be a wreck within days. I try to close my ears and take Henry's hand to stop him from following a pair of dogs down the street. This school stuff is getting a little out of hand, but I can't help myself getting a bit anxious again: I need to do something, not just stand around and eavesdrop.

As I pull Henry back into the playground, I'm playing out various scenarios in my head. Maybe join the golf club myself, play a round with Totham? Use the opportunity to network with people who might give me freelance work? Perhaps I should join the PTA after all? A parent-governor position has just become vacant – perhaps I could take that up. It would look good on my CV, and it's the sort of thing that Totham would look upon favourably.

'Mummy, it's Tim. I can see Tim,' Henry shouts, just as I feel a tap on my shoulder and see Tony's face beaming at me.

'You left your camera bag behind,' he says breathlessly.

'Oh, I'm so stupid, so sorry to make you come after me. You're a star. Look, there's my eldest,' I say, nodding towards Tim, who is walking with Dominic, Claire and Mia, belonging to Julie, Karen and Paul respectively. Tim keeps looking round at Claire – I think he has a crush on her but I won't say anything as Jenny has ears like an elephant and will tease him mercilessly if she suspects.

'So this is it, is it? This is what it's like in the playground?' Tony says excitedly, scanning the crowd of parents eagerly watching the doors for their children to run out and hurl themselves at their mums, which is what Tim used to do to me until about a year ago. Tony seems in no hurry. Good, maybe we'll run into Julie. It might not be a bad idea for all of them to meet, *casually*, before Sunday.

'Yes, do you like it?' I say, still keeping one eye on the door and noticing Jenny emerging with Alexander Rose, Julie's other son, and Cara Wilton, Paul's youngest, karate kit in hand.

Before he answers, we're bombarded with children offloading their book bags and gym kits. Paul comes up to say hello, Julie and Jamie close behind. Jamie is only a temporary face here, since Karen is still in Scotland, but now that I come to think of it, I don't think I've ever seen Jessica at the school run.

Everyone's talking at once about the day's events in the playground, karate and kick-boxing, recorder playing, who was naughty in choir today and isn't it great that Tim, Dominic and Mia could all be going to The Oaks together, and a chorus of 'Can we have a quick play in the playground, Mummy?'

'No time for play,' I say, trying to sound authoritative in front of Tony. 'Jenny, you have art class. Tim, you've got homework to do, and Henry,' I say, looking at his little expectant face, 'you've got tea, bath, bedtime story and bed.'

The children all ignore me and run off to play, including Henry, who wriggles out of my reach and runs after Jenny and Cara, who slow down and take a little hand each, leaving the grown-ups watching helplessly.

'Five minutes then, but just five,' I shout after them feebly.

'So,' I say, turning to Tony, 'this is Paul, Paul, Tony.' They both shake hands. 'This is Jamie, who's married to one of my best friends, Karen.' Jamie and Tony smile and shake hands. Then I turn to Julie. 'This is my friend Julie,' I try to make the introduction sound exactly the same as the previous two, although I can feel myself smirking mischievously as I say it, going slightly red and a bit hot under the collar. No one seems to notice and everyone shakes hands and smiles.

'Tony is one of the other students at my photography course,' I explain. 'He's a chef, and I've invited him to lunch on Sunday.'

'Great,' says Paul, 'we'll have an even number.' He grins at me, winks and walks towards the children, leaving Julie and Tony looking at me disdainfully. OK, so this is awkward, but Julie, shooting me a brief dagger look, dispels the tension by asking Tony where he works. Tony visibly relaxes and they shart chatting while Jamie tells me he's off to New York as soon as Karen is back tonight, but will definitely be there on Sunday.

After ten minutes the children are finally rounded up by Paul who ushers his two and Jenny into the BMW, heading for karate class. Jamie waves and drives off with Claire and Simon, and Tony suddenly remembers the meter and rushes off too, turning once to wave goodbye. This leaves Julie and me alone with the rest.

As Julie walks towards her Beetle, she looks at me askance.

'So, Lily Dearl, you're not trying to set me up with that man, are you?'

'Would I do that?' I say, trying and failing to sound innocent.

'Yes, you would. And you're about as subtle as a brick. Poor guy. First meeting and it's in the playground surrounded by mums and screaming children; and it's not exactly the best first impression. I didn't even look good today,' she says, appearing polished and bright in orange and green and long brown boots.

'You look great. You always do. But I'm glad you didn't know in advance – you'd have got all nervous and dressed up in something ridiculously vampy and scared him off completely. I thought it was all completely natural and now he's already met your children. He's so nice. I've known him for a month now and he seems a genuine sort of guy, not psychotic or anything. He doesn't have a mother fixation, isn't overly materialistic, drives a second-hand Mini, has a small house in Hartford, owns his own restaurant, is a good cook, loves travelling and hasn't been married before.' I run out of things to say and sneak a look at her.

'OK, so he sounds too perfect,' Julie interrupts. 'Too perfect.'

'Well, find out. Chat to him at lunch on Sunday. It's not as if you're going on a date. If he's that hideous or boring, just leave it. There'll be enough distractions to not look awkward or rude. And at least you'll get fed,' I add cheekily.

'Oh, OK,' says Julie, smirking at me. 'And he cooks, which is something. I've never had a man cook for me before.'

'And he's sexy,' I say, nodding approvingly.

We giggle and I'm almost a bit envious. I definitely thought there was a spark when the two met. But hey, what do I know. I can't even relight my own flame.

Chapter 5
Tea Party

I've turned into Karen overnight. I've become Action List Woman. I'm usually a Post-it note taker with a liberal smattering of mental reminders, but this week I've actually bothered to print out a 'to do' list on the computer and am religiously trying to tick off everything. The lunch party looms large, so that accounts for at least thirty-two items, then there's the course work and the other usual stuff. Plus, trying to bring Julie and Tony together has given me a new impulse to inject some romance into my own love life as well. So, first order of business: a nice outfit, some underwear. And a bikini line with sparkles.

*

Tatiana, my gorgeous half-Swedish, half-Polish neighbour two doors down and owner of the best local boutiques (appropriately but unimaginatively named Tatiana's) recommends a beauty therapist in Kensington.

'Darling,' she says in her whispering voice, gracefully wafting from clothes rail to clothes rail like a ballerina, occasionally striking a dramatic pose, 'you must go to Frederick's in town, if you want something special. They do diamanté hearts, flowers, champagne bottles, tigers, butterflies, bees. They wax you into any shape you want and have a menu of choice with drawings.' She holds a brown chiffon dress against me as I stand there with my shopping bag and empty buggy. 'Very you, darling. Very, very you.' She does a little twirl around the mannequin and then takes my hand, leading me to another rail of clothes. 'And while you're there, why don't you have your nails and hair done, darling? Indulge yourself for a few hours? You're always so busy rushing around everywhere, and it would be so good for you, don't you think?'

I nod lamely in agreement, fondly remembering my time at *De Rigueur*, when I was always immaculately turned out. Tatiana makes me a little dizzy sometimes with her pirouetting and posturing but I enjoy my visits to her shop. We talk about fashion and designers and I name-drop dreadfully as I recount the horror stories of tetchy models. She in turn has all the latest gossip on local celebrities who come into the shop and buy totally unsuitable clothes, generally refusing her advice. Currently, one of her favourite subjects is the supposed liaison between Francesca and celebrity chef Randy Hasbro. Apparently they spend a lot of time vigorously denying that they're having an affair, but Tatiana tells in hushed whispers that he recently bought a slew of what she calls 'barely there' clothes – outfits designed more for the bedroom than anywhere else – and she's certain they're for Francesca. Talking to her is like a brief peek at my old life, a world of labels and glamour, gossip and superficiality, which, in small doses, is life-enhancing. As is the small fortune I spend in her shop on lots of barely there thingies for my night of passion.

At Frederick's a few days later, an Australian girl called Jottie recommends two diamanté hearts entwined just below the bikini line on the left-hand side, and a Brazilian. She is very gentle with me but it still fucking hurts. I don't swear a lot normally, unlike Karen, who puts Ben Kingsley as psychotic gangster in *Sexy Beast* to shame (I couldn't watch him in anything since without thinking he was going to burst into one of his tirades), but I think I shouted, 'That fucking hurts,' in a range of variations when she ripped off the wax. I looked at myself in the mirror when I got home, and it was all raw and throbbing, but by Sunday morning it has calmed down. The hearts are still intact too, and I don't look as though I've got herpes any more which I consider a good omen. Tonight is going to be the night, after everyone is gone.

But first – Sunday lunch. The fish are fed, the house is cleaned, new linen is on the beds – just in case someone wants to take a peek or the kids play hide-and-seek and find some dirty knickers where they shouldn't. The toilets upstairs and down are shining and the kids are cleaned and looking smart casual – for at least ten minutes, half an hour if I'm lucky. I've managed to get Jenny into a dress after asking nicely ten times and then shouting on the eleventh, and although she's not very happy about it, she compromises because it's red and she likes red.

I've spent five minutes in the shower putting on a face mask while simultaneously shampooing and conditioning my hair and examining my diamantés once again. Mike hasn't seen them yet but I want to wait and surprise him tonight. Each time in the last couple of evenings that I've tried to entwine my thigh around the door before entering the bedroom or come in provocatively stroking my negligee, Mike is either gently snoring or the phone rings just as I'm about to reveal myself. Tonight will be different, though, because the children will hopefully be out like lights, we'll be buzzed on champagne and I will have a sparkling secret. I just hope the diamanté will survive the action I'm happily anticipating. I remember when we first moved in to the house together, before the children arrived, that key-in-the-door moment when I'd get home first and hear the front door open, knowing it was Mike. I would rush to meet him, there would be lots of writhing, pinning up against walls, giggling and the occasional ornament breakage. Which is probably why I habitually keep my hallway empty of ornaments, although there's no chance of any of that nowadays.

I pad down to the kitchen for one last once-over. I've raided Waitrose for chicken, herbs and peppers, which I know the kids will like as much as the grown-ups. Paul, Karen and Julie are similar to me in that respect – they all feed their kids what they eat, albeit in smaller portions. I'm not saying Henry has never had a fish finger, but he wants to have food that Jenny and Tim eat and tells me regularly that he prefers his fish with eyes on.

I've got breads and dips and bowls of olives and root vegetable crisps (although everyone always goes for the beetroot variety, so I don't know why I bother buying the rest) and loads of still water in glass bottles (not plastic as I read somewhere that it gives you cancer, though Karen says everything in excess gives you cancer, even worrying about cancer too much probably gives you cancer). I've known everyone long enough to know who's allergic to what. Jessica doesn't eat dairy or wheat because it makes her puffy and irritable – so Paul tells me – Julie eats anything, even if it's bad for her, and Karen has a fondness for sweet things, so will probably end up fighting over the desserts with the kids.

I did ask them all to bring a dessert in the end (everyone was very insistent about contributing) and I think it might turn into a bit of a competition as they each know they're up against a professional.

I've been fiddling with the last bits and pieces and when my eyes now fall on the big clock, I jump in shock. The first guests are due to arrive any minute. I race upstairs to get dressed. I love colour, especially in the depths of winter, and my wardrobe is a shock of oranges, pinks, browns and mauves. I've also got a small selection of too-good-to-wear beautiful clothes that I collected during my fashion-editor days, which I keep like love letters to look through and remember how things were when I was the polished professional surrounded by needy models, needier designers and impossible deadlines. I allow myself a moment to gaze at that side of my wardrobe and stroke the garments. I doubt if I'll ever wear the Chloé bright-orange-and-brown silk flares or the wonderful lime-green Chanel wool jacket or the vintage Dior black-and-beige dress which I can only get into when I've been ill for a week and haven't eaten for a few days. I shake my head and quickly reach for an old favourite from the other side of the wardrobe, a stripy green-orange-pink-and-brown signature Paul Smith silk dress with a little mauve cardigan and brown suede boots. Henry is dressed in top-to-toe junior Gap and looks rather trendy in brown and blue. Tim is wearing an oversized sports shirt that would look more at home on a rugby pitch than at a Sunday lunch. He's sulking a little as lunch is eating into vital could-be-doing-sport time and Mike had to speak to him sternly this morning about occasionally forgoing sports to do something with his family. He's appeased slightly by the offer of extra pocket money if he helps with handing out the nibbles. Jenny, who overheard Tim and Mike's conversation, has negotiated £3 for herself from her dad if she does the same.

'Where are you, Jenny?' I call, walking down the hall. I haven't seen my daughter all morning since the red-dress debate, and am wondering if she's decided to change back again into her combat gear.

'In my bedroom,' shouts a voice, 'deciding if I should swap any of my dolls with Claire, Mia or Cara, and if so, what I should ask for in exchange.'

'Anyone seen Henry's other sock?' I say, leafing through his sock drawer, knowing I've got a better chance of finding it than anyone else in the house.

'No,' Mike calls from the bathroom. 'I think he eats the things.'

'I don't eat my socks, Mummy,' Henry says, lounging on the bed and looking at me questioningly.

'I know, darling, Daddy is just joking. Has everyone tidied their rooms?' I ask, hoping for a yes, but getting a deafening silence.

'In that case, please get a move on. Everyone will be arriving soon.' I find Henry's other sock under-neath his pillow on top of one of his teddy bear's heads.

'His ears were cold and he needed a hat,' Henry explains, taking the teddy from my hands as I liberate the sock.

Karen and Jamie are the first to arrive with Claire and Simon.

'Jamie, lovely to see you,' I say, giving him a big hug. He looks absolutely shattered, but I don't want to say anything because I personally hate being told I look tired, because, even if I didn't feel tired before, that is bound to make me feel exhausted.

'Lovely to see you too, Lily. Just back from the Big Apple. Brought you some Hershey's Kisses,' he says, handing me a large family-sized pack of chocolate.

'Hi, hon,' I see Karen behind him, wearing what I know is her favourite Paul & Joe outfit, with Simon and Claire on either side, grinning nervously. 'Pavlova, something Carlotta made with strawberries,' she says, handing me a silver-foil-wrapped tray.

Claire is only ten but looks stunning already and she's feisty, like her mum. Simon is seven and in the year above Jenny. He's more like his dad with a dark, cheeky glint in his eyes. He's very easy-going on the surface, but Karen tells me he worries and is quite meticulous about everything, which she thinks is unusual in a boy, especially one of his age. 'He does an inventory of his toys each month, Lily,' she complained once, 'and he gets very cross if anything has gone missing.' He's probably copying her list-making habit, which can't be a bad thing. They're always in neat Mini Boden and Gant outfits and well-groomed, slightly too preppy for my liking. Although when I look at my own kids – Jenny's dress is already dishevelled and Henry has now got two different-coloured socks on, maybe the right one is on his bear's head again – it makes me sigh. A bit more organisation would work wonders here, I guess.

Mike greets everyone and shows them into our sitting room, which leads out to the garden beyond. The kids skirt nervously around each other for the first few minutes, and then Tim suggests that Simon comes up to his room. The girls follow on with Henry and all trail up the stairs.

'Be good!' I shout, knowing they won't be.

While Mike's asking Karen and Jamie what they'd like to drink – champagne – Julie arrives with Dominic and Alexander. She is wearing an ankle-length, chocolate suede skirt, short crimson boots and a long tight-fitting 'God Save the Queen' jumper. She likes to mix and match texture and shade, so the effect is dramatic rather than busy and she dresses her two boys, with their light brownish hair, roughly tousled and just above shoulder length, the same way. If the Fields dress preppy, then the Roses are designer hippy.

'Where's Tim?' asks Dominic, looking towards the sitting room as though the grown-ups are merely an obstacle to the potential fun. 'Upstairs in his bedroom,' I quickly move to the side so as not to get caught in the rush towards the stairs.

'Shoes off,' I shout after them, looking at Julie, who hugs me and whispers expectantly, like a child waiting for Father Christmas to appear down the chimney, 'Is he here yet?'

'Soon, I think. Paul and Jessica haven't arrived yet either, but there are Karen and Jamie,' I usher Julie in as Mike offers her a glass of champagne and a wide grin.

'Pavlova,' she says before she takes the champagne, handing me a silver-foil tray. 'Raspberry, as I know that always goes down well.'

'Ah, pavlova,' I reply, trying to decide quickly if I should mention that we have one already or just wait until all is revealed on the buffet table. I decide to hold my tongue.

'You look lovely, Julie,' says Mike, 'and you do too, darling,' he says quickly.

I smile and give him a quick kiss on the cheek. Fingers crossed Julie won't be the only one getting lucky tonight.

The doorbell rings.

Cara Wilton, Paul and Jessica's youngest, is standing in the doorway, pretty in an apricot dress with white flowers.

'Mummy and Daddy are just trying to park the car. They'll be here shortly and we're very sorry we are late but Daddy couldn't find the car keys and then Titan did a poo on the pavement outside our door, and we had to tidy it up and that took a long time.' Cara draws breath and waits, expecting me to say something. 'So that's it then,' she prompts.

I clap my hands. 'Delighted to see you, Cara. Would you like to join the others upstairs in Tim's room? Jenny and Claire are there as well.'

Cara considers this option for a second before replying, 'Yes, that would be very nice, thank you. Could you let Daddy know where I am, please.'

This six-year-old going on sixteen walks past me, quietly slipping off her shoes without asking, and walks upstairs, calling regally to the other children, 'I'm here. I'm here.'

I turn round and see Jessica with Mia and Paul with Titan.

'Hello, Lilian,' says Jessica, looking immaculate if slightly overdressed in a navy Balenciaga suit. I hate being called Lilian. Not even my mother calls me Lilian, but for some reason Jessica always does. She's admitted to Paul, although never told me to my face, that she thinks of death when she thinks of lilies and she doesn't like the association. Well, I guess I should be pleased about that if anything. To be honest, I think a lot of people would classify Jessica as a grade A bitch. Not to her face, needless to say, but she's hard as nails, too bright and polished, slightly brittle. She's not really friends material, but I think she has as many soft layers as hard, more artichoke than onion, and I quite like her. At times anyway.

'Hi, Jessica, how are you?' Unlike Jamie, she doesn't look as though she's just stepped off a translatlantic flight. How does she do it?

'Oh, fine. Just back from New York and off again tomorrow, I'm afraid. I'm only home for the weekend to remind the family that I exist,' she says, smiling brightly over at Paul.

'I've brought some Hershey's Kisses for the children,' she then says, giving me a hand-wrapped parcel 'and this is something for dessert. It's the only thing I know how to make reasonably well.'

'Great,' I say, not daring to peek and hoping against hope it's not pavlova.

'Now Mia, off you go upstairs with the others,' Jessica

says, gently shoving her daughter towards the stairs. She looks as though she's dying for a coffee. And a drink.

I go into the kitchen and check that everything is ready, putting Jessica's silver-foil parcel next to the other two. Let's hope the kids like meringue. And mountains of Hershey Kisses. The chickens are cooking nicely in olive oil with a smidgen of soy sauce and herbs, the nibbles are being handed round by my helpful husband. Mike has a bowl of olives in one hand and a bottle of champagne in the other as each couple debates who is going to drive home and who is going to drink. Still no Tony.

When the children hear that Titan has arrived, all seven storm downstairs to see him. The deafening noise almost drowns out the sound of the doorbell, but Julie looks up and catches my eye. Not so indifferent after all, huh?

'Sorry I'm late, Lily. I had a mini crisis at the restaurant, but it's all sorted now, and I've prepared two desserts: profiteroles for the children and something light and simple for the adults.'

I look at the silver-foil parcel and I know in my heart of hearts, it just has to be another bloody meringue.

'Thanks. Pavlova, lovely,' I say, trying not to sound ungrateful.

Tony laughs. 'It's not, actually, it's a coconut cake from the Caribbean, very light and slightly tangy. I thought your friends might go for pavlova, so I decided to make something a bit more unusual.'

'Oh, good,' I brighten up and pull him inside, whipping off his coat. 'We've got a table full of meringue.'

The children and Titan have taken over the sitting room and the adults have migrated into the corner, where, from what I can gather, they're talking about New York, with Julie politely listening in.

They all look up at the unfamiliar face and the room momentarily quietens down.

'Everyone, this is Tony. He's on my photography course and he's a chef,' I say. 'And the only one in this room arriving without a pavlova,' I add. There's a bit of a pause, then everyone laughs, shouts 'Hello' and the guys come forward to shake hands.

I try to gauge Julie's expression to see if there's a hint of embarrassment, but she's playing it cool, knowing that we're watching her.

I gravitate towards Karen and Jessica by the olives, keeping my eye on Tony, who is now saying hello to Julie. My cunning plan may work after all. Give it five minutes, and if she doesn't join us it's a good sign.

'How's the golf going?' I ask Karen, breaking up an awkward pause in her conversation with Jessica. Karen and Jessica are more than chalk and cheese, they're like the same magnetic poles unable to ever connect. Karen speaks volumes on the subject if you let her, but I'm determined to defuse the tension.

'Oh, I didn't know you played golf,' says Jessica, genuinely surprised.

'It's for Jamie really,' Karen retorts dismissively. 'He's got a family membership at the local club as so many of his clients play the game.'

'That's great. Jamie's lucky to have that kind of support. Most big deals are done on the golf course or over lunch these days, very few seem to be agreed in the office.'

Karen as dutiful wifey partner is the wrong thing to say. I hastily offer them both an olive.

'That may be the case, but I find the game a bit dull. Oh and Lily, you'll never believe this. Have I got news for you: I've been outted,' Karen then says dramatically.

Jessica looks shocked.

Karen giggles, enjoying the expression on her face. 'Oh, grow up, Jessica. As a non-attendee of mass, of course. The priest keeps a register and Claire's and my names haven't appeared on it for quite some time. Obviously only devoted members of the congregation get to attend their precious school, so Claire's officially taken off the waiting list.'

Jessica's eyes narrow. A school conversation. That is probably something she's particularly good at. 'Well, my parents were Catholic and I didn't go to a Catholic school because my mother hated the nuns. Not too much of a loss, I think. Always praying and singing, when they could have made much better use of their time. So where are you trying for?'

'Probably The Oaks,' Karen says, shrugging her shoulders, obviously finding the conversation exceedingly tedious and turning round quickly to peek at how Julie and Tony are getting on. 'They prove you don't have to have money to get the best education.'

'I agree that paying money doesn't guarantee you're giving your children a better education, but at least the private schools are a little more accountable than their state counterparts. The right schooling is very important,' Jessica intones, grabbing a passing vegetable spring roll from a tray which Tim is now diligently handing round to guests. I don't see Jenny helping with the food so she's not going to get her money.

'You've got to choose the right pre-prep schools which feed into the right prep schools which feed into the right public schools. The strategising starts before you've even given birth these days.' She pops the spring roll into her mouth but continues to talk. 'It's a ridiculous system but that's the way it is and there's nothing anyone can do about it. There's still an old-boy network in the private sector, where one headmaster knows another and all of a sudden you find your child is selected when you've been told the waiting list has been closed for a year. And it isn't enough just to be well-connected or to have the funds to pay for a private education, your child has got to pass the entrance exams, too.'

'What?' interrupts Karen, taking another swig of champagne and sighing, having just missed Tim's tray as he wanders towards Julie and Tony who are talking animatedly. 'It's not enough to be well-connected and rich any more, you've got to be bright as well?' she comments sarcastically. Karen's attitude gets more pronounced with each glass of champagne, so I surreptitiously beckon Mike over with the orange juice. Mimosas for Karen, I think.

'Exactly,' says Jessica blithely. 'Every school wants to maintain its academic grades so even the aristocracy have to pull up their intellectual socks these days.'

'I don't think the state system is any better,' says Karen, shaking her head and irritably waving the juice away. 'It's supposed to be more transparent and honest, but actually it's just as much about whom you know. And you've got the added complication of state schools being told to change feeder schools every so many years, so you may have chosen one school because it feeds into another, but your best-laid plans could be scuppered if the system changes. It makes it very difficult for parents to decide where to send their children.'

Jessica nods vigorously in agreement and I can see that Karen doesn't like that complicity one bit. 'There's an awful lot of political hypocrisy on this subject. I think it's ridiculous that the government spouts on about the sound and admirable choice of state education, and then send their own children to private schools. Politicians are happy to encourage other people's guilt in the matter, while their private beliefs make a mockery of public policies.'

In answer to my beckoning eye-rolling, Tim hurries over with the spring-roll tray, which is now almost empty. Karen and Jessica pinch the last two. I use the interruption to change the subject.

'It must be nice to see the children again after such a long time,' I say to Jessica conversationally, handing Karen the tray with Waitrose mini Indian mix that Mike has just brought over from the kitchen. 'You must have been away for ten days this time.'

'Yes, but it's always wonderful to come back,' she says, looking lovingly at Cara and Mia, who are still terrorising Titan.

'Does Jamie often travel for work too?' she then asks, noticing Jamie playing with Claire and Simon, aided and abetted by Henry, who is pretending to be a Power Ranger.

'Yes,' Karen says, obviously dying to get away from Jessica now, 'and he's off again next week, to Sweden.'

'Ah, lovely country,' says Jessica and a brief, embarrassing silence ensues as we all munch away. I can hear the children telling each other bad jokes, and Julie finding something Tony says very funny. She has such a dirty laugh that everyone starts to giggle. I look over and mouth, 'How's it going?' behind his back. Very smooth, Lily, very smooth.

But she mouths back, just as he nips into the kitchen, 'Wonderful. He's lovely. I have a date next Tuesday!' She beams like the proverbial Cheshire Cat, happy.

'So how's work?' Karen says to Jessica, taking surreptitious slurps from her champagne flute. She's moved over to the window, but I've tugged Jessica along and followed her.

'Oh, the usual. But tell me, Karen, how will you get

Claire into The Oaks? It's so late now and waiting lists will be full?' Jessica takes a small sip and squints as she gets a bubble up her nose.

'Well, I don't know, I'm sure that . . .' her voice trails off. She clearly doesn't want to have this conversation now. 'Tony and Julie look as though they're getting on well,' she then says evasively, smiling over at the couple.

But I'm intrigued as well now. 'Yes, yes, they seem to be doing fine. What *will* you do, Karen?' Admittedly, I have a vested interest in this question.

'Oh, I don't really know. We'll apply and see what happens. Claire's grades are good and I can only hope she'll make it. I think the best thing is not to really get caught up in the hysteria of all of this and just hope for the best. The girls' comprehensive over on Rowan Avenue wouldn't be the end of the world either.' She shrugs, affecting a nonchalance that is partially her personality and partially for Jessica's benefit.

Jessica does her the favour and immediately takes the bait. 'But Karen, you must take this much more seriously. Yes, it might be too early to decide their future for them but the least you can do is give them as wide a range of experiences as possible. Schooling and strategic planning are key to getting into the right diverse network of people. I don't think I would have been the successful person I am, financially and career-wise, without getting into the right school and mixing with the right element.'

Oh-kay. I think Jessica would get along just fine with Lottie and Hetty at the sports club. Before I have a chance to speak, though, Karen does.

'The right element? What the hell is that, Jessica? White, middle-class bankers? Private schools, if that's what you're thinking about, are so homogenous these days that, no matter what their level of academic excellence might be, your children will never experience anything that remotely resembles a cross-section of society. I'd be more inclined to sacrifice a little bit of the academic side and see my children grow up among a diverse mix of people, *real* people. And I think they'll be just as successful as yours.'

'Plus,' I add before Jessica replies, 'people have very different definitions of success. To some people, success is making a lot of money, but it's questionable whether it adds to your happiness. It might make you happier if you're already a content person, but it doesn't do anything for a fundamentally miserable person.'

'It can make them more comfortable,' says Jessica, frowning slightly, thankfully sidetracked from Karen's attack. But Karen's not going to let her get away with it.

'I talk to wealthy, miserable, supposedly successful, privately educated buggers all the time,' she says, frowning at Jessica, who, surprisingly, now looks almost amused. She's really enjoying this, I think. Maybe that's why she's drawn to Karen – she's one of the few who will stand up to her. 'They define their success and status in life by how much they earn and the title on their corporate door. The only ones who possibly see them for who they are are their children, and a lot of these supposedly successful business people don't see their kids very much because they're too busy making money. And when they do have time with their children, they spend it buying them stuff to appease their guilt at not seeing them enough. So, in the end, even kids define their parents by how much they earn and how much stuff they get from them.'

I can't look at Jessica's face, and I also find this just a tad hypocritical and traitorous – Karen is a working mum herself and should know how tough it is. I interrupt quickly, before Karen insults Jessica further.

'We're generalising here,' I say, trying to keep the conversation friendly. 'I think we've got to be careful about inflicting our values on our children rather than letting them learn their own lessons. Also, I think what works for one child won't for another – some kids thrive on challenges early on in life and find their way later on, while others don't and then feel a failure because they haven't made their first million by the time they are thirty.'

Karen bursts in again, obviously fired up by the subject. 'I totally agree, Lily. I'm not saying for a minute that you need to dump your child at the gates of the next inner-city public school and wave them goodbye through the metal detectors, and I'm just as keen for Claire to go to a decent, safe, involved school, where teachers spend more time teaching than disciplining and where I don't have to worry about their minds or bodies every day. But I just can't see the long-term sense in monitoring their education so carefully and closely and, yes, obsessively, always keeping an eye on the prize of academic achievement, networks and success twenty years down the line. All those parents at Somerset drive me crazy, talking about their children like their little robots, needing to be guided and pressed and formed at all times, always striving for perfection and success.

'Children need to make their own choices and experience a breadth of opportunity, and by pigeonholing them by *our* definition of success and our idea of who the right people are, we're limiting them, not nurturing them.'

Karen suddenly stops to draw breath and I have a feeling she's almost expecting applause, but Jessica just sighs, looking deflated (and a lot more human), as if she's heard all this a million times before.

'Well, I'll have you know, Karen, that despite the fact that I apparently buy my children's affection and am an emotional cripple as a result of having a strategically planned education, and that I don't know what I want or who I am, I have a healthy, happy family, a comfortable lifestyle, an adoring husband, two beautiful children, some lovely friends, and a challenging and stimulating job that I enjoy. I am a very contented woman, which rather screws your argument, ladies,' and with that Jessica turns on her heel and joins Paul, who is playing with the children.

'Yeah,' whispers Karen, 'and a chip the size of a fucking elephant. Stuck-up, smug cow. Paul's the reason those kids will grow up balanced, not her. What does Paul see in her?'

I feel almost sorry for Jessica, although I'm inclined to agree on the hysteria front. All these women busy getting their children into the right schools, using ever more extreme measures. I bet most of them haven't asked their children what they really want. Fifteen entrance exams just so they meet the right people?

'Well, as you said, Karen, what works for one family doesn't for another, and it obviously works for them.'

I hope Jessica's not too hurt by what we said. How you choose to bring up your child is one of those taboo subjects that shouldn't really be talked about or challenged because it's too close to the bone.

I look at my watch, realising I've left the chickens in for way too long, and rush out into the kitchen.

The chickens are fine and, as I bring the platter to the table, I can hear calls of 'Everyone line up, please,' from Tim, as Jenny calls out, 'Can we go in height order, please, smallest first, so that means Henry first.'

I stand back and watch everyone compliment the chicken, laugh at the three huge meringues on the table and marvel at Tony's coconut cake and chocolate profiteroles, which look fabulous. Then I smile as I notice Henry has changed into his red Power Ranger outfit and is rigorously policing the queue, making sure everyone gets their turn at the buffet table by whacking them on the shins with a light sabre if they push in.

I watch us all, talking and laughing, Tony and Julie flirting, Karen and Jessica courteously polite, the guys talking about rugby, shares, DIY. I can't help it, but my mind is still buzzing with all these school debates. For some strange reason I thought we'd steer clear of that subject today. Then the full reality of it all suddenly hits me in a flash of ice-cold realisation. All of us might be friends, good friends, but we are all in direct competition with each other now. Even Karen has ended up going for The Oaks for Claire. I've never really considered us overzealous competitive parents or the type who accost other people in the playground about what school their children are trying for, which tutors they're using, how the interview went, is that school any good and who else is going there.

But what happens if one child gets in and another doesn't? Or if everyone else gets in and only one doesn't? I watch the progress of my little red Power Ranger, walking over gamely, copying his older brother, offering a plate of food which consists of one profiterole and two raspberries, and wonder what this competition will do to our friendships.

Throughout the rest of the day and into the evening, as I pamper myself, all three children fast asleep and the house quiet apart from me and Mike (who, I hope, is waiting expectantly in bed), I can't stop wondering what will happen if Tim can't get into The Oaks because

Claire, Dominic or Mia have taken a place that had his name on it. But, I think to myself, forget about it tonight, Lily, you have a wonderful man in your bed and here's your chance for that night of passion. Plenty of time to think about The Oaks tomorrow.

I do the provocative leg movement around the door in black thigh-high stiletto boots (Karen's suggestion). They're extremely difficult to walk in and I've already got the heels stuck between the wood panels on the floor a few times, but when I sashay into the room, tottering only a little, Mike almost falls backwards out of the bed. Great, so at least he's still awake. I do a swirling come-hither gesture and he is grinning at me delightedly, drawing back the duvet and tapping the bed beside him.

'Would you care to join me?' he says, stroking the sheets.

'I might, I might not,' I say, thinking, *right*, girl, don't mess this up. You've got the suspenders, the sheer stockings, the boots, the semi-transparent negligee, you smell of Jo Malone and your sparkle hearts are intact. And you have a man who is ready, eager, slightly pissed and waiting just for you.

I walk to the bed and sit on the side, leaning over slightly on my elbow, my hand resting on my chin.

'Where would you like me to start?' I say, looking suggestively towards his side of the bed and the duvet.

'Here,' he says, pointing to his lips.

I lean over and kiss him very quickly on the lips, stroking his cheek.

'Where else?' I ask.

He pulls the duvet down a little and points to his chest.

I lean over and kiss him quickly on the chest, moving my hand on his chest slowly down towards his stomach.

'And where now?' I say expectantly. This is working so much better than I'd hoped it would.

Suddenly, I hear a faint but all-too-familiar noise.

'Mummy! Mummmmmyyy!'

Henry. Mike and I freeze in mid-kiss, not daring to move, hoping against hope it'll just go away.

But he doesn't do us the favour and after a fifth insistent 'MUMMY!' I reluctantly climb out of the bed and pull on my dressing gown.

'If you fall asleep, Mike Dearl, I swear I won't talk to you for the rest of the week,' I whisper threateningly as Mike falls onto the bed, throwing back his head in despair.

I can hear Henry banging the side of the wardrobe in frustration. 'Mummy!' I totter down the hallway as quickly as I possibly can before he wakes up everyone else and my night of passion – already seriously endangered – goes down the drain altogether. I throw open the door and half-jump into his room as one of my stilettos gets caught on the rug.

'Why did you take so long, Mummy?' Henry asks accusingly, eying me balefully. 'I've been calling you for hours. My bed is all wet. And I'm thirsty.'

I just about manage not to snarl at his reproachful little face, snatch him out of his bed, change his sheets at lightning speed and totter to the bathroom to refill his little cup, and then tuck him back in. He's already looking sleepy, snuggling down with his bear. I turn off the light and quietly sneak out of the room. Just as I reach the door, I hear a sleepy voice from the bed. 'Goodnight, Mummy. And don't forget to take off your shoes before you go to bed.'

I totter back to our room, slowing down to sashaying mode once more as I approach our bedroom door. 'Hi, darling,' I whisper seductively. Silence. I peek around the door and there is my husband, sprawled across the bed in his underwear, fast asleep.

Damn. So much for my night of passion. I sit on the side of the bed carefully, looking sadly at my long black boots. They're quite itchy, if the truth be told, the suspenders are digging into my thighs, and I've already got a ladder in my stockings, despite my best efforts not to snag them. I tug on them impatiently and suddenly some of my sparkles fall onto the sheets. Ominously, one of the hearts is broken.

Chapter 6
My Friend Fancies You

'Aaaargh!' I sit bolt upright in bed, shivering in a cold sweat, and stare at the wardrobe in front of me.

'What's the matter, darling? What's the matter?' Mike says groggily, putting his arm around me.

'Oh nothing, just a stupid nightmare,' I answer, still shaking from a spectacularly vivid and spectacularly horrific dream.

'I was in a TV studio, something like a daytime chat show, with a TV presenter – I think it was the one who interviewed that annoying woman a couple of weeks ago – and she introduced me as the worst mother in England. That was it,' I say, nodding foggily, trying to clear my head. 'She said something like "Hello and welcome to *The Morning Show*. Today we're going to meet the worst mum in England."'

Mike looks at me, more awake now and distinctly bemused, so I try to explain.

'They have all these labels for women like "Rear of the Year" and "Yummy Mummy of the Year".'

Mike looks blank, and then laughs disbelievingly.

'Well anyway,' I continue impatiently, 'Tim couldn't get into any school in the country. I'm not just talking The Oaks, Mike, I'm talking any school in the whole country. And voters from all round the country had voted me the worst mother in England because it was all my fault. And they had that annoying, pompous time-management woman giving me advice about where I'd gone wrong, the sanctimonious cow. And Jessica was on the other sofa, and the presenter introduced her as a "friend of the family" and a family psychologist who looked a bit like Quentin Tarantino for some reason, and they kept nodding and saying I was in denial. I couldn't work out what I was in denial about, but then the presenter looked at the TV monitor and said, "And after the break, we're going to meet Tim Dearl who wants to divorce his parents. See you after the break." That's when I screamed, turned into a vampire and lunged at the time-management woman. There was blood everywhere and then I woke up.'

'Sounds grim. Why all this sudden anxiety?' Mike asks solicitously but, I'm convinced, secretly laughing his head off.

'Oh, just all that stuff that Jessica was saying yesterday

about networking and the importance of getting into the right school. She said that things like joining the golf club are really important and point-scoring in the local community isn't just nice, it's necessary if you want your child to get the right education.'

'Oh, don't be so silly,' Mike laughs. 'She's way too dramatic if you ask me. Let's keep this in perspective, Lily. We can't obsess about it, you know, make Tim all anxious.'

'I'm not being obsessive, Mike,' I say defensively. 'What I'm saying is that we've got to be careful. There's nothing wrong with a bit of forward planning. And maybe Paul, Julie, Karen and I can do something *together* for Somerset and the local community; something that will help our kids' chances and keep us all together in this competition. We've at least got to try,' I say, sighing deeply as I look at all the diamanté sparkles on the duvet. 'And such a shame about last night,' I say, with a pang of regret.

'Oh, there's always another night,' he says, kissing me affectionately on the lips. He obviously doesn't know that diamanté hearts come at a bloody painful price.

'Why don't you arrange to have a coffee with Karen, Paul and Julie after drop-off today and talk through some ideas? You've got a lot of brain power and determination between the four of you. I'm sure you can think of something. Now, let's go back to sleep? It's only six in the morning.'

But I can't sleep. That ridiculous dream is still too vivid for me to settle down comfortably, so I get up, shower and dress and send texts to Paul, Julie and Karen, asking if they're up for a coffee later on this morning.

It's nine fifteen and I've arrived at Letchbury café too early, slouching on the oversized brown leather armchair by the large bay window and slurping a double espresso to clear my head. A lot of school mums are here, as it's just down the road from the Somerset, and I wave to a group in the corner. It's actually a nice change from our normal slightly fancier coffee bar, and it's close enough for us all to squeeze in a meeting after the school run.

It's a grey morning and the clouds are low. People look miserable in the rain, battling against the wind outside the window, but there's a log fire in the café and inviting but fattening cakes on the counter. The shrill ring tone of my mobile startles me out of my reverie. It's Mum. I only know it's her because the *Superman* theme tune sounds and that's the one I've given her.

'Hello, Mum. Are you in the country?' I ask hopefully. A few people lift their heads and glance in my direction.

'Yes, I am, darling. Have I called at a bad time?'

'No, no,' I say in more hushed tones.

'Did the children get the postcard?' Her voice is so clear she sounds as though she's in the next room.

'Yes, they did, thank you. It sounds wonderful, although Tim was concerned that you put yourself in unnecessary danger going to a place with a live volcano.'

'That's what life is all about, darling, and it was a calculated risk. It's not due to go off for another couple of years. How are you?'

'I'm fine,' I say, telling her about the photography course and my next assignment and about Tim's interview at The Oaks and how our interview with Dr Totham went.

'It all sounds very promising, darling.'

'There's only one problem,' I drop my voice even lower, whispering into the phone. 'Julie, Paul and Karen are now all trying for The Oaks, so we're in direct competition. Mum, I find myself not wanting to tell them anything about the interview or give them any tips that might help their chances. Bit of an awkward situation.'

Mum is quiet for a moment and then replies, 'Lily, they are your friends and that's what counts really. It's funny, these days friends are so much more like family – at least you can choose them – and they're much more forgiving. So don't worry too much, I'm sure it'll all be fine.'

Before I can answer she says, 'Oh, darling, sorry, I've got to go. I'm off to Spain next week to see a friend in Barcelona. I've been invited to do some salsa classes and I'm really looking forward to it. Love you, darling. I'm sure things will work out for the best in the end but I'll call again soon. Big kiss to everyone.' She clicks off.

'Bye,' I say, slightly disconsolately, but she's already gone. My mother is amazing, she's so clear-sighted and balanced. And she's a writer, mainly of children's books, although she tells me she doesn't think children read any more. 'They're too interested in Game Boys, Xboxes and PlayStations.'

Mum thinks Tim, Jenny and Henry have enough imagination for the whole of Letchbury, though, thanks in no small part to her colourful bedtime story-telling which has become quite gruesome on occasion and given Jenny an unhealthy fixation with vampires and werewolves. I wish I could see more of her. We some-times joke that if she did see more of me, we'd get on less well than we do, but I don't believe that. Next time we speak I'm going to ask if she'd like to come to a photography exhibition with me. I know she'd enjoy that.

The others show up one by one with their coffees, sinking into the soft chairs. For a moment, nothing but the sound of cups and plates can be heard.

'Yesterday was lovely, Lily,' says Karen finally, opening her eyes and munching on her croissant. 'Thank you so much for the invite. Jamie was saying how nice it was to be with friends rather than just work acquaintances.'

'Yes, I'm pleased with how it went,' I reply, finishing the last froth from my coffee and getting my pen and pad out. 'I think all the children enjoyed themselves.'

'Tony was handsome and looks fit. Nice body,' says Paul in his usual direct way, throwing a furtive side glance at Julie, who now has a moustache thanks to a particularly creamy hot chocolate.

She doesn't notice and immediately falls for the trap. 'Yes, he is nice, isn't he? So lovely. And interesting too. He used to work in the City, you know, and left because he hated it, so decided to work for himself. He got some money behind him, left and set up his restaurant in Hartford.'

'You seeing him again?' Karen asks, leaning forward slightly, trying not to seem too eager for the gossip.

'Yes, we're seeing each other tomorrow. It's his day off and he's cooking me a meal.'

'Oh,' says Karen, clapping her hands. 'How romantic. If I asked Jamie to cook me a meal, I'd be lucky to get burned toast.'

'So, that's a date then?' I ask, unable to quite wipe the triumphant grin off my face.

'Well, I guess so. I don't know yet. He is sweet,' says Julie, looking slightly dreamy-eyed, something I have never seen her in all the time I've known her.

I would love to gloat some more, but sadly we've got work to do.

'Right,' I say, sitting up straight, which is difficult in these armchairs as they're meant to be slouched in, 'great that you were all able to make it. I thought it would be a good idea, as we're all now hoping to get our children into The Oaks, if we work collectively on an idea to help all our efforts.' I pause to gauge everyone's reaction. Nods all round. Interested faces. So far so good. 'It's not too late yet and anything's better than sitting around and waiting. One fact I learned from listening to Dr Totham is that he's very community-minded, and he likes the parents to give something back. I don't know about any of you, but Mike and I do nothing for the community – maybe that's exactly what would make a difference?'

'Do you really think they care about such things?' Paul asks, sounding intrigued but not yet fully convinced.

'Well, Christine Hawes – you know her, don't you, Lily?' says Julie over her hot chocolate. 'She told me that in some areas of the country there's a points system schools use, which takes into account not only the amount of community service your child does, but how much the parents do. I don't know if we have that round here, but it sounds as though Dr Totham subscribes to the general idea of it.'

'Well, there aren't really any other options. He plays golf, but that doesn't give us a lot of scope, it's not like we can all turn up at the golf club suddenly. And he probably likes money. And since we can't exactly bribe him . . .' I trail off uncertainly.

'I think it's a great idea,' Julie says quickly and decidedly. Paul nods, slowly at first, then more vigorously.

I turn to Karen, who's been sitting quietly all through it.

'How about you, Karen, are you in?' I say, expecting a nod.

'Well, I think it's a good idea not to sit around and mope . . .' Karen says hesitantly and you can already hear the 'but' coming. 'But I'm so snowed under with work right now, and I really don't know whether I'll be able to contribute much. And, as you know, Lily, I'm not really that keen on all this school hysteria in general,' she says apologetically. 'I would –' A loud ring from her mobile cuts in and she picks it up immediately, looking relieved at the intrusion and excusing herself with a nod.

'That woman is permanently attached to her mobile,' says Paul as we watch Karen walk outside the café.

I'm confused and slightly hurt by Karen's reaction. Isn't she anxious about Claire? She had strong enough views on the subject yesterday. My disappointment must show on my face.

'You know what Karen's like,' Julie leans forward to pat my knee. 'She's never been much of a team player. She likes to do things by herself; that's why she does the job she does. She probably sees us as competition.'

'I don't think so,' I say, feeling the need to defend my friend. 'She cares as much about it as we do, she just puts a lot of emphasis on work and, well, perhaps she's got a lot on her plate. We've got to respect that,' I say, even though I don't totally subscribe to that myself. I pull myself together and resolve to talk to Karen when I next see her and ask outright about why she doesn't want to help. I know Karen's a self-starter and that she's competitive, focused and work-orientated, but she's also a good friend and she wouldn't do a friend down, except perhaps – and this is the suspicion nagging at the back of my mind – for her family. I banish all such thoughts and try to focus on our plan of action.

'OK, let's huddle closer. No need for everyone to eavesdrop.'

'Charity money, something at the school, for the school, something appropriate for kids, but raising enough at the same time,' Paul says reflectively.

'So not a naked *Calendar Girls* style poster of all the PTA members,' Julie says absent-mindedly, thinking hard. 'Although that would go down a storm in the local community.'

We laugh, quickly trying to erase the various mental images.

'It's got to be something big and public enough to raise our profile in the community quickly, so that Totham gets to hear about it,' I add, scribbling. 'Raises our profile and profile of school.'

'The point is,' Julie wisely points out, 'there are parents at Somerset School who have been involved in the community and helping out for years, and we can't afford to put their noses out of joint. There's going to be a lot of resistance to us newcomers arriving and thinking of something when other mums have lived and breathed this community and school stuff for years. We need a real flash of inspiration, a good original idea to impress not only Totham, but to get past Ms Treadwell and the PTA. Otherwise, they'll see through us straight away.'

'What makes Totham tick?' says Paul. 'Write that down, Lily, because that should drive our thoughts.'

I scribble furiously.

'It's all about community, doing stuff in and for the community. How about organising a fair?' I say, pulling at straws.

'No,' says Julie. 'The idea's not original enough. The

school already has a summer and Christmas fair and you'll be stepping on the toes of the PTA. We need to keep the likes of Jane Anderson on our side. Plus, I think Linda Black is in charge of organising the Somerset fairs and I'm not sure you'd want to take *her* on, Lily. How about organising a spa day?'

'No,' I say, shaking my head, 'too difficult to do and it won't generate enough publicity in the local community. We could organise a fun run, but the weather may still be too cold in early spring.'

'Back to the nude calendar,' Paul says half-seriously. 'We could strategically place rulers and schoolbooks to hide any embarrassment. You could take the photographs, Lily, and it's guaranteed to get a lot of local coverage.'

'Coverage being the operative word,' Julie mutters as we all sit back and contemplate our options. I look at my pad. The words 'Raises our profile and profile of school' and 'What makes Totham tick?' shout out at me but say nothing of substance. I add 'community' for good measure. Whatever we do, Totham has got to be impressed by it. He likes golf. But I couldn't organise a golf tournament to save my life. What am I good at? What do we know how to do? I know about being a mum – that's pretty much all I know these days – and about photography, and I used to know a lot about fashion, and Julie . . .

'Yes!' I say out loud. 'That's it.'

Paul and Julie turn to me with hopeful faces. 'What?' they say in unison.

'We'll organise a fashion show! We'll organise a fashion show for the school and use the mums as models. I've still got contacts at *De Rigueur* and have kept in touch with Angela, Angela Flexor. She's now the editor and would be able to suggest designers who want to target the yummy-mummy market or their kids. We can invite lots of celebrities to the show as well, Letchbury celebs anyway, and that will guarantee press coverage. The fashion world is so into parents and all things parenting at the moment – it's fashionable to have a bump, to be a mum, but above all it's fashionable to be a well-dressed, trendy, sexy mum. This is it.' I slap my pad down hard on the coffee table, smiling as if I've discovered the answer to world peace.

'That's a brilliant idea,' says Julie. 'I'll handle the publicity and I can help coordinate the mums and designers. I can even ask Tony if he'll help with the catering.' She smiles and bats her eyelashes.

'I can help with the logistics and sponsorship, Lily,' says Paul. 'We're going to need money from the local community to do this, and we'll want to do it well. We don't want to fall on our faces here, because it'd be a very public humiliation,' he says cautiously.

'We won't, we won't,' I say, fired by the thought of organising an event I know I'm capable of doing well. 'Julie and I will work on the mums and designers. Paul and I will arrange the sponsorship, and you two can be in charge of the venue, catering and any media coverage we can get. I've got a whole photography class who will be game to do the pictures if I ask them.

And Karen can help a little bit with everything,' I say hopefully.

Julie raises her eyebrows but says nothing and gets out her diary. 'We're going to be stretched for time,' she says, flicking through the pages, 'and there's no guarantee Totham will get to know about the show, or care about it if he does. We have to be realistic: this may not even have any impact on his decision,' she says. 'Aren't we closing the stable gate after the horse has bolted, Lily? And what happens if he thinks all fashion is pure nonsense?'

'What else can we do?' I say, feeling slightly deflated by Julie's seeming backtracking. 'None of us wants to sit around just waiting for the letter, not having tried everything we possibly can.'

'You're right,' says Julie, closing her diary again, 'Let's think about what we want to do this fashion show *for*. Our agenda is selfish – we want, and need, to impress a certain headmaster – but what are we going to put any monies raised towards?'

'Well, since we need to get Ms Treadwell's permission to organise the show in the first place, why don't we ask her what *she* would like to do with the funds?' I say, getting out my own diary to check for dates.

'I think the library needs renewing, but she might also want new computer equipment. Whatever, I'm sure she'll be delighted, and we also need her support with the PTA. We must, at all costs, keep them on side if this is going to work. There was one group of mums in Year Three who tried to organise a bring-and-buy sale last year without advising Jane Anderson, so Jane got Linda to organise a parents' outdoor theatre event on the same day and no one came to the bring-and-buy. It can get nasty out there if you don't ask permission,' Paul says ominously.

'OK,' Julie folds her arms and sits back in her armchair, looking around the table. 'I like our plan. Let's get moving.'

'I've got an appointment to see Ms Treadwell this afternoon anyway,' I say, checking my diary. 'I don't know what it's about, but I can mention it to her then.' I leaf through my diary. 'It looks like we've got to have the show in late May to give ourselves enough time to organise it, and hopefully that's not too late to influence Totham. We'll invite him, of course, or is that too unsubtle?'

'Lily, this is no time for subtlety,' says Julie. 'Of course we should invite him.'

'So is everyone in the country in the last two weeks of May?' I ask hopefully.

'I think Jessica is away the last week, but here the third,' Paul scrolls down in his palm pilot, 'but you can definitely count *me* in, I'm not going anywhere.'

'I'll call Tony. And I bet the PTA mums would be happy to make cakes and stuff; they seem to thrive on that sort of thing,' Julie says loudly, marking the weeks in her diary.

'Yes,' I say cautiously, and wave them closer again. No point in broadcasting our plans around the whole café. We all jump a mile when there's a sharp rap against the window. It's Karen, smiling and waving, pointing down the road, miming that she'll call later. Apparently she's about to take off. I point to our diaries and try to mouth something through the window but quickly give up. She grins cheerfully and gives me a thumbs-up, although I can't quite work out what for, then takes off at a trot. I sigh and busy myself with my papers, studiously avoiding avoid the others' eyes.

'I don't want too many cooks organising this event,' I then pick up our conversation smoothly. 'We've got to keep things simple and the focus needs to be firmly on *our* efforts rather than anyone else taking the recognition, because then the opportunity to shine in front of Totham is lost. If we keep Ms Treadwell, the PTA and parent governors on side, but do all the organising ourselves, we can't fail.'

At two o'clock that afternoon I'm waiting in Ms Grant's office. Ms Grant is Ms Treadwell's secretary and she reminds me of the creepy neighbour in *Rosemary's Baby* who keeps offering Mia Farrow weird milky drinks and cookies to sedate her so the Devil can make her pregnant. For this reason, perhaps, I've never been able to bring myself to drink any of the tea, coffee or biscuits she's offered me over the years. Sadly, she's the power behind the throne and rules Ms Treadwell's diary with a rod of iron. Nothing gets in there without her knowing; and I am currently inked in between two and two thirty, but have made a concerted effort to be five minutes early, just in case.

Somerset School is a one-storey modern building, with fourteen classrooms, two halls, one gym and a very large playground with a climbing frame (built with money raised by the PTA), a vegetable garden and a one-acre playing field, bordered by mature chestnut trees that shed their conkers in the autumn and turn the area into a war zone during September.

The large bright reception, which is all glass, is bordered by the school library (which, Paul is right, is in serious need of renovation), and Ms Treadwell's office. You can't get to Ms Treadwell unless you go through Ms Grant's office, a fact I think she rather relishes. Although there's a music room next door and as Mr Fletcher, the music teacher, is very vocal in his appraisal of his pupils, Ms Grant's office is never quiet, so I'm not surprised that she's constantly irritable, poor woman.

While I wait patiently, deciding to advocate using the donation for a refurbishment of the library as it's something that Henry and Jenny would benefit from as well, and listening to someone tentatively playing the violin in the next room, I look at the various posters and notices on the wall opposite. One advertises a charity event called 'Jeans for Genes', where the children are allowed to wear jeans in exchange for contributing to a charity that funds research projects on human embryos and foetal tissue. I wonder how the teachers explain that charity to four-year-olds.

There's another fête being organised this summer and a request for helpers by Linda Black, as well as a spa day, again organised by Linda and Jane. Thank goodness we didn't go for that option. Just as I start on another piece of paper about an outing for Year Five, Ms Grant calls me in.

I've only been in Ms Treadwell's room a few times since my children have been at the school. None of them have been especially naughty, which is the reason for most parents being summoned, and I know that with three children at the school, I've gotten off lightly not being involved in PTA stuff. And any family with more than two is expected to at least have a stall at the Christmas fête so I must be a very black sheep altogether in the PTA's books.

Ms Treadwell's office is the antithesis of Dr Totham's. It's weird as they're both heads of schools, but their personalities, and the personalities of their schools, are highlighted by the way they decorate their offices and greet their visitors.

Totham's room was quite bare of photographs, but full of books, and had a wonderful view overlooking the sports field. Treadwell's room is full of photographs, with piles of papers by the side of her desk and a large bookcase to the left. There's a rather charming little table and chairs to the right, and some books, which Tim tells me are for children who've done especially well in their reading. They go to see Ms Treadwell and are asked to read for her, and then they get a gold-star certificate and a boiled sweet. Jenny caused a bit of a giggle in the staffroom the other day, when, apparently, my daughter entered into a discussion about Daleks and how they were persecuted for wanting to protect their race and how Dr Who was only interested in it for himself and didn't Ms Treadwell think this was unfair. Jenny got two boiled sweets that day.

'Very nice to see you again,' says Ms Treadwell now, offering me a seat, a simple wooden chair upholstered in white linen instead of the heavy brown leather chairs in Totham's office. Ms Treadwell is fifty-four and due to retire shortly. She's tall and handsome, with silver-grey hair, and always immaculately turned out. She has a disconcerting habit of smiling in a knowing way, as though she can read your mind, which, as she's been a teacher for the past thirty years, she probably can. Despite all the paperwork, reports and requests for information sent from what she calls 'headquarters' about standards, changing standards and testing, she manages to know all the pupils by name. She's what my mum would call a 'good egg'.

'Nice to see you, too,' I say, shaking hands and sitting down in the seat offered.

'Would you like some tea or coffee?' asks Ms Treadwell. 'I always feel like cabin crew when I ask that,' she adds jokingly.

'No, thank you,' I say quickly.

'Just a cup of weak tea for me, Dorothy,' Ms Treadwell calls into the other office. 'Thank you for coming, Mrs Dearl. Couldn't your husband join us today?' she asks, looking towards the door.

'Oh, I didn't get the message that you wanted to see

both of us,' I say, feeling a little concerned. 'Why? Is anything wrong?'

'Oh, no, no. It's just that I asked Ms Grant to request both of you. There must have been crossed wires somewhere,' she says, looking a little annoyed. 'There's nothing sinister I want to talk about, just to let you know that every year the pupils choose their Boy of the Year and this year it's Tim.'

I clap my hands and let out a squeal. This is turning out to be a brilliant day after all.

'I have only just told Tim himself, so obviously you'll want to congratulate him when he gets home tonight, but I wanted to tell you personally.'

'Oh, Mike will be so thrilled.' It really would have been nice if he could have been here.

'Yes, Tim's very popular and you should be proud of him. There will be a special assembly at some point in the next few weeks and we would like you and your husband to be there if possible.' She smiles.

'He wouldn't want to miss it for the world,' I reassure her, and make a mental note to remind him.

Ms Treadwell continues. 'Tim has been such a credit to you and to us. Which school is he going to after us?' she asks, as Ms Grant brings in the tea and leaves again without looking at me.

'We're hoping he'll get into The Oaks,' I say, trying to sound more confident than I feel.

'A fine school. I don't know the headmaster very well, but the deputy, a Mr Elliott, is superb. I would highly recommend the school with him at the helm.'

She sighs, tapping the pile of papers she has stacked to her left.

'Do you still enjoy teaching?' I ask curiously, although I can tell she's dying to get back to work.

'Oh, I don't teach much these days, Mrs Dearl, but I hover around the classes a lot, and I always take assemblies and make sure I know how every pupil is doing. In a school of five hundred that is just about possible,' she says, taking a sip of her tea, which I think must be awful because she winces slightly.

'Yes, well, Tim has always been very happy here, Ms Treadwell, as has Jenny. And Henry will be in Reception next year.'

'Ah yes, Jenny Dearl. Very bright child. I like her sense of justice. Very strong in one so young.' She smiles, obviously remembering the Dalek conversation. 'She'll probably be a judge when she grows up.'

'Oh God, I hope not,' I say. 'She'd have everyone beheaded, knowing Jenny.'

We both laugh. Ms Treadwell picks up her cup to drink, then looks as though she remembers that it's undrinkable and puts it down again.

Now is the opportunity for you to strike, Lily. Ms Treadwell is warmed up, so go for it, girl.

'I would also like to take this opportunity to ask something of you, Ms Treadwell,' I say, looking her straight in the eye. 'We, that is myself and three of my friends who also have children in Tim's year, would like to organise an event to raise money for the school.'

Ms Treadwell looks up in surprise.

'Really? What a lovely idea. What sort of event?' she asks, leaning forward slightly, her eyes sparkling in the light.

'I used to be fashion editor of a magazine called *De Rigueur*. I don't know if you've heard of it?'

I pause for any sign of recognition, but get none, so continue, encouraged at least by Ms Treadwell's expression.

'Well, I thought it would be a good idea to hold a fashion show, using some of the parents as models, and invite up-and-coming designers to produce clothes that the mums and dads could wear on the catwalk. We would manage the event in its entirety, from auditioning models, to identifying designers, choosing the venue, the catering, the publicity and sponsorship, and maybe the monies raised would go towards paying for a new library for Somerset School,' I say without drawing breath.

Ms Treadwell smiles, taking her time to think over what I've just said. 'That sounds a wonderful idea,' she says at last, sounding genuinely excited. 'But may I ask, why now?' Her eyebrows are arched in a knowing kind of way.

I look down at my hands, then up again, and decide on the spot to tell her the truth.

'Well, Tim is very bright and sporty, but I fear that's not enough. Competition is so tough and it seems that not only is he to be judged worthy, but his parents are as well, and their sense of community spirit is part of the package. Frankly, I must admit, my contribution over the years has been minimal. We want to do something for the school and we want to do something for our children. Even if our children don't make it to The Oaks, at least we'll feel we've given something back to a place that's been such a big part in our children's lives,' I say, hoping I sound as gracious as I feel.

'Ah yes,' Ms Treadwell sighs, looking quite agitated for the first time. 'Entrance policies are getting more bizarre by the year. Changing catchment areas, strict entrance exams, scholarships which seem impossible to win, it's ridiculous. This target-driven education system puts children into an academic straitjacket from a very early age. Very little makes me lose my temper, Mrs Dearl, but the admissions system in this country and more importantly in this area is moronic,' she says, more animated than I've ever seen her. She looks at her teacup and takes a sip, winces again, then takes a deep breath, her voice calm again.

'We're not deaf to the conversations in the playground about schools and how many entrance exams pupils are being entered for. Some are being given extra tuition and are unable to do their homework because their tutors give them so much extra work. We have lists of tutors who work with us to ensure they complement what we're doing at the school, but we've had children falling asleep in class from sheer exhaustion. It's sad, but it seems increasingly necessary in a more fiercely competitive environment,' she says, her eyes meeting mine.

'Well, I'm not going to ask Tim to go through all of that. It may be too late but we wanted to try to do something ourselves.'

'I applaud your initiative and understand your motive,' she says wryly, 'but I think you should first speak to Jane Anderson and get her and the PTA on side. Their support is vital. Highly emotive, these playground politics, I find. It's been ever thus,' she says, drawing back her chair and standing up. Some of her phrases and mannerisms are strange and when she sighs and comes out with her little worldly wisdoms, she reminds me of my mum. 'Perhaps we could even get the children involved in some way,' she then adds, her eyes lighting up. 'They would love it.'

'That's an excellent idea,' I reply, encouraged by her enthusiasm.

'We could have a children's fashion show and perhaps organise a competition to design an outfit for . . .' she gropes for an idea, '. . . for mufti day. Our children are very creative and I know there are some budding designers out there. The school uniform is eminently practical but very dull, and I think they would be inspired by dressing up a bit, don't you?' she says, giggling almost like a schoolgirl herself.

'Sounds brilliant,' I say delightedly, getting up to shake her hand.

'Mind you, I suggest you let Jane Anderson come up with that one when you talk to her. There's nothing like letting someone else think they thought of something to get the ball rolling. I remember my late husband,

Norman, always saying to me, "The best way to keep someone on side is to let them think you're on their side when really they're on yours." It's just looking at something from a different perspective.'

'Do you have any children?' I ask, surprised by my impertinence.

'Yes, two. Both have left university and are all grown up. One is travelling the world, filming wild animals for a cable TV company and loving it, although he'll probably be eaten by a lion one day, and the other is a teacher somewhere in Asia. I don't see much of them but they love their lives and are passionate about what they do,' she says, beaming with pride. 'They were naughty at school, of course. Teachers always have the worst children, you know. We make dreadful parents; bags of patience with other people's children and absolutely none with our own.'

'Thank you for your time,' I say, leaving Ms Treadwell at her office door and smiling brightly at Ms Grant, who stares at me suspiciously.

As if Jane Anderson has read my thoughts, I bump into her in reception.

'Ah, Jane, would it be possible to have a brief word with you?' I ask, in the hope that I've caught her while I'm still on a high from Tim's nomination and Ms Treadwell's enthusiasm.

'Well, it'll have to be brief, I'm afraid,' she says pompously, looking slightly flustered. 'I've just popped in to drop off some papers concerning the school fête this year, and the minutes of the last PTA meeting, and I've got to walk Poncho and then come back and collect the children.'

'Well, would it be possible to join you on your walk?' I ask, determined to take action.

'Yes, of course,' she says, 'as long as you don't mind slightly frisky dogs. Poncho is very aggressive at the moment. We've had him neutered and it's obviously made him a bit depressed,' she explains, sounding almost embarrassed.

The extremely capable and rather intimidating Jane Anderson makes Karen look like a dawdler. I don't know if she went to public school, but she talks a bit jolly hockey sticks and I can imagine her in tweeds and green wellies, going hunting and shooting in the country. She just looks the type. Well, she looks like a horse and she laughs like a horse, so that's probably my logic. Julie, who lives down the road from her, tells me she has a large house, a large husband and a large bank account, plus four children. Jane is well-respected and well-connected in the local community, and if she doesn't know something or someone in Letchbury, they are not worth knowing.

'Congratulations on Tim being Boy of the Year, Lily. You must be very proud,' she says as we walk out of the playground, heading towards the gate where Poncho, Jane's red setter, is waiting impatiently. I'm a bit disconcerted that Jane knew the news before I did, but I say nothing. I need this woman on my side.

'Thank you,' I say graciously. 'We're very proud of him.'

'I'm sure you are,' she says, taking Poncho's lead. He's a bright-eyed shiny specimen of a dog, who doesn't look cross at all, just ready to do a 100-yard dash as soon as he gets the chance.

We walk towards the park, Poncho straining on the lead and dragging Jane to the left and right as I try to open the conversation. I take into account Ms Treadwell's advice and broach the subject of the fashion show carefully.

'Jane, I need help with something and I couldn't think of a better person to approach,' I finally say, trying to avoid being entangled and tripped up by leash or dog as we enter the park gates and more open territory.

'Really?' replies Jane, looking as though she's the one needing help at the moment as Poncho spots a squirrel and forces us to head for the nearest chestnut tree.

I tell Jane about the fashion show, outlining very carefully what we're planning to do. No mention of Totham or The Oaks, of course. Just a straightforward charity show.

'And how do we come in?' asks Jane sceptically. I hope she's buying into my newfound school activism after years of dodging her requests. But she is obviously still listening, despite being drawn towards a pond by Poncho.

'I wanted your opinion on this one, Jane. Do you think it would be better to have professional models? Or perhaps some of the mums might be interested . . . ?' I leave her to fill in the gaps.

'The mums as models!' She laughs out loud, all

wariness gone. 'That could be fun. I know some models are oversized but, well, these really would be . . .' She stops, having pulled Poncho to heel, laughs to herself again and thinks for a moment.

'I like that idea. I think you should use the mums. Do you know what I think you should do? Why don't you audition the mothers and see which ones would make good models? I would help with the selection, of course.' She ponders for a while, staring into space. 'And then the children. You should get them involved somehow. Perhaps let them have their own fashion show. I think that's a good idea, although I should imagine the parents will be more competitive about their children than they are about themselves, so you've got to be firm there, Lily, but I think it's a fab initiative. Really fab.'

I'm jumping with joy inside. Almost there. Jane bends down to stroke Poncho. 'Who's been a naughty boy, then?' I watch in disgust as she rubs noses with her dog. The things I put up with in this school quest. Honestly.

'Do you think it would be a good idea to have a competition amongst the children to design the ideal mufti-day outfit?' I suggest, starting to feel confident. Hold it, Dearl, don't get ahead of yourself.

'Competition?' Jane says, abruptly standing up. Perhaps I should have let her think of that idea, too.

'Of course, you may have a better idea?' I say, quickly trying to sound conciliatory.

'No, no,' she says, pulling Poncho away and walking

back to the path. 'That's a good idea. The children will love it,' she says.

We walk for a few minutes without saying a word. Then, as though she's been writing an agenda in her head as we've been walking, 'I'll advertise for mums who are interested in taking part by putting posters around the school and getting the children to take home information in their book bags. Then I will ask Ms Treadwell to announce the competition for mufti-day outfits in assembly next week.' She stops abruptly and turns to me.

'I wish you'd been on the PTA earlier – you'd have been a good one for these events. Well, there's still time, isn't there?' She smiles triumphantly. Another victim for their coffee mornings, cake bakes and Christmas plays.

'Do you know where and when it's to be yet?' she asks.

'No, I wanted to ask you first, it's the courteous thing to do,' I say, trying not to sound too brown-nosy.

'Right, well, you'd better get that sorted, Lily. You know these things need a lot of organisation. Some of those mums will get nasty if they're not chosen, and I'll need to speak to Linda Black, who officially organises most of the main events. But leave that to me, Lily. I'm telling you, sometimes there are almost fisticuffs in the PTA meetings. It can get very heated.' She sounds half-excited, though, so I'm sure she secretly enjoys all that.

I try to get rid of images of Linda and Jane in boxing gloves, whacking each other over agenda points. This is awkward territory. I want to have Jane's input, but I want her involvement kept to a minimum. Still, her influence is useful because she knows everyone and she is a bit of a force of nature of her own which I'm sure will come in handy. I guess it's a small price to pay if it will help Tim.

Collecting the children soon after this conversation, I let Jenny chase Henry around the playground for a bit as I rush to Tim and give him a huge hug, congratulating him on being nominated Boy of the Year. He's beaming with pride and for once doesn't care about being hugged by his mum in public.

'I've called Daddy and he's just delighted, Tim,' I say after I've managed to stop hugging him. 'Very well done, darling. How do you feel?' I ask, half-concentrating on his answer, half-aware that Jenny is now playing dodgems with Henry's tricycle around the playground.

'Very pleased, Mummy,' he says, 'although it means I've got to boss my friends about, which I don't really like. I don't want them to think I'm better than them.'

'They won't,' I reply. 'They were the ones who nominated you so they know you'll have responsibilities, and they obviously think you can handle them.' Jenny has just managed to narrowly swerve away from Linda Black. Linda is now scowling at my daughter and, realising who the little girl belongs to, turning her baleful gaze on me, the irresponsible mother.

Over supper that night, a special family supper in Tim's honour, rather than their usual tea, everyone is buzzing with excitement at Tim's new role at Somerset, Jenny asking if she's allowed extra playtime as she's related to him and Henry asking if Tim now has to wear a crown. Mike is delighted, whispering to me that perhaps we should drop an anonymous note in to Totham, as it will undoubtedly help our case at The Oaks. I can't quite see how we can do that without being too obvious, but it's worth a thought.

Over dessert we talk about the fashion show. Tim is enthusiastic and thinks it will be fun. Jenny thinks it's pointless, until she learns that she might be able to design her own outfit and suddenly becomes interested, wanting to start scribbling immediately. Henry isn't sure what a fashion show is and finds Jenny's explanation of men and women walking up and down wearing new clothes to show them off to other people who wouldn't look as good in them as the people wearing them, totally illogical.

'Are *we* going to be models?' asks Jenny, who would ordinarily rather eat porridge than wear a dress.

'There will be an audition for both mums and children,' I explain. 'And I'm going to be very busy for the next months, so will all of you please be very helpful around the house?' There's always the hope that if I sow the seed now, their bedrooms might remain vaguely tidy, although that's probably too much to hope for from Henry, who prefers to sleep under his bed than on it at the moment, and takes all his toys with him just in case aliens invade.

*

When the children have all had a bath and been tucked up in bed, I go back downstairs to a still-beaming Mike. I haven't seen him this happy in a while.

'Our son Boy of the Year, Lily,' he says, brimming with pride. He grabs a bottle of champagne from the fridge (yes, I've always got one handy on the basis that you just never know!) and opens it with a flourish.

I take my glass through to the sitting room and snuggle up on the sofa, telling him bits and pieces of my day and asking him if he had a good one.

'Certainly not as eventful as yours,' he says, giving me a kiss.

This is looking good.

'Do you fancy another glass?' I say quickly, noticing that Mike has already emptied his.

'Yes, that would be lovely,' he replies, lying back on the sofa and closing his eyes.

As I go to the kitchen, I remember that Karen doesn't know anything about the actual fashion show yet. I waver, as a night in with Mike is such a rare occasion, but curiosity about her strange behaviour earlier today wins and I decide to give her a very quick call. I don't doubt her motives – Karen's too straight for that – but something is definitely up. Well, as I listen to the ring I *know* something is up. She doesn't answer, nor does her answerphone. Karen always, always answers her phone, day or night. Something about being a journalist, I guess. Perhaps she's working. Or spending precious time with Jamie? I leave a lengthy voicemail, explaining all about the fashion show, Ms Treadwell and Jane.

And now, back to business. I return from the kitchen, full of hope and two more brimming glasses of champagne, to find my prince asleep, gently snoring on the sofa. My night of passion will have to wait for yet another day.

Chapter 7
Swot Face

'Don't you just hate men who want sex all the time?' Tamara is bemoaning the downside of having a husband who's discovered the delights of Viagra, and I am seriously considering getting Mike a prescription. The conversation isn't made any easier by the fact that our class is in a studio full of naked models today – well, four to be precise – there for us to shoot. It's a very surreal experience. There is a woman in her sixties who has the facial expression of a bulldog, a man in his twenties who looks cold and drugged up, a woman in her forties who obviously wants to show off her liposuctioned body (Tiffany tells me she can spot the scars a mile away) and a girl in her twenties, who is obviously a student and over whom all the men in the class are salivating.

'It's ridiculous, Lily, Terence wakes me up at three in the morning sometimes, without even asking. He says it's not his fault, and that his nether regions have a mind of their own now, but that's all bollocks. He's just bored and feeling randy. I'm the woman he's met during his mid-life crisis. He was trying to buy a Ferrari on the Internet last week, and he's booked himself a scuba-diving holiday in the Seychelles,' she says, fiddling with her lens pointed at the druggy man.

'Are you going too?' I ask, still making a mental note about the Viagra and wondering when I'll have time to buy it today and if women are allowed to buy it over the counter or if it has to be a man.

'No, I've got a wedding to go to,' Tamara replies, looking the models up and down. 'Anyway, Terence will find himself surrounded by honeymooners all boring as fuck, bonking all the time and saying nothing to anyone, just looking smitten and beautiful. He's also taken up rally-car racing and wants to learn to kite surf. Now I ask you, why does a man in his mid-forties want to learn to kite surf?' she asks now, studying the liposuction model intensely. 'There's a website for married couples who aren't having sex and want extra-marital affairs – I was reading about it the other day – but there's nothing out there for women who are stuck in a marriage where the man wants sex all the time and the woman needs a break. Perhaps I should start one.'

I don't want her to ask me about my sex life, or lack of it, so I quickly change the subject.

'Would you like to come to a fashion show in May? I'm organising a show in aid of my son's school. We're using some of the mums as models and the children will be modelling too, including some clothes they've designed themselves. It might be boring for you, but it's something different at least. You could take pictures?'

Tamara looks at me as though I've offered her the crown jewels. 'Oh thank you, darling, that's very sweet of you. I would love to come. Can I bring Terence and the children, if we have them that weekend?'

'Of course. Although you'll need to watch them – the mums and kids have already started to go completely mad over it. There might be fist fights, screaming matches and stuff like that,' I say warningly.

She looks even keener.

'Are you asking anyone else in the class?' she asks, lowering her voice slightly as if it's a forbidden treat only the initiated can be allowed to partake of.

'Yes, I think they'd enjoy it, don't you?' I say, looking round at Christine, Ella and Tiffany, who's pointing out the liposuction scars on the female model, and at Tony, who's chatting animatedly to Gilbert and Leon about whether they should make the models look their best or just emphasise their major points, whether they're positive or not.

'I wonder if Tiffany will be willing to do hair and make-up for the model mums?' I say, thinking aloud.

'I'm sure she will,' says Tamara. 'I'll mention it to her, if you like.'

'Don't worry, I'll speak to her later on,' I say, making a mental note to ask her.

'You look lovely today,' Tamara remarks as we're putting away our equipment and Gilbert asks the models to do the same. I've worn my Chine short suede skirt, Belstaff leather boots and jacket today, with opaque tights, so I look a little like a trendy rock chick. It's three seasons out of date, but I think it's just come back in again. I'm pleased I've held on to the stuff and it still looks quite good, even if I do say so myself.

'Thank you, Tamara. I'm meeting an old friend from work today and it's rather swanky there, so I thought I'd better put on some designer labels to ensure they let me in the door.'

'Oh, it's that sort of lunch, is it?' Tamara smiles. 'Good luck; you certainly look just the part, Lily.'

I'm enjoying my photography course more every time I go. I like the people and the conversations and the break from my usual routine. Tamara talks about sex and clothes, Tiffany talks about plastic surgery and nutrition, Tony talks about food, and Adam talks about his mother a lot, but he's very funny with it. It seems she makes him do all the housework, despite the fact that she could easily get a cleaner. Christine and Ella are fellow mums but they don't talk about their children much; perhaps they, like me, need a break from the school-selection nonsense that's starting to give me a headache. I haven't had any more 'worst mother in the world' dreams, but I haven't been sleeping too well either.

As I'm leaving, I tell Tiffany about the fashion show and ask if she'd be willing to help out with the hair and make-up. She's delighted and whips out her leopard-skin-covered diary. Tony chimes in to say that Julie has already asked him to help out with the catering and that he's happy to do anything. I refrain, with great difficulty, from asking how it's going with Julie or when they're next meeting and, sadly, he doesn't offer any information.

The offices of *De Rigueur* are in a leafy side street off the King's Road. I have never seen a person within a square mile of the building who isn't implausibly attractive. They all look and walk like pedigree dogs at Crufts, waiting to be judged for their shiny coat, sparkling eyes and whitened, straightened, capped teeth. I feel positively casual, despite the effort I've made today, as I walk in and ask for Angela Flexor, doyenne of one of the UK's leading fashion magazines, but also a good friend who isn't anywhere as scary as she likes to pretend. I called her to arrange one of our catch-up lunches sometime last year and she managed to squeeze me in for an hour and a half. Well, it's turning out to be fortuitous timing. I've emailed her with news of the fashion show, and she's emailed back – or rather got her assistant to email me – that she would like to know more and to help, if she can.

The building is a tall, narrow column on the edge

of the square, with large glass windows that reach up to the third floor, revealing the lift and groups of immaculately groomed upper-crust boys and girls, waiting for someone wealthy and eligible to snap them up. I'm sure there are more assistants than are necessary, but they all look young, hip, trendy and very earnest, carrying bits of paper and files around. I only ever had one assistant when I was fashion editor at *De Rigueur* and that was Angela. She definitely owes me a favour.

I was born in Ilford, so was never really considered a suitable filly, only a potential bit on the side for the clients and publishing directors. I tried to get on by working bloody hard, delivering results, keeping my friends close and my enemies closer. Even though people envied me my glamorous job, I seemed to spend most of my time at work, where most of the men were gay or married, and had hardly any time for romance. Then, one evening, Angela dragged me out to play at Marbles, a private members' club across the road, which would always let you in if you were glamorous and female. It was a cold, wet Monday in October and I really didn't want to be there, a claustrophobic red-wallpapered room, packed with black cocktail dresses, black trouser suits and inane conversations, the harassed-looking waiters carrying steaming mini black choc ices and permanent smiles.

I was one of the few not wearing black; in fact I was wearing an outfit similar to today's: short suede skirt, long boots and biker jacket. Mike was obviously into the designer-boho-chick-who-doesn't-give-a-toss look and he fell in love (he said) at first sight, across the crowded room and all, even though it took him fifteen minutes to extricate himself from the blonde he was talking to. All I can remember about that evening is talking to a young man whose name I forget, a successful film producer (although I'd never heard of him) who then introduced me to another equally boring man, a TV presenter who read the news on autocue really well and had never met a *real* fashion editor before. He came out with stuff that even Jenny the style hater could have delivered with more verve at four years of age. Then I got lumbered with a celebrity cook, who specialised in Caribbean cuisine and told me that everyone knew her there. I was just on the verge of telling her how little I cared, when Mike came over. I wilted and cook, presenter, producer and all the other wannabees in black melted into the background.

The first thing I noticed about him was his shirt, which was a vivid red in a sea of black, and his warmth. It felt as if I'd not so much met my soulmate as met someone with soul. Mike had loads of rich brown wavy hair, cut just about the shoulder, sparkling wide-set eyes, an easy open smile and a gently flirtatious way, without presuming I was interested in him. He didn't use any classic chat-up lines, or at least they weren't ones I'd heard before. We didn't talk about fashion or advertising, in fact I don't think I knew what he did until our third date, and even then he only mentioned it because I made a comment about a poster campaign. I think we talked about colours for the first half-hour and what we liked. A weird and wonderful conversation in quite surreal surroundings. I was fascinated by what he said, the way he spoke, and the way he thought, and we talked so much that we didn't even sleep together until our fourth date, which was unheard of in those days, especially in the fashion world. Angela would reliably inform me that men would expect it on the third date and if they didn't get it you wouldn't see them again. Mike obviously hadn't heard of that rule, or if he had, he broke it for me. Our second date – to Glastonbury – was memorable for totally different reasons. We walked in a crop circle, and although I don't believe in the supernatural, I was fascinated by all that stuff about aliens, energies, stones and ley lines. We ate at a local pub, where we met and chatted to a lot of Hell's Angels who were passing through. Despite their appearance, they were a lovely bunch (I talked to far more aggressive people in my office every day), although they did tell Mike and I that if we ever wanted someone dealt with, they could be of assistance.

He didn't kiss me, not even a peck at the end of our date, but I was hooked. Our third date was in Cornwall, at the Minack theatre, where we sat on hard stone seats for hours and watched *A Midsummer Night's Dream* to the sound of crashing waves. The winds were bitter but provided a good excuse to cuddle up. Mike had gallantly booked two separate rooms in the hotel, which I found enchanting, albeit a little old-fashioned. I remember not being able to sleep properly because I thought he'd knock on my door at any moment and all night I was ready, waiting in anticipation, barely dressed in Lejaby and Wolford sheer silk hold-ups, covered in Jo Malone scent and Dermalogica oils. But he never arrived. By the fourth date, I was so hungry for a kiss, I was climbing the walls, and thought I might have to pounce on him during a performance of *The Rocky Horror Picture Show*. My lust was masked by the fact that everyone in the theatre looked horny, dressed as they were in black and suspenders. And that was just the men. I wore a short black skirt, which I got from Topshop, and a little black bustier from Chine, with fishnet stockings, Lejaby suspenders and shiny black thigh-high boots. We did the 'Time Warp' again and again and again, all the way back to Mike's house. A three-bed Victorian house in Ealing, which took me by complete surprise: high ceilings, original cornicing, and so beautifully and stylishly decorated it wouldn't look out of place in one of *De Rigueur*'s home shoots. He said he'd drive me home, as I lived in Barnes at the time, but that first he wanted to show me the house. I remember walking around his sitting room in high heels that were killing me, black suspenders, a bustier and a long cream sheepskin coat, ready to explode with sexual frustration. I desperately tried to concentrate on what he was talking about, while trying to show him as much as possible without making it too obvious, although in that outfit, how could I not be obvious? By midnight I was still looking through his etchings, all of which were very good, and I had resigned myself to another evening of no kissing. Suddenly I had a terrifying thought that he was gay and I had got the chemistry all wrong. Then in the hallway, he suddenly turned to me, pushed me up against the wall, lifted me up as though I was as light as a feather, pinning my thighs on either side of his waist, and said, 'I can't do this any more.' And before I could ask, he gave me the most overwhelmingly passionate kiss I have ever experienced to this very day, and proceeded to make love to me on the stripped wood panelling, both of us still dressed in suspenders, stockings and high heels.

Our meetings were sexual, spontaneous and rigorous after that, even when we moved in together. I remember the day we moved into our first house, we managed to lock out the guys delivering the furniture because we got randy in the bare, empty bedroom and while we were having sex on the floorboards, they were banging on the door.

The arrival of Tim, Jenny and Henry has meant that the days of stockings and high heels have had to be suspended for a time. But as I approach the big front door, watching all the pretty preening editorial staff waft in and out, their noses high and their hair tied in tight pony-tails, I can't help but smile to myself, remembering those first frantic years before domesticity and children.

Jacob, the fifty-something receptionist, looks incongruous amongst all the young nubile glamour, and sits like a cross uncle overseeing those who enter and leave. He looks as though he's from Essex like me, but in fact, he's an Eton boy who's lived many lives and taken so many illegal substances that he's completely pickled and only good for meeting and greeting those who are even more drugged and wired than he is. He's been here for over twenty years and has become the company mascot.

'Hello, Lily,' he says, chuckling to himself as I walk through the large swing doors and nearly knock myself out. These used to be a lot heavier, but someone has obviously taken some WD40 to the hinges.

'Hello,' I say, trying to regain my composure while being stared at by all the bright young things.

'I'll tell Angela you're here,' he says, picking up the phone. 'How are you, then? You coming back to join the team?'

'I'm very well and I may be re-entering the world of fashion sooner than I expected,' I say, trying to sound mysterious but probably just sounding slightly pompous.

'Good,' he says. 'Lily is here for you, Ms Flexor. Would you like me to send her up or will you be coming down? . . . Right . . . Right. I'll let her know you're coming then. Thank you.'

Jacob puts the phone down and smiles. 'She's on her way, Lily.'

A few men sit on upholstered benches on either side of reception, looking at their reflections in the mirrors behind us, straight through the people sitting there. Front covers of *De Rigueur* are pinned up behind the reception area with anal precision. I remember overseeing each front page when the editor was on sabbatical for six months finding or losing herself in South America, only then realising just how many people she had to please for each cover shot. I met loads of celebrated supermodels, Dominica and Fi, Danni and Toto, complete drug heads who have stuck more needles in themselves than an acupuncturist. At least they were professionals – it's the celebrities who think they are models who are the worst. The models are always bigger than the labels they wear; with celebrities, regardless how well known they are, the brands always wear them. I stare at the various front covers, trying to remember where I was when each one was taken, and sighing at the amount of retouching we had to do on some of them, when Angela appears.

Angela is only five years my junior, but she entered the world of journalism later in life, having had a successful career in Sales. She'd married well, divorced better and decided to do something creative with her life. She took evening classes in journalism and, much like Tamara (but with a great deal more success), decided to make money out of her hobby. I took her on because she was so down-to-earth that I thought it would do our snooty offices some good. She was a breath of fresh air, a grafter, and I knew she'd make a very good editor one day.

The Angela Flexor who greets me is totally different from the woman I first met all those years ago, dressed in T-shirts and combats.

'Hello, darling!' She speaks with a high-pitched voice that could break a champagne glass. 'So very pleased to see you,' she adds, wafting serenely past Jacob and giving me two air kisses.

'You haven't changed a bit,' I say, grinning and keeping my tongue firmly in my cheek but sticking it out a bit so she can see. She's lost weight, but that's usual in this business, and she's wearing a black Gucci number with petrol-blue velvet knee-high boots which I'm sure are Jimmy Choo and must cost well over £500. Her hair is cut into a very short bob and dyed black, while her skin is alabaster pale. The make-up is natural and muted, and she smells of Dior. I ignore her cheek and give her a bear hug, probably creasing her immaculate black cocktail dress, which wouldn't look out of place at a sophisticated soirée.

She grins at me. 'Like the boots? Jimmy's, you know.' She does a little twirl.

'Very nice,' I say, quietly pleased that I haven't lost my touch and recognise style when I see it.

'Well, shall we go, then? We have a lot of catching up to do, and I want to know all about this little project of yours.'

As we walk out, I hear some of the bright young things whisper to each other excitedly. They've obviously recognised Angela, but don't have a clue who I am.

On our way to the restaurant – Olivio Harbour, Anglo-Asian fusion with a nod to modern European, so Angela tells me – we catch up. Well, she talks first and I listen.

'Oh, Lily. Nannies. Aren't nannies a pain?'

I'm not sure if this is rhetorical, so I say nothing.

'You don't have one, right? Well, they are dreadful, take it from me. The young ones are the worst. They all want to fly first class. We offer them their own annexe and a car – a Mini Cooper S, no less, they can even choose the colour – and now they want to fly first class. Well, really, it's just too much. When they're with the children, that's a different matter, but when they're just meeting us somewhere, then they can go economy. I think that's fair, don't you, Lily?'

I have no clue what to say to that but she doesn't give me time to answer anyway.

'You're best out of the nanny circus. But schools – don't get me started,' she says, reminding me that she pays £10,000 a term each for her children, Felicity and Horatio. 'St Edmund's has this open day when various schools in the area come in and promote themselves – you know, bring in the old boys who've all done good and hand out the glossy brochures. I attended one event because I was helping out. Felicity was only six and they said that it wouldn't be too early to start looking. Honestly, they're worse than the Scientologists; they never get off your back! Some were more sporty, others more academic and all guaranteed that their child would mix with the right sort of children. And I think we're the poorest people there, Lily!' (They own a five-bedroom detached house in Knightsbridge and a house in Port Grimaud.) 'I went to the houses of some of the other parents – and their mansions. I daren't invite any of them back.

'And the travels . . . I've been travelling all over the place. We were going to shoot in Thailand, but then they had the bombing, so we rescheduled and then they had the flood, and then we rebooked to go to South America and a volcano erupted. It was OK for hundreds of years and then it bloody erupted just as we're due to arrive. How bloody inconvenient is that? We ended up in Tunisia and all the models got food poisoning. A mystery, as they don't eat anything as far as I can see,' she says, giggling to herself.

I smile. I've always loved Angela's irreverent monologues, and I feel an urge to be part of all of this again: the travelling to exotic locations was always the best bit.

'How are the children?' I ask, trying to bring her back down to earth a little.

'Oh, they're fine. It's Felicity's birthday soon. But enough about us, how is it going with you? How's that gorgeous husband of yours?'

We turn the corner and I talk about my children and Mike, then start on my plans for Tim's school and why I want to organise the fashion show.

She listens intently while we're walking, nods repeatedly, then says, 'Why don't you send him to boarding school?'

'I'm not sending Tim to boarding school, Angela. It may be OK for your children, but we've asked Tim and he doesn't want to board. He wouldn't be happy. Also, we can't afford it.' She glosses over that.

'Oh, they don't know what's good for them at that age, Lily. They're so young,' she says, taking my arm and pulling me along to Olivio's at the end of the street, just past a coffee shop on the right. Angela would probably get on well with Jessica. They share the same views on educating children, but I'm not going to argue the point because Angela is much, much nicer than Jessica. And I need her advice.

Angela is off again, talking about boarding schools and shoes, and how a recent survey reported that an astonishing number of women own over a hundred pairs of shoes, and wouldn't life be simple if footwear was the panacea, a generic prize that instantly ensured a warm glow inside.

I laugh and nod when my eye suddenly catches a familiar face in the window of the café. This is odd. I could be wrong, but I'm fairly sure that the woman sitting there with a coffee, opposite a man wearing a hideous pink-and-blue blazer, is Karen. I haven't seen her much this week, because she's been travelling and Carlotta's had to do most of the school runs, so I can't quite work out why she's here, lounging around in a Chelsea coffee shop? And who the hell is the bloke? It can't be Jamie, mainly because he has decent fashion sense, and Karen seems totally and unsuitably engrossed in this man, leaning towards him, smiling and laughing,

'Do you know those people?' Angela asks, noticing my frown and peering into the window as well. 'Disgusting jacket. I wouldn't allow someone into my café looking like that,' she adds.

'I thought I recognised that woman,' I say, pulling her along quickly, half-wanting to go back and tap on the window. But I'm not sure I should. I haven't really spoken to Karen much in the past couple of weeks. She wasn't at Daisy's last week, and we've been mostly playing phone tag ever since the meeting at the Letchbury café. And yet, here she is now, with Hideous Blazer man. I shake my head, still frowning, but force myself to push it to the back of my mind. I've been looking forward to this lunch for ages, and I'm dying to talk to Angela about the fashion show.

'We're here.' Angela smiles as the restaurant door opens and a tall, slim, smooth-suited man meets and greets us like long-lost friends.

Lunch – tiny quails' eggs, guinea fowl that must have died hungry, a soupspoonful of translucent soup, a handful of salad and a thimbleful of coulis poured over an eggcupful of sorbet – makes me ache for a steak and a family pack of Minstrels. Angela name-drops all over the place and talks about her life, which sounds quite tiring to be honest. She's brilliant on the fashion show, though, and offers lots of helpful tips, suggests free copies of *De Rigueur* at the venue and promises to ask some of her contacts to contribute towards a goodie bag, which could be offered to all those attending. I tell her about my life, how much I'm enjoying my photography course, and about the characters I've met there, like Tamara and Leon.

'You must do a column for us, Lily,' says Angela after she's downed the eggcup of sorbet (even she looks up at the waiter as if to say, 'Any more?'). 'You have such a good understanding of people, you know what makes them tick. It could be anonymous, of course, but you could write a column on . . . on . . . trendy school life:

the mums, the politics and comparing private to public, state to boarding. You could define them by their fashion sense, or lack of it, and be our parental expert,' she says, clapping her hands, delighted with her idea.

'Oh, go on, I think there are probably enough of them about already,' I say, inordinately pleased by her suggestion and leaning over for a roll which is only marginally bigger than an eggcup itself. 'Although I'd most likely be attacked at the school gates for my shocking exposés of PTA goings-on. It's more than my life's worth. Thanks so much for the offer, though, Angela, I'll definitely think about it.'

'OK,' Angela nods, looking at me as though she's won me over already. 'Don't you miss the buzz of the office, Lily? The fizz of it, the excitement, and the wonderful superficiality of it all? It keeps the brain cells ticking in a way that *Teletubbies*, dirty nappies and play-ground puff don't, you know that. I couldn't have done what you do, Lily. I would have been so dreadfully bored. I would have had affairs all the time just to fill the hours.'

Angela's last, unintentionally patronising comment brings back Karen and her mystery man again. She couldn't be having a fling with Hideous Blazer man, could she? Or is that the reason she's been so busy and distracted? I suppose having an affair does take up a lot of time, plus you've got to work hard to cover your tracks. And she wouldn't tell me because she'd know I wouldn't approve. But she loves Jamie, I know she does. I saw them at lunch the other week and they looked so happy together. OK, Jamie was with the kids a lot but he doesn't get to see that much of them. I sigh.

'Right, Lily, now back to this fashion show of yours.' Angela raps her knuckles on the table. 'I think I can help with the clothes as well. There are quite a few designers who are re-focusing and broadening their portfolios to attract the yummy-mummy market and their children. Think Gucci and mini-Gucci, Prada and mini-Prada,' she says, asking the waiter for two coffees.

'I think we're looking more mini-Marks & Spencer or, at a push, mini-Gant,' I say, thinking about the model-mum potential and their offspring. 'We're not talking supermodels here, Angela, we're talking mostly full-time mums.'

'Fine, fine,' she says, dismissing my comment. 'I'll think about it this afternoon and email you with some contacts. I think I know a few people who would be perfect for you: Smokey, Fifi, Pooky and O. They're all good and Pooky does clothes for men, too, and owes me a huge favour.'

I laugh slightly self-consciously. I haven't heard of any of them. 'Sorry, Angela, don't think I know Pooky?'

'Oh no. Up-and-coming designers who are very *De Rigueur* and will actually be featured in one of our autumn issues. So you'll catch them before they're hot. Perfect, Lily, I'll make the introduction so it'll be easier for you,' she says, smiling at the waiter as he brings up two thimbles of espresso. Doesn't anyone ever eat or drink in this place?

Then, for half an hour, Angela relaxes back into the

person she was over a decade ago, and talks about her parents and how proud they are of her, and how she misses the children sometimes and how the gloss of the all-black parties is starting to tarnish a bit, and how she might give up her crown some day soon to travel or do something else 'more real', as she puts it.

'Everyone thinks this job is so glamorous, Lily, but it's not all glam and glitz, is it?' she says, slouching a little in her seat. 'Oh yes, it's one of the top jobs, but it doesn't really feel real. It's so nice to see you. I still remember you giving me a chance when I started. I hadn't much glam and glitz to offer, just determination, but you saw past all that. Now, everyone treats me like their best friend, but it's good to know who your real friends are,' she continues, grabbing hold of my hand, which I find quite touching.

After Angela has gone an hour over her tight schedule by chatting about life pre-fashion, she promises we'll see each other more often this year and invites me and the family down to her place in France, on the condition that I keep Jenny on a leash. The last time we were invited, my daughter set the geese free because she learned (by accident) how foie gras was made. Angela was not pleased.

'So,' she says as we walk out of the restaurant. 'I'll talk to the designers and also see if they know anyone who can provide a catwalk, marquee and sound system at cost. Otherwise it'll get too expensive. If they know I'm in the audience, you might even get it for free,' she says, winking conspiratorially, leading the way back to the main road. I take a brief look in the window of the café as we pass, but Karen and her mystery man have gone.

I hug Angela in front of the large doors of her office, creasing her black Gucci number again. As I watch her stride through the foyer, I can already see her reaching for her mobile and starting to talk, reminding me forcibly of Karen.

As I'm heading back to the station, I try her again but once more there's no answer and her voicemail clicks in.

'Hello, Karen, this is Lily. Hope you're well. Just wanted to catch up and let you know what's going on with the fashion show. Big kiss.' Well, technically she doesn't know much about the fashion show yet but maybe this will be an incentive to call me.

I click off, confused but more determined than ever to make the fashion show a success. As Angela said, it's good to know who your friends are, and despite her curious behaviour, I'm still counting Karen as one of mine.

Chapter 8
Bundle

Supermodel mums wanted for fashion show in aid of the Somerset School library fund. No previous experience required, just ability to walk – possibly in high heels – and smile at the same time. Dress rehearsals in April, fashion show scheduled for 24 May, venue TBC. All those interested, please attend the auditions in Ms Constantine's classroom, to the right of the junior school corridor, at 1:30 p.m. on Friday, 16 March.

Ms Treadwell, Jane and I are standing looking at the notice which has been up for a week outside Ms Grant's office and has been sent to all the parents in the PTA newsletter via the children's book bags.

'Jane and I received quite a few queries from parents wanting to know if "supermodel mums" meant someone who set an excellent example as a good mother or a supermodel who happens to be a mum,' said Ms Treadwell wryly.

It's 16 March and to say that the notice has generated a lot of interest would be an understatement.

'Ms Treadwell,' Jane whispers, turning round to survey the queue of women, some extremely heavily made up and wearing evening wear, sitting patiently and expectantly in the school corridor, 'perhaps I should have added "casual dress" on the notice.'

We flee into the classroom, the science room to be exact, with two huge posters of the human body and its muscular structure on the walls alongside a life-sized skeleton, which Tim tells me is called Herbert, dangling from the top left-hand corner behind Ms Constantine's desk. Like all the classrooms at Somerset, the room is very bright, with huge windows looking out over the fields and the clear, blue skies outside. The children's desks have all been pushed to the side so that we are able to ask each applicant to walk up and down and evaluate their stride and general attitude. I feel as though I'm one of the judges on *UK's Next Top Model*, unworthy creature that I am.

'And thank you for organising the children's fashion side of it so well, Ms Treadwell,' I say as we sort through lists of names, realising that she's taken a lot of the politics out of this competition by reassuring parents that everything is above board and that every child will be considered fairly and squarely. I'm just relieved that Ms Treadwell, and not me, will be judging that competition.

'It's a pleasure, Mrs Dearl. We're holding the auditions for that one tomorrow,' she says with a smile. 'The children, admittedly mainly the girls, have been very excited about the prospect of being on the catwalk and designing their own outfit. Everyone in the playground is talking about the fashion show. There have been a few cuts and bruises as children have argued about who has the most beautiful mummy and most handsome daddy, and unfortunately I think there's been quite a bit of supermodel-style behaviour, but we're trying to curb the tantrums and keep it as orderly as possible,' she adds. 'The boys have been fine, really. They're not interested at all. They have their football.'

I look at the throng of mums outside the classroom, half-hoping to maybe even see Karen's face there, if only for her jokes and teasing, but she's not there. I saw her only briefly today as I dropped off the children. She was kissing Claire and Simon goodbye, waved at me and immediately put her mobile to her ear. I'll call her later.

'Right,' says Ms Treadwell decisively, turning to face me and Jane. 'It's nearly half past one, so we'd better get started or we will be here all night.'

'Yes, but before everyone comes in,' I say sitting down, 'let's decide quickly how many models we are looking for.'

'Why don't we aim for around ten and hope that it

will become blatantly obvious when we see who's suitable?' says Ms Treadwell. 'And do we yet know what the mums will be wearing?' She looks at me expectantly.

'No, Julie and I are meeting the designers just after the Easter break, so in about three weeks. We thought if we pick ten, then the designers can either pick two or three, depending on their busy schedules and we're taking pictures of the mums to bring along, so the designers can select the ones they'd like to dress. We thought that would be easier,' I say tactfully, knowing full well that if the designers had the choice they would all choose the emaciated-looking ones.

'Good idea,' replies Ms Treadwell, smiling as if she has read my mind.

'And if there are any dads auditioning,' I add, 'that would be great as well, as one of the designers works with men's fashion. All in all, the show should probably last about forty-five minutes in total, with a ten-minute interval halfway through, so that everyone can have something to eat and drink. The evening should be fun for all of us, not give the mums hernias trying to dress and undress in double-quick time.'

'From what I hear, some of the mothers waiting are very well-rehearsed in getting their kit off quickly, Lily,' says Jane, so completely unexpectedly that Ms Treadwell and I both burst out laughing.

'Make sure to point those ones out to me, Jane,' I say, nudging her cheekily. 'Might come in handy.'

Ms Treadwell looks at us more seriously. 'Now, ladies, just a last word of caution. This all has to be totally above board. Some parent-governor mothers have already complained that the fashion show would encourage competitiveness, superficiality, anorexia and spoilt behaviour, in the playground and at home. I'm afraid Linda Black is the main problem. She's always up in arms about one thing or another.'

'Did you know,' Jane leaned forward conspiratorially, 'that her husband tried to sue the school a few years ago because we chose their daughter as one of the elephants in the school nativity? He said we were causing their daughter psychological damage.'

She smiles at me and despite her friendliness I shiver slightly. 'Just leave Linda to us, Lily. If she approaches you in the playground, be nice and smile and talk about the weather, and don't feel intimidated in any way.'

I'm starting to feel a bit anxious about all this. Intimidation in the playground? Talk about the weather? I'd been so sure that once I got the PTA and Ms Treadwell on side, that would be all the politics I'd have to deal with, but there's obviously a lot I don't know about.

'I don't want the fashion show to cause problems for either of you,' I say hesitantly.

'Don't worry, Lily,' says Jane, 'we'll deal with it. The initiative is excellent, the library could really use a makeover. And the children's competition for designing an outfit nurtures creativity and encourages entrepreneurship. Women like Linda are just jealous because they didn't think of the idea, and we did,' she says, folding her arms. Well, I did actually, but I think it's wise to say nothing as Ms Treadwell catches my eye.

'Right, Mrs Anderson,' she says, turning to Jane, 'I've asked Ms Grant to wait five minutes between mums so we can debate each woman's merits. You understand the politics of the playground better than any of us, so I'll leave it to your better judgement who absolutely needs to be included on the catwalk, and who' – she pauses briefly here – 'should we say, we'd be able to gracefully reject without fear of retribution.' Jane nods and smiles, with the look of a woman who has experienced and survived many a political storm in a coffee-morning cup.

'I suggest we give each mother a mark out of ten and make a note of their key points to make a first list of candidates,' I say, handing out A4 pads and pens. 'Then we can see if we have a balance between slim mums and shapely mums. This is, after all, a chance to show designers that they need to dress real women rather than twigs. OK, I think that's it. Ready?'

'Ms Grant,' calls Ms Treadwell, projecting her voice across the classroom without shouting, 'can you let the first one in please?'

The door opens on Andrea Jeremiah who has a son, Daniel, in Tim's year. She's a Sweaty Betty mum, as Julie would call her, always picking up and dropping off her two boys in a tracksuit top and leggings. She's an ex-model and I remember her from some of *De Rigueur*'s fashion shoots – always professional and polite, never late or drunk. She hasn't lost her looks or her figure, thanks to regular trips to Letchbury Spa to have facials (so I'm told) and has a personal trainer who encourages her to run fast round Letchbury Park three days a week. Her whole family is bright, athletic and loud, constantly tanned and, coming from California, still has that irritating West Coast twang. The PTA have unkindly and very openly nicknamed her the school floozie – unfairly I believe, and mainly because most, if not all, of their husbands, fancy her.

'Hello, Andrea,' I say with a welcoming smile, even as I feel Jane freeze up next to me. She may be political dynamite but she will be ideal for the designers, so I've got to give her a ten. Cleverly, Andrea has dressed down in black opaque tights and kitten-heel shoes, a simple skirt and jumper that's just tight enough but not so much that her chest juts into your face.

'Could you walk up and down,' I say, 'and do a turn?'

Andrea smiles and gracefully, silently turns. She twirls and sashays as though she's walking on a cloud, not in a classroom, holding her shoulders back and her chin high. Her smile shines from her eyes, her mouth gently pouting. She keeps her eye line steady but doesn't look any of us in the eye. She turns again and finally comes to a halt in front of us, standing directly in front of Ms Treadwell.

'Thank you, Andrea. We'll be making our choice this evening and calling the selected mums tomorrow morning. The show, as you know, is on 24 May and there will be a dress rehearsal a week prior to the event. Will you be available?' I ask.

'Yeah,' she nods enthusiastically. 'I'll definitely be in the country. And I'd be delighted to represent the school. I think this is a wonderful, absolutely fabulous idea, I really do. And if there's any way I can help, let me know. Thank you for, well, thank you,' she says, quite modestly in my opinion, because in her *De Rigueur* days she wouldn't have got out of bed for less than five grand a day.

When she's gone I say nothing and wait for Jane or Ms Treadwell to comment.

'Well, she's ideal,' Ms Treadwell finally admits graciously, 'but she's not exactly the most popular mum in school, is she, Jane?'

Jane bobs her head up and down, clearly trying to formulate the least offensive answer for Ms Treadwell's sake, so I say quickly, 'Well, what do you say we heavy-pencil her in for now and see who else there is? Andrea is relatively well-known as a model, so she would also be a draw.'

'Well, OK then,' Jane finally speaks. 'If you think so. But get her to wear the simpler stuff or I'll never hear the end of it.' She sighs.

'I agree,' nods Ms Treadwell. 'If she makes the others look bad, that wouldn't be good for school morale.'

I wonder if they ever had these problems on *UK's Next Top Model?*

Next in line is Tina Gerard. She's one of the PTA members and very outdoorsy, with dark hair, and she looks as though she could sling a good right hook. When we ask her to walk and turn, she scowls and proceeds to trot like a man: striding along flat-footed, legs slightly apart and pelvis forward. I notice that her eyebrows need plucking. She runs a lot of marathons so has chunky thighs and no definable ankles. Nonetheless she gets a definitive yes from all of us, probably out of fear more than anything else.

Then there are Tracy Francis (no waist, nice smile), Tanya Reed (all tits and lips, no chin) and Antonia Marlow (jolly hockey sticks, looks like a rabbit and laughs like a drain). We mark them down as not quite right for the show.

Ella Fritz, one of the two mums who attend my photography class, is next, looking absolutely terrified. She's wearing a black cocktail dress and high heels that even Andrea would find difficult to walk in, let alone turn. The black makes her look even thinner than usual and she's wearing an awful lot of make-up, with more of a clown-like effect than anything else. Her hair is tied back tightly in a pony-tail, and when she tries to smile it comes out as a weird crooked grin. Ella might be thin enough to be a model, but her posture is terrible. I'm concerned that the designers will revolt if we include her, but I'm also aware that her fragile self-esteem will take a bashing if we don't. And I like her. Not that that should be my prime criterion, but I do. After her tentative walk and twirl, and lots of Japanese-style bowing on her part as she exits the room, we discuss her.

'Can we put her on the catwalk?' Jane asks matter-of-factly. 'I'm worried she'll be too self-conscious if we pick her and even more self-conscious if we don't.' Jane and Ella are quite close friends, outside the PTA at least.

'We're not counsellors or psychologists here, Jane, we're just choosing models for a fashion show, to raise money for the school library, and if we look into every case too deeply we might as well start interviewing them *Miss World* style, you know, asking if they had a wish, would it be world peace and all that,' Ms Treadwell says firmly, scrawling notes on her pad.

'I agree with both of you,' I say diplomatically, 'but I know, the designers like to work with someone who's very slim. At the moment we only have Andrea and Ella, all the others are, well, on the larger side.'

'We need more generously proportioned models, too,' Jane bristles, obviously taking slight offence because she can't be under a size 16 herself.

'I agree,' I say, 'but at the moment, that's really all we've got, with a few notable exceptions.'

My point is taken and Ella Fritz is included on the list.

Ironically, the next one to walk through the door is Christine Hawes, the other Skinny Lizzy in my photography group. She's not wearing black and isn't anywhere near as nervous as Ella but manages to do a twirl, walk and look genuinely happy to be there. She's a yes.

Charlotte, who hasn't had any comeback from the wheelie-stick man, is given a polite no because Ms Treadwell thinks she's not right. I do know that she's heard about the incident from some of the other mums, so maybe she feels that Charlotte would be a bit of a loose cannon in something related to the school issue? Harriet Jones, a very pretty mum in her mid-forties, with a son in Tim's year, is also a no, mainly because she's unable to commit to the dates. And a very disappointed Ms Constantine is also declined, Ms Treadwell having to explain in quite a lot of detail to the fifty-something science teacher that the fashion show is only for the mums. She leaves the room mumbling to herself, but watching her quite sturdy frame slam the door shut, we all feel we've made the right decision.

Suzanne Morrison, who looks immaculate in an evening gown and full make-up, twirling with flair, obviously for a moment forgetting her angst about school selection, is definitely in. And Daniella Frost looks a yes as soon as Ms Grant opens the door. With her long legs, long body, long arms, open smile and shiny red hair, she looks like a cross between a pedigree red setter and a sexy spider. The designers will love her.

After a few Mrs Pepperpot types and even a turn by Ms Grant – she always wanted to be a model apparently – Sally Day walks in. She's still living with her mum and the catchment-area angst has her looking tired and stressed. Mousy, about five eight in height, with light brown hair and a wide smile, she seems the least likely candidate.

After she goes and Ms Grant closes the door, coming in briefly to announce that Sally is the last of the mums and there are no dads on parade, we all sit back exhaustedly.

'Well, obviously Sally's a no,' Jane says and starts shuffling together her papers, then getting out her compact to dab her nose. It's hot and stuffy in here.

'I disagree,' I say, forgetting the promise I made to myself to hold my tongue and try to be conciliatory. 'Sally has potential. Wouldn't it be great to transform one of these women so they could hardly recognise themselves? It might give them a huge confidence boost.'

Ms Treadwell laughs, clearly as glad as Jane and I that the parade is over. 'Lily, I think we're probably aiming too high there,' she says. 'The most we can hope to do is raise funds for the school library. To aspire to turn a wallflower into a rose, well, I don't know about that.'

'Maybe we *should* consider her,' says Jane after a pause, perhaps remembering her loyalties. 'Sally has always done a lot for the school, helped out with fêtes, assisted on trips, and bought raffle tickets for prizes I'm sure she didn't want to win. She was brilliant at the harvest festival.'

'Well then,' says Ms Treadwell, 'it seems we have more than enough female models to choose from, and no men. How very disappointing.'

'I know Paul Wilton might be game. He's helping out with the organisation, but he's fit,' I say, once again opening mouth before engaging brain.

Jane giggles. 'That's nice to know, Mrs Dearl, I'll make a note of that,' she scribbles furiously.

'I know another guy called Tony Herald. He's at my photography class and he's offered to do some of the catering, but he might be interested as well,' I say, standing up briefly to stretch my legs and think on my feet.

We spend a good fifteen minutes talking through the candidates' physical and political merits. It's not a conversation I'd ever like to see leaving this room and I hope to God no one is eavesdropping. In the end we decide on Tina Gerard (because she's deputy chair and Jane owes her a favour), Jane herself (because she's Jane), Daniella Frost, Suzanne Morrison and Andrea Jeremiah (because the designers will love them), and Christine, Ella and Sally because we know they'll get a lot out of it. I nominate Julie in her absence, because she says she'd love to have a go and I confirm Paul as the token male, hoping he'll take it in good spirits. We decided against Tony in the end, as he'd have to focus on the food. I'll be organising and MCing on the day, so have, regretfully, declined the chance to be on the catwalk.

'I'll call those who were unsuccessful myself,' says Ms Treadwell. 'They'll be placated by the knowledge that they won't have to make fools of themselves in front of everyone.' She laughs.

'Thank you both so much for your support. We couldn't have done it without you. It's a minefield out there and you were amazing,' I say gratefully.

They both smile, surprised. 'We do this sort of thing all the time, Lily,' says Ms Treadwell philosophically, putting away her papers. 'We're old hands, aren't we, Jane, at making everyone think they've won when really no one has. But when something like this comes along, a new initiative that's fun and which the children can get involved with as well, then the school benefits and everyone wins.'

'I totally agree, Ms Treadwell,' says Jane, brushing herself down and bending her knees slightly so they crack. 'Ooh, my joints. What was I saying? Oh yes, do you have a venue yet?' she asks, putting on her coat.

'No, but we're looking. We're hoping to find a large field locally for the marquee.'

'You could always use our field,' offers Ms Treadwell helpfully, 'but it may be too muddy. Putting up the bouncy castle for the last school fête was a real hoo-hah, wasn't it, Jane?' Jane nods vigorously. 'Horrific. Anyway, it's a good fallback but I'm sure if you ask around at the local sports, tennis or golf clubs, they may have something to offer.'

'Great, yes, I'll sort something out. At least we have our models now,' I say, as we hustle out the door. Four o'clock on the dot. Mike is working late again tonight, and all the children have been organised on play-dates and teas, just in case we were going to run over.

As I drive home slowly, relishing the fact that no one will be clamouring for my attention for a while, I think about the venue again. Perhaps we could consider my sports club, or one of others' – perhaps they'd like to sponsor the event in some way? I must chase Angela about the marquee, lighting and catwalk contacts she promised, and then I've got the designers to meet week after next. I giggle, thinking of their names. What sort of mother would call their child Smokey Popham?

Just as I get out my phone beeps and when I pull it out of my bag, I see that Karen's sent me a text. *Hi hon – sorry so frantic lately, catch up soon, promise. x.* I don't want to call again, to sound desperate and pestering, so I'll leave it and sit in tonight, working on preparations for the fashion show. I've also got some course work to do, taking photographs of children asleep, which mine never seem to be.

It's grey and gloomy and I'm thankful for the rare moment of silence that greets me as I walk into the house. The sitting room is warm and cosy, with its large sprawling sofas and magazine-covered coffee table, and I switch on the lights which always flicker a few times before coming on. Just as I dump my papers on the dining-room table my phone rings.

'Hello, darling, it's Mum. I'm in New York. I'm staying here with friends. You know the Greens? Anyway, I'm calling to see how you are?'

I tell Mum all about the auditions, which she finds hilarious. She agrees with my decision to include Sally Day in the final line-up and thinks that Linda Black sounds like a possible but not an insurmountable problem.

'I'll definitely come too and applaud your efforts, Lily. I'm so very proud of you. Oh, gotta go. Speak soon, my love,' and she goes, leaving me once again to my silent house.

Chapter 9
Eggheads

It's the beginning of April and the Easter break at Somerset School. As well as organising the kids for their various football, hockey and rugby games, Easter egg hunts and play-dates, from which the children usually return completely shattered, there is also the long-standing Easter holiday break in Cornwall which we do every year. I've booked a four-bedroom cottage not far from Penzance, which has lovely views over the bay. The children love to go to the beach and hunt for bits of driftwood, then Tim tells the other two children gory and imaginative stories about the wood, which he says comes from ships that have been smashed on the rocks, raided by pirates, possibly

Vikings, and how all the sailors were cut to pieces and fed to the sharks. Henry now wants to be a pirate or a Viking, although I don't think he's quite sure what a Viking is. Jenny wants to be a shark. I know a psychologist would have a field day with my children.

I have a soft spot for Cornwall, because that's where our honeymoon was. We got married four months into our relationship, something that was very un-PC in those days; now, of course, getting married at all is un-PC, even more so staying married for decades. I didn't care. I was still at that stage when every time I heard Mike's voice, smelt his aftershave or felt his touch, my heart missed a beat. I'd always thought that sort of stuff only happened in cheap romance novels, but I swear I could feel the electricity every time he walked in the room. The thought of him made me breathless. I didn't care about work or eating and skipped out every morning in the shortest skirts and a big smile. We had a simple wedding ceremony in a small chapel in South London. Everyone in the office wanted it to be in Tuscany and feature it in the magazine, but we just wanted family. No one cried and everyone went to Le Manoir afterwards and drank too much champagne and fine wine and ate wonderful food, and made speeches about two people who were so much in love, so right for each other and so lucky. No soppy poem about 'What love is', which I seem to hear at every wedding I go to these days (and used to hear at the ones that have ended in divorce a few years later).

We drove down to Cornwall in his red Spitfire, his first ever car, which was an old rust bucket, breaking down a few times en route. We barely had any summer that year, and it should have been horrible, but we didn't feel the cold. We had so much fun. Mike would whisk me off in the early morning and tell me we were going somewhere, like a secret cove or a hidden garden or a peak with the most amazing view, and it was always simple and wonderful.

I remember making love in the hallway and the kitchen, on the sink, on the cooker, in the sitting room, bathroom, downstairs cloakroom, all of the three bedrooms, by the windows and on several window ledges. I don't know if Cathy got really intimate with Heathcliff on the moors, but we did. I found my Mr Darcy, Heathcliff and Mr Rochester in Mike as well as my emotional, physical and intellectual equal. I remember not being able to tell anyone about the honeymoon when we came home – what we had seen, who we had met, what we had done – because it was too private, and I'm not poetic or clever enough with words to express such complete happiness. The memory of that wonderful time always makes me smile inside, but these days there's also a faint sense of regret. Because despite knowing that the breathless, passionate, heady, electric feeling of your honeymoon never lasts, I quietly mourn its loss.

Needless to say, our Cornwall breaks are very different these days. We still have fun, but it is family fun. We visit the exotic and colourful gardens, most of which start with Tre-something. Then there are the castles, where King Arthur was supposed to have visited or stayed at some time and where witches have cast numerous spells, and the small, quaint hamlets where modern-day witches are still supposed to live. In the castles, the children fight imaginary dragons and ogres and win their victories gloriously with lots of blood and noise. Then there are the visits to the steam railways, the seal and otter sanctuaries and the bike rides, and, of course, the beach, where the children like to collect crabs, play hide-and-seek, create ingenious sculptures with sticks and stones, and scrawl their names. They'd live and sleep on the beach if we didn't physically drag them away at the end of the day.

In the early evenings we play Monopoly and Scrabble, Articulate and Cluedo. Jenny gets very competitive and aggressive, and for some reason I'm always the murderer or the victim. We have Easter egg hunts, kindly leaving a few behind for next year.

Our annual Easter holiday in Cornwall is the one and only time in my life when there is no diary, no time management, no clocks, no wake-up calls, no schedule, and the only occasion I ever feel I have all the time in the world for myself and my family. And it always goes by all too quickly.

When we get back, the fashion show is literally just around the corner and we need to organise everything with military precision. We had agreed to meet again after Julie and I have seen the designers, so two weeks from now, and there's still a lot to do. I put a typed colour-coded schedule on the kitchen wall for everyone, including myself. For once, I'm just as busy with my own stuff as with everyone else's, and my family will have to help out. I might even have to log onto Ocado at this rate.

I finally saw Karen, albeit briefly, at kick-boxing but although she was full of chat, she didn't mention anything out of the ordinary. If anything, our meeting left me both more reassured and more anxious.

Fortunately the photography class has been taking a long break for Easter although I have homework to do – the theme being 'my family at leisure'. I don't think any of us has time to chill, I ponder, as I contemplate the schedules which seem to have Tim in two places at once, including a new Sudoku club some geek parent at the school has agreed to oversee. And Jenny is triple-booked on Thursday afternoon. How did this already go wrong?

Mike had helpfully offered to look after the children while Julie and I do our designers visits, but he's already said he has to work on one of the dates after all so I'll have to take Henry with me when we visit Fifi and O, which could be interesting. Angela sent me an email to say that she has spoken to all the designers directly and that they've all been briefed to be as helpful as possible. I'm so grateful to Angela; she really has pulled out all the stops for us. Knowing her, I suspect she promised them a mention in the next magazine, or to include one of their designs in a fashion shoot.

Rather than drive to each location, we're taking the train and then the underground. Like me, Julie commuted into town for years, so we know how to look through people and avoid making eye contact, smiling or speaking above a whisper. We manage to navigate the tube looking as desperately suicidal as everyone else without letting the depressing atmosphere get to us.

'Which one are we seeing today?' Julie whispers as we arrive at Liverpool Street station.

'Smokey Popham. She's got warehouse offices in Spitalfields and according to Angela wants to bring glamour to middle England,' I say, stepping out of the carriage and minding the gap, although the station lacks the electronic voice to warn us. I've got the photographs of our model mums for the designers to choose from, and Smokey has first choice.

Liverpool Street station looks more like Bluewater every time I visit. I used to come to the City sometimes when the publishers wanted to schmooze one of their financiers. The station is all glass, chrome, noise, shops selling meaningless electronic gadgetry and hairdressers saying they'll serve you while you wait – which I've never quite understood. There are sushi bars, stocking shops full of back-office boys, and extortionately priced florists and chocolatiers that are heaving on Christmas Eve with suits who forgot to ask the secretary to get a present for their wife, lover or nanny.

I've heard that there have been a few spontaneous iPod-induced raves lately, but nothing today, sadly, and as we walk through the wide, white open space, with anonymous commuters zigzagging in between each other, I realise I don't miss anything about this place at all.

Spitalfields has changed considerably since my *De Rigueur* days. When I last saw it there were loads of little shops around a large space, where local residents used to play tennis or something. Artists, poets, writers and actors lived in the warehouse flats around the area, and it was very bohemian, slightly grubby and rather quirky. Then the City boys made their money, bought up the warehouses and renovated them and the area, taking away the dirt and some of the soul.

'God, I hardly recognise this place,' says Julie, staring at a stall in the market selling designer handbags at £500 a go. 'Surely you should get designers selling cheap here,' she adds, not daring to touch any of the products for fear that she might be charged.

We walk past the Spitalfield market traders who are having fun trying to bargain with the City traders, and head towards Smokey's studio.

According to my notes from Angela, Smokey Popham is in her twenties, a six-foot stick and a bit of a diva, although her name reminds me of a porn star more than anything else.

After a few failed attempts to find number seven Haven Park, we eventually locate an innocuous wooden door painted bright green with the word 'Popham' in stylised orange print emblazoned across the top. Under 'Popham', there's a typed notice in a glass cabinet with the words 'No junk mail, fuck off'.

Julie giggles. 'I like her style,' she says, pressing the intercom. A thin, tinny voice echoes back.

'Who is it?'

'Julie Rose and Lily Dearl from Somerset School. We've come about the fashion show. I think we're expected,' Julie says, trying to sound friendly but confident.

We hear the intercom click and then a 'burrrr' sound from the door. Two seconds later we realise that we have to push before the 'burrrr' finishes and I manage to lunge at it just in time.

There's a long flight of dark narrow stairs and I'm grateful I'm not with Jenny or Henry on this visit and that we decided against wearing heels. There's a musty smell in the air, like damp washing, so strong it's making me feel woozy. 'Not a particularly good first impression,' I whisper to Julie as we reach the top of the stairs.

It's fortunate that I whisper the last comment, because waiting for us at the top is an extremely tall, extremely thin woman dressed in a knee-length sixties velvet dress, the same green as the door, thigh-length black boots, with dyed black hair and heavily made-up green eyes. Smokey Popham looks like a sexy stick insect and she is staring at us intently for a moment before ushering us into the room.

'You must be the *mothers*.' Emphasising '*mothers*' as though we look as alien to her as she does to us. She sashays her way towards a huge open space with huge white walls and floor-to-ceiling windows looking out over the market. Her walk is so graceful that she looks as though she's on rollers.

Not sure in which direction she is going to turn, we wait for her to make her way towards the sofas, hideous in green, brown and orange, and we all sit down. To our left there are rails of clothes all various shades of green, brown and orange, flanked by a large oak desk with a vase of arum lilies and a four-poster bed, which, despite it being eleven o'clock, still hasn't been made.

'It's interesting that you chose the orange sofa,' she says unexpectedly as we make ourselves comfortable. 'People who choose orange are followers, people who choose green are creative.' Is that so? I think grimly, remembering this kind of attitude all too clearly from *De Rigueur*.

'What are people who choose brown?' Julie asks, sounding genuinely curious.

'Those who couldn't get to the orange or green sofas first,' she replies curtly. I laugh, although from her face I don't think she meant it as a joke. This is clearly going to be a scream, but it's all for a good cause, so I persevere.

'First of all, Smokey,' I hesitate slightly as that was the name of my family cat and it sounds ridiculous; it's a bit like calling a woman Tiddles, 'thank you very much for meeting us. Angela Flexor highly recommends you and we're in need of a talented designer who produces clothes for real women, rather than . . .' I am about to say 'stick insects' but it doesn't quite seem appropriate looking at Smokey, so my voice trails off. I start again.

'The show is on 24 May and we would ideally like you to choose three models to dress out of this selection of ten.'

She gives Julie and me another one of her intent stares. 'Are they all like you?' she then says sceptically.

'No,' replies Julie who's obviously getting a little irritated by Smokey's attitude. 'Far worse.'

Unexpectedly, this comment makes Smokey warm up a bit and she even smiles a little.

'I'm sorry if I come across as curt today, ladies. I've got a very large and important collection to finish, and I'm working on it day and night,' she says, gesturing to the four-poster. 'I've been subsisting on coffee and rice cakes for the past week, so apologies if I'm a bit tetchy. Angela is a good friend, and I'm doing this as a personal favour to her. It's very nice to meet you,' she adds, turning her beady eyes on me. I shrink back a bit and she continues, 'I admired your writing and sense of style when you were on the magazine.'

I'm quite taken aback by this sudden recognition, but realise I would have been working on the magazine when Smokey was in her early teens and probably poring over the glossies just like I used to, dreaming of one day being on the masthead and jetting off to wonderful locations with models and beautiful clothes. That illusion is quickly shattered, of course, when you realise you're working with bad-tempered models (with horrendously bad breath because they don't eat), in a world that attracts even more flakes than TV and more egos than the City.

'Why, thank you,' I reply graciously and somewhat mollified.

We show Smokey photographs of the mothers and their measurements, all taken with oaths of strict confidence. Predictably she chooses Daniella, Ella and Christine. All three women with long bodies, long necks and even longer legs, they look not unlike Smokey herself, albeit thankfully a good four to five inches shorter. I've always thought that designers like to dress their own body type, and that's why most male designers make clothes for women with no hips or bust.

'I would have chosen this woman as well,' she says, pointing to Andrea. 'I've seen her before, but I'd like to try these three out, if I may. I don't think any of the others would work.'

She hands me the book of photographs. 'I would have liked to have dressed you, Lily,' she says, using my name for the first time, 'but you're quite a bit curvier than I usually design for these days, so perhaps another time.' In your dreams, lady, as I smile noncommittally and rummage round in my bag to avoid giving her a swift kick on the shin, which probably would have hurt me more than her, come to think of it.

She gets up, smiling serenely, and ushers us over to the clothes rails, where she starts picking out a series of outfits.

'Just bear in mind that these women are not professional models so they need clothes that are easy to put on and take off quickly,' I say, remembering many professionals ripping skirts and tearing tops in their rush to return to the catwalk.

She nods and holds up some exquisite dresses, a trouser suit that I know will look wonderful on Christine, and a bright orange poncho top with straight trousers that I wouldn't mind trying on myself.

As we're looking through the clothes, she says, 'I'm very sorry, I haven't asked if you'd like anything to eat or to drink?'

'Oh no, we're fine,' Julie says, sifting through some wonderful saffron- and ochre-coloured skirts. 'We'll have to get going soon. Well, actually, I wouldn't mind a cup of coffee,' she adds, looking at a dress that I can tell from her face she's dying to try on.

'I might as well have one too in that case,' I say, enjoying myself immensely. It's at moments like these that I wonder how my life would have panned out if I had turned into Angela, sent the children off to boarding school and stayed at *De Rigueur*. Maybe I should have pressed more firmly for a part-time slot. Well, I guess that wouldn't have been the same, really.

'Of course,' says Smokey, 'just a minute, and if you'd

like to try that on, you are very welcome, but it may be a little tight. I think it's the largest size we have.'

She turns and heads towards a spiral staircase in the far corner of the room, which I hadn't noticed before, leaving Julie staring at her back open-mouthed.

Despite her best efforts, Julie can't fit into the dress, and frantically mutters something about losing weight and can we skip lunch today.

'Of course it doesn't fit, Julie,' I say. 'It's minute. It's a size six, my daughter could wear it.' We try to smooth out the wrinkles and hide the dress between the others on the rail.

When Smokey returns with a tray of coffee, I'm amazed to see a plate of chocolate digestives too, then we sit and talk about fashion, magazines and so on. Smokey asks what I've been doing since leaving the magazine and I ask if she found it easy to become a designer.

'Oh, it's a long story,' she says. 'I went out with someone who worked in the City and he financed this,' she says, gesturing around her. 'I'm no longer with him, but I've decided to stay because there are people with money literally just outside my door, desperately looking for a sense of style, who will and can pay,' she says matter-of-factly. 'I write poetry, too,' she then says. 'I get models to recite it when they're walking sometimes. It's very effective.' She points to a nicely bound folder on the coffee table. I flick it open politely.

City of miles of interchangeable squares
Full of meaningless suits and control freak bulls and
  bears –

I can make out the first page, then quickly put it back
down.

'Mmm,' I say, thinking quickly. 'I don't think we'll
manage to get our mums to recite anything – they'll
need all their focus on the rhythm of the music.'

'Well, it was a great pleasure meeting you anyway,'
Smokey says when we're finished and shake hands at
her green door, street noise echoing in the interchangeable square below. 'Everything will be fine for
the twenty-fourth.'

As Julie and I walk back through the market, I'm actually quite relieved to walk away from Smokey's slightly
claustrophobic attitude. We weave our way through the
crowds quickly, heading for the tube station.

'How are things with you anyway?' I ask Julie,
dodging a few office girls with trays of Caffè Nero
coffees.

'Oh good, busy. And I've been seeing loads of Tony.
He's great.'

'Sexy, too,' I add nonchalantly. I want so much more
info than 'great' – Have you done it? for starters. None
of my business, though, but she has a sparkle in her
eye, which suggests that perhaps she has.

'I know,' she says and smiles as she gets out her tube
pass, accidentally jostling a couple of suits.

'He's all-round lovely, and he listens, really listens, Lily. He makes me feel as though I'm the only person in the room when I'm talking to him and it's quite intoxicating. Eddie never did that. It was a bit like being on a phone with me talking and him not being able to hear a word, and it was very frustrating,' she says, scowling back at the men she's just pushed aside.

'What was Eddie like when you married him?' I ask as we find our seats on the train. But she's not to be drawn, maintaining her usual discretion about her divorce. 'We just had slightly different ideas about life,' she says. 'I didn't respect the money, the people or the lifestyle he bought into. It was all superficial, too materialistic. It's sad really. He was a creative soul when I first met him. He should have been someone like Smokey, with his own design studio, but he got sucked into the system. Maybe losing all his money would have been the making of him. I tried to help, of course, with the divorce settlement, taking a chunk of it when I did,' she says and I laugh. 'We get on fine now. And the girl he went off with in the end was so totally different to me and so totally right for him.'

'In what way?' I ask, my curiosity getting the better of my manners.

'Short, rounded and normal,' she sighs, 'and much more his type than me. She's always polite to the children, which is all I really care about. She wears the trousers, checks his text messages and emails, that sort of thing, and the only way he asserts himself is by bringing in the money. But enough about me. Anything new with you?' she asks, firmly changing the subject as we push our way out of the train and through the queues of people buying bagels and double lattes.

'Nothing much. All the fashion-show stuff at school.' I tell her about selecting the mums with Jane and Ms Treadwell before the break and she loves it, laughing so loud in her hoarse, slightly naughty way, that several people turn round to look at her censoriously.

'I haven't heard much from Karen, though,' I say. A little hesitantly, because although I love Julie and Karen equally, I've always felt the slight coolness between them.

'She's been so busy recently,' Julie says, almost reading my mind, 'all she ever seems to be doing is talking to that mobile of hers, or making excuses about why she can't help. Mind you, there are times when I am a little jealous of Karen. She's managed to keep her career, marriage and family intact, and she has you as a best friend, so she really has it all,' she says, squeezing my arm.

I think about Karen's mystery man and wonder if there isn't something missing after all. I decide on the spot not to tell Julie about him, because although it might make her feel that Karen's life isn't as perfect as it seems, she might accidentally let it slip in the playground, and then the whole of Letchbury would know within a week.

'Well, one down, three to go,' I say as we exit the station. Julie starts to talk about Tony and their dates again and some of the funny things that have happened to them, and I remind myself that I must try once more to seduce my husband. And soon, otherwise it could get very frustrating being with a loved-up Julie for the next three days.

Chapter 10
Hit and Miss

Our trip to meet Fifi Lord, the red-haired, thirty-something trendy kiddies' designer, who is just about to launch a range for adults, goes very well, mainly because Henry completely and utterly enchants the woman.

'Oh, my, isn't he gorgeous,' she says, squeezing his cheeks, which he hates but tolerates because I've bribed him to be good.

Fifi is based in Chelsea, which is thankfully more child-friendly than Spitalfields, and her offices are busy, noisy and full of models. Dressmakers are coming and going as she has her own designer clothes shop for up to seven-year-olds on the ground floor. The shop is full of Chelsea mums, crisp, nice-smelling, immaculate, full-breasted, tiny-waisted and dressed in clothes that look as if they've been bought that day. Julie and I, despite looking quite trendy in our Chloe outfits, feel very much last season.

Never mind, we talk to Fifi while Henry noisily tries on a range of hats and scarves from the huge pile Fifi has kindly provided for him to play with.

'I wish I'd brought my camera,' I say, looking at my son as he twirls, giggles, pouts and does a John Travolta *Saturday Night Fever* impression in front of the huge mirror propped up against the wall.

Fifi chooses Jane and Tina from our model mummy book, trying to target women with curvier figures, 'real women' as she puts it. She is excited about branching into adult clothing, but we ask if she could also provide clothes for a children's fashion show and give her details of the children chosen – two boys and two girls from Tim's year, including Tim himself (Boy of the Year).

Our next visit is also in Chelsea and goes less well. 'O' turns out to be not one person but a conglomerate of designers. The O office is a huge glass-and-chrome building and Julie whispers furtively that the waiting room reminds her of the reception at her divorce lawyers – very stark and white, with large squares of Warhol- and Hockney-type portraits of all the office employees. None of the portraits is smiling, which makes them look even more sinister. 'I don't like it here,' says Henry as soon as we walk out of the lift.

The room has three white leather sofas, horrendously slippery floors and a glass coffee table with such sharp edges that it must be the most unchildfriendly room in the city. A woman who looks as though she's an accountant rather than a design assistant comes to collect us and leads us into another lift without saying a word.

'Don't worry, darling. We won't be long,' I say to Henry, not wanting to explain that the receptionist is a stuck-up cow and hasn't even deigned to look at the grown-ups, let alone a little boy of three foot.

The woman shows us to a boardroom, which is just as stark and cold as the waiting room, with large windows and a whiteboard at one end. There are no paintings, only a large, long, glass-topped table with about fifteen black leather chairs and five people in black suits sitting at the opposite end. I can't tell which one is the boss, as Angela didn't specify, but all the men are tall and emaciated, with short dark hair and Roman noses.

'Would you like to sit down,' asks one of the men in an unexpectedly squeaky voice. The man, who I presume is the overall boss, manages a faint smile, which suddenly hardens as he sees I have a little person in tow.

'Oh, I didn't realise you were bringing a child. Are we designing for a child? We don't really do children at O.'

'I'll take Henry outside,' offers Julie, 'so you can do the talking, OK?' She takes Henry by the hand and whispers in his ear, 'I've got a Kinder egg in my handbag, would you like it?'

The last I can hear is a loud and enthusiastic, 'Yes please, Julie.'

I walk towards the group, still uncertain if the man who's just spoken is the head.

'Hello, I'm Lily Dearl,' I say, introducing myself and offering my hand.

He doesn't offer his, instead he pulls out a chair and I sit, place my mummy-model portfolio neatly on the desk and explain the background and purpose of the fashion show. When I've finished I wait for questions or a response but am greeted by silence and no noticeable facial expressions. It's a bit like talking to mannequins. So I prompt, 'What do you think?'

The man who spoke before, who may or may not be the boss but is obviously the spokesperson for the others, finally speaks after a brief, embarrassing pause.

'Thank you for your presentation. We have spoken to Angela about this. We were thinking along the lines of *Desperate Housewives* meets *Suburban Sluts* with lots of torn black leather and bondage gear. We are thinking coffee-morning foreplay, threesomes in the afternoon and vigorous debauchery behind the blinds. The awakening of suppressed middle-class sexuality, straining to break out of the quiet desperation of failed aspiration and overwhelming, suffocating mediocrity.'

I'm speechless for a moment, then have a sudden and overwhelming urge to snort, trying to erase the image of Jane Anderson and her formidable side-kick Tina walking down the catwalk in ripped bondage gear and spiked heels, and of threesome Suzanne, Christine and Ella knocking on each others' doors for a quickie in the afternoon while watching *Richard and Judy*. The team seems oblivious to my reaction and the man continues.

'From a marketing perspective this will create a lot of interest and controversy, and generate PR coverage for both you and us. There's no money in this, Angela tells me, but we're business people, and this is a way we think everyone can come out of it with something.' He pauses, flicking a pencil in between his fore- and middle fingers.

I have to get out, and quickly.

'I'm afraid this isn't the sort of profile we're looking for,' I say, 'but thank you so much for seeing me.' I get up and make a break for the door, muttering things about schools and playgrounds and cake bakes. Nodding and smiling and forcefully shaking everyone's hand, I finally escape.

Never in all my days at *De Rigueur* did I encounter such weird people. I met many Smokeys and Fifis – wild, eccentric creatives – but not people like these. Turning our mums into sluts indeed. I'm shown the door by the receptionist and leave without saying another word.

'How did it go?' Julie asks as we each take one of Henry's hands and start his favourite game: one, two, three, swing, one, two, three, swing.

'I think we've drawn a big fat zero from O, if you will excuse the pun,' I reply.

We chat about the show all the way home, comparing notes and coming up with yet another massive 'To Do' list especially now that we'll have to ask the other three designers to take on at least one more model while

Henry keeps up a running monologue at the window. He's been in such a good mood all day, only getting fractious when we're driving home from the station waving to Julie as she peels off to the left.

'I need the toilet, Mummy,' he says urgently from the back.

'Can you wait until we get home? We're almost there,' I say absent-mindedly, running through venues and empty town fields in my head. Julie has drawn a blank on suitable locations and it's getting close to crunch-time. Where can we hold this event?

Another desperate 'Mummmyy' from the back seat pulls me back into reality. We've been stuck in traffic for a few minutes now, so I'm going to have to stop somewhere and let Henry go by the side of the road. I pull out of the traffic and into the bus lane, hoping against hope that the camera clock is a few minutes slow. No such luck. A bus driver is honking at me angrily and pointing to the camera a little way down the road, so I decide to cut through and quickly do another left turn. Down Rosehill Lane and past Rowan Road, then down Nucleus Drive.

'Just hang on a minute, sweetie,' I frantically look for a place to pull over. Just then, I'm passing Karen's house. Salvation. The lights are on inside, so even if Karen is not home, Carlotta is bound to be and she'll let Henry use the loo, I'm sure.

I jump out and unbuckle his seat belt, then help him out of the car.

Despite his urgency, Henry wants to ring the bell, so

I pick him up and let him pull the cord. Karen has always wanted to get rid of the old-style bell, but it came with the house and the children love it. Jenny calls it a posh pull-me bell, which they had in olden times.

I'm just beginning to despair, when, after a minute or so, the door opens. I'm all ready to greet Carlotta and am surprised to see Karen stand before me, casual but stylish in jeans, white shirt and navy gilet, hair slightly crumpled, pen in hand. She looks just as surprised, but pleased, I'm relieved to note, and ushers us in.

'Lily!' she says, beaming and giving me a big bear hug that I find quite affecting. 'I didn't know you were coming over.' She takes my coat, then notices Henry who's twitching next to me.

'I'm so sorry to barge in, Karen, but Henry needs the toilet badly and I was wondering if we could . . .'

'Of course you can,' she says. 'Use the one in the hall. Henry, you know where it is?'

'Shall I come with you?' I offer, but Henry shoots me a scowl.

'I can go myself, Mummy.'

He totters off in the direction of the toilet, busily undoing his trousers en route so that by the time he reaches the downstairs cloakroom, the things are round his ankles.

'Would you like a coffee?' offers Karen now, towing me in the direction of the kitchen, which is a dream of beech and marble surfaces (the real stuff, not the fake).

'Yes, please, that would be lovely. It's so good to see you, Karen. It's been so long.' I gratefully sink onto one of the kitchen stools around the island. This is a fortuitous meeting, I have to say. Maybe I'll even get some info on Mr Blazer. 'We've got so much to do with this fashion show, I've got lots to tell you.' Maybe she'll reciprocate.

Karen's house is immaculate, thanks to Carlotta's fixation with Mr Muscle on everything three times a day. A mixed blessing Karen says, try cooking on a cooker with no temperature gauge marks, or any indication of whether the oven is grilling or roasting. Admittedly Karen's house is easy to keep clean, lots of polished wood floors, large open spaces and loads of natural light. Her philosophy in life is that domesticity kills creativity so she doesn't spend much time on housework (which, if you ask me, is easy to say if you have a Carlotta yielding Mr Muscle 24/7). All the walls are covered in a shade called Stargazer Yellow, which was sent to her free from Fox and Bell when she wrote glowingly about their products for an interiors magazine. She's not above using her title for her own ends occasionally. Her house always looks cheerful and upbeat even in the winter, a bit like Karen herself really.

By comparison, my home is cluttered. I have family photos everywhere around the house, as well as pots and little painted eggcups that the kids have kindly made for various Mother's Days, Father's Days and Easters over the years. Karen doesn't believe in ornaments and only has vases full of huge sunflowers and lilies (even out of season) in her sitting room, some large paintings and a few dramatic and posed photographs of herself and her family on the wall leading up to the landing. The only rooms in the house that look lived in are Simon's and Claire's, which are gloriously messy, covered in posters, books and Silver Surfer comics.

'Would you like the real or instant stuff?' she asks now.

'Oh, instant is fine for me,' I say happily. I hadn't realised until now just how much I've missed seeing my friend these past few weeks. I love her irreverence towards life. She doesn't take herself or anything else too seriously and that always gives me such a sense of perspective. Julie, as temperate and considered as she usually is, can also be a bit too intense, whereas Karen, hot-tempered at times, is usually optimistic and bright and a real light in my life.

Henry comes in and asks if he can watch a bit of TV and given that I'm trying to get Karen to talk I relent and put on *The Incredibles* for him, then settle back onto my chair. Karen bustles around the kitchen, chopping up some fruit for Henry and dumping biscuits on a plate as I update her on what's been happening at home and at the photography class. We speculate a bit about Julie and Tony and I tell her all about selecting the models and meeting with the fashion designers. When I describe the parade of mums she laughs so hard that she splutters instant everywhere.

'Oh, I wish I'd been there,' she gasps. 'It would have been worth organising the whole show just to see

Ms Grant prance down the science room.' I laugh with her, but can't help but secretly bristle at her last comment. So she'd only help with the show for her own amusement? I decide to go in for the kill.

'I also went to see Angela recently, and we went for lunch by the *De Rigueur* offices. We went to this ridiculous restaurant just off the King's Road, Olivio's, do you know it?' I say nonchalantly. If I've hoped to catch her offguard, however, my efforts are in vain. She just shakes her head and offers me milk and sugar.

'How is Angela?' she says then. 'There was a massive profile on her in the paper the other day.'

I sigh. Either there's a completely harmless explanation for her meeting with Blazer Man or she's unwilling to take me into her confidence.

As we talk on, I'm half-hoping, half-expecting Karen to offer to help out with the fashion show, but despite her general enthusiasm about the project there's no hint of her offering support. Instead she talks about how frantic things have been, with various editors out of the office and with Jamie travelling to and from New York a lot. Apparently, their sexual relationship has been based on transcontinental text sex and phone sex. She makes me laugh about a few of the times he's obviously mistyped something at a crucial moment, and completely destroyed their momentum.

'Talking of sex,' Karen then says, grinning, 'do you think Tony and Julie are OK in that department? I've been so out of the gossip loop recently,' she sighs, sipping coffee. 'I'm so sorry. I know I've been a bit of a rubbish friend lately.' She smiles at me ruefully and I feel a wave of sympathy towards her. I remember doing a five-day job, but add two kids to that and an absent husband – no matter how good your nanny is, you've got no spare minute for anything else.

'Well, Julie doesn't talk in such graphic detail about her sex life as a certain someone,' I nudge her, 'but I think there's definitely a spring in her step. We've been working together a lot on all this fashion-show stuff, and Tony is even helping out. So what are you working on at the moment, then?' I ask.

'A few different things. I just did a big piece on that Sugar Daddy scandal. I'd done an exposé on sexual innuendos on the Internet and chose Sugar Daddy as an example of lecherous men gone mad. He was known on all these sites as an amazing lover, with a magical tongue and a sideline in decorative butt plugs. Don't you remember?'

I nod nervously, hoping Henry doesn't catch the end of that sentence. I don't want to attempt to explain to anyone, let alone my youngest son, what butt plugs are. Karen continues, oblivious to my concern.

'Well, it turned out that he and Ted Banson, you know, the local MP for environmental issues, were one and the same person. He ended up just admitting to it during our interview, said he was a very lonely man and that I was persecuting him just for being lonely. Bloody politicians, always wanting to blame someone else for their own screw-ups.'

A sex scandal! Maybe Mr Blazer was really Ted Banson

aka the Sugar Daddy? I'm just about to start on another line of questioning when Henry inadvertently rescues Karen by coming in, announcing that he has forwarded through all the scary bits and the movie is over and can we go home for tea?

Karen laughs and ruffles his hair.

'I have some work to do anyway and the children should all be home pretty soon. It was lovely to see you, Lily, and you too, Henry. Let's get together some time soon.'

I hug Karen goodbye, slightly annoyed that Henry so rudely interrupted my cunning and subtle interrogation and that I am absolutely none the wiser about Karen's movements these days. She's so elusive, and so noncommittal whenever I do see her. Cheerful and nice and bright as always, yes, but her frank candour and her ability to always squeeze in a coffee and a chat with me seem to have gone. As I tuck Henry into his car seat and drive off, waving Karen goodbye, I feel I've somehow managed to lose a friend.

I think about her all evening, trying to figure out what is niggling at me, then finally push it aside, trying to narrow down my action list to something achievable and focus on my visit to the last designer tomorrow.

The next afternoon, for the third time in a row, Julie and I catch the overland train into London. Pooky Hasdammami's studio is in Canary Wharf, overlooking the Thames.

We have Jenny with us as Mike had to work after all,

but I think she might like it. I half-expect to find another O-type character in the soulless tall glass-and-chrome buildings, but thirty-something Pooky is slim, with bright, sparkling eyes. Her clothes are more conventional than Smokey's, but more quirky than Fifi's. She is warm and charming and pays more attention to Jenny than she does to us, which I like.

We run through our usual presentation about the fashion show and mention that there will be a few high-profile parents in the audience, as well as fashion buyers (thinking of Tatiana). Pooky nods enthusiastically throughout, agrees immediately to take four models then looks at the photos of Sally Day, Andrea and Julie, smiling cheerfully at Julie as she does so, positively beaming when she gets to Paul.

Jenny seems to be entering into the spirit of things, and as she looks through the rails of clothes with Julie and me, she seems to be fascinated by Pooky and what she says. Perhaps there's a chance my daughter will develop a feminine streak after all? It's strange – when I knew I was having a girl, I thought I'd have loads of fun dressing her in pretty things, a bit like a doll, but that never happened. Jenny has always resolutely wanted to wear dungarees and trousers and gets in the sort of mess even the boys have never managed to. But perhaps it's not too late.

'You would make a wonderful model,' Pooky tells her as Jenny holds a bright purple skirt up against herself. 'You can be my supermodel, my muse,' she adds, obviously indulging her.

'Can I?' she says, wide-eyed. 'Can I really?'

'Well, I can't see why not. I'm definitely in the market for a muse. Admittedly I was looking for someone a little older, like your mummy maybe,' she says, winking at me and smiling, 'but you seem perfect,' she returns to my daughter.

'Oh, Mummy's far too old for you,' says Jenny, swirling about in the skirt.

After Julie has stopped laughing, we sit down and talk logistics. Julie and I have worked out that each of the designers needs to produce two outfits for each model. Fifi has sent an email to say that she's sorting out a wide selection of outfits for the children as well as those for the adult models, now adding Suzanne to her lot and that she'll be happy to judge the winner of the budding school-age designers a week before the show, which should give her enough time to make the design up into an outfit. The winning child will then be able to wear his or her own entry.

'I think this is a wonderful idea of yours,' says Pooky as we sip our herbal tea (there's no coffee or PG on offer).

'Well, we've got to do all we can,' I say brightly. If she only knew. We all pull out our diaries to schedule the fittings, and I make a note to contact Ms Treadwell when I get back home to update her on who's wearing what.

As we say goodbye to Pooky and head for the station, Jenny skipping in front of us and occasionally breaking into a run, I feel for the first time as if I'm actually achieving something that could make a difference not just for Tim's future but for all of us. And myself, if I'm really honest. Meeting the designers and Angela has reminded me what I miss about the fashion world. As we walk down to catch the train, I get a brief pang of regret. My days at *De Rigueur* were extraordinary. Yes, there were ridiculous deadlines, petty politics and sleepless nights because paginations didn't work or models had fallen sick at short notice, but it was such fun. The characters I met would put the likes of Pooky, Smokey and Fifi in the shade. I once travelled to three continents in ten days, and was given so many designer handbags at one fashion show in Paris that I ended up giving about a thousand pounds' worth of them to friends and family. Beats a bunch of flowers any day! No day was the same, except the mornings. The hell of commuting amongst sweaty armpits on the tube, and the rude anger of people, were draining but as soon as I entered the office, all the hassle was worth it. Yes, I made the decision to see my family grow up, and that's worth a huge amount in itself, but sometimes it just doesn't seem quite enough.

Chapter 11
Hide'n'Seek

'I'm full,' says Henry, wide-eyed, nodding his head and rubbing his tummy at the breakfast table.

'You haven't eaten anything,' says Jenny, taking his still-full bowl of malted Shreddies and starting to eat them herself.

'I've got a little tummy, I don't need much,' says Henry, staring at his sister sternly.

'You don't have much trouble with chocolate, Henry,' says Tim, tapping his brother on the head.

Tim and Jenny talk about two kids in Tim's year who, apparently, haven't been out much lately, doing tutoring and stuff after school – Freddie and Dominic, it transpires, Sally Day's and Linda Black's sons. I'm half-tempted to ask Tim whether the rumours are true and Charlie's dad is really selling a body part to get him into a good school, or how Freddie's mum is getting on with her mother, but I hold back.

It's the morning Tim is to be announced Boy of the Year in assembly and Mike is going in to work late so he can be at the presentation, along with me and Henry. I've got the responsibility of taking the photographs while he's got the video camera. The children don't usually see this much of their dad in the morning, so when Mike comes downstairs looking his usual smart self in a blue suit, they all look delighted and get up to hug him.

'Is everyone ready?' he asks.

'Yes', says Tim. 'Let's go.'

'Go,' Henry echoes, getting up to find his boots.

Ten minutes later and we're still not all ready, mainly because I haven't decided what to wear. I want something suitable for the presentation, but not too special because I have to run lots of errands afterwards, then meet Julie and Paul at the café around lunch-time for a fashion-show update meeting, then I'm going on to the golf club with Paul, where I have to be professional and businesslike. I finally opt for a simple Chine skirt and jumper with boots, slather on some make-up and hope that it'll do.

'What do you have to do as Boy of the Year, Tim?' asks Henry, holding on to his brother's jumper as he follows him to the hallway and out the door to the car.

'I have to be an example to everyone in the school,' says Tim, sounding scarily sensible even to me. 'And I can boss people about,' he adds with a cheeky grin, apparently having reconciled himself with the notion.

'You boss me about already,' says Jenny, pushing after the two boys and jostling Tim a bit in the process.

In the car on the way to school, I half-listen to the kids' conversation. The latest playground craze seems to be something called pat ball, a kind of tennis against the wall that everyone's wildly excited about. Then I zone out, my mind buzzing with the excitement about Tim and anxiety about the golf-club meeting and how we'll make the fashion show pay if they don't offer us a large-ish donation.

'What are you thinking about?' asks Mike, as he turns out of our road, sensing that I'm distracted.

'I've got the meeting with the golf club today,' I say, sighing.

'Oh, are you getting us membership?' he smiles.

'No, but I thought you were going to do that? Isn't that what you promised Dr Totham?' I say, slightly miffed that I seem to be putting all my efforts behind the fashion show when Mike can't even find the time to join a golf club.

'I've been so busy with work lately, haven't gotten round to it,' he says, munching his last piece of toast and beeping someone who's dared to cut him up.

'Dad, it's bad to talk and eat at the same time,' says Tim, watching us as if he's expecting an argument and wanting to change the subject, 'It confuses your oesophagus,' he then explains as if that makes it clearer. 'Or is it epiglottis? I can't remember which.'

'Does it really?' says Mike, not really hearing, then turning back to me. 'I'll do it this week, Lily, I promise. But if you get the time, why don't you do it while you're there?'

'I'm going to talk about the fashion show, and I don't want to confuse things. I will, however, tell the guy, Masterton I think, to expect a call from you and that you've been meaning to apply for ages. OK?' I say, realising Mike won't call unless I continue to prod him.

'Yes, dear,' he says slightly indulgently, which pisses me off even more. 'And by the way, you look lovely today,' he adds quickly to make amends.

We find a parking space and pay until eleven, although Ms Treadwell has told us it will only take half an hour.

As we walk into the playground, all the children are just starting to pile in and instead of saying goodbye in the playground as usual, we follow them, feeling like grown-up schoolchildren ourselves. The reception quietens as the children head into their respective classrooms, leaving Mike and I standing alone with our children. I've asked that Henry can see his brother's certificate, and I keep hold of him while Jenny and Tim hug Mike and me goodbye.

'See you in a few minutes, Dad,' Tim calls out to Mike before disappearing down the corridor.

We make our way to Ms Grant's room to find her sitting behind her computer, typing what looks like a copious list of children's names. She smiles and stands up as we enter, a lot friendlier than usual, shaking Mike's hand and all. Perhaps she doesn't get many handsome men in her office.

'Ms Treadwell will be out in a minute. She's just seeing another parent at the moment,' she says, directing us to some chairs by the door.

Harriet Scott's parents, whom I know vaguely from parents' evenings and the playground, are also here for their daughter's appointment as Girl of the Year. I don't know Harriet very well, but I think she's got a soft spot for my elder son, a fact that he was blissfully oblivious to until Jenny went up to him in the playground one day and, in a loud voice in front of his friends, told him that Harriet fancied him and wanted to have his babies.

We nod at the Scotts and are about to say something when all of a sudden we hear loud voices from the headmistress's office: she seems to be having a rather heated conversation with someone. I vaguely recognise the tone, but can't quite place it. Then the raised voices suddenly go quiet.

A few minutes later, just as Henry starts fidgeting, the door opens and Jane Anderson walks out, closely followed by a very stern-looking Linda Black with Ms Treadwell on her heels. Jane looks a little surprised to see us, but smiles warmly, while Linda looks as though she's just swallowed a bitter pill.

'Good to see you all here,' says Ms Treadwell to us and the Scotts, closing the door to her office behind Jane and Linda (a touch more firmly than necessary, I notice). 'And you, too,' she adds, smiling at Henry who obligingly smiles back.

'If you would like to follow me,' she walks ahead briskly, then ushers us into the empty assembly hall. The hall is sometimes used as a gym and there are ropes and climbing frames balanced along one wall, and benches piled up against another. There is a large curtained stage at the front of the hall, the other wall being a glass window from floor to ceiling, allowing the bright spring morning light to flood in.

'Please take a seat on the stage by the piano. You don't have to say anything, just watch and if you want to take photographs, please could you do so towards the end of the presentation?' she says, noticing our cameras and video equipment.

The hall is starting to fill up now, starting with Reception. The four-year-olds look like babies in uniform; some of them with thumbs in mouths, barely toddling, staring at everything as though they've happened upon aliens invading the earth. Then the First and Second Years come in, looking more confident and self-assured. The girls whisper to each other in huddles and I vaguely recognise some of them, while the boys stride along as though they're the only ones in the room. I see Jenny and Cara too, and Julie's Alexander and Karen's Simon in the Third Year, and then finally the Fifth Years, with Claire, Dominic, Mia and, lastly, Tim, who looks nervous because he's biting his bottom lip.

After an initial hum, a few coughs (and the sound of a whoopee cushion, which is immediately confiscated), Ms Treadwell stands up.

'Good morning, boys and girls,' she says, nodding regally.

'Hello, Ms Treadwell; hello, everybody,' the children reply a little more slowly.

'Today is a very special assembly, because today we are announcing the Boy of the Year and Girl of the Year for the year ahead.'

All the Reception class children say, 'Ooh,' and there are a few excited whispers from the rest, quickly shushed by their teachers.

'It's a very special honour. These children have been elected by their friends as well as the teachers for being young people they look up to; people they like and will follow. It is my great pleasure to announce that Harriet Scott and Tim Dearl will be your new Girl and Boy of the Year. Would Tim and Harriet like to come up to the stage to receive their awards?'

Tim and Harriet both stand and walk towards the stage as I surreptitiously click away with my camera, and Harriet's parents do the same. I am trying to remember Gilbert's advice about focusing and framing the image, but it's all a bit of a blur. Both children look nervous and after they receive their certificates and shake hands with Ms Treadwell, they are asked to remain on stage, and everyone claps. I can hear Jenny whooping in the audience and Henry is jumping up and down, waving at his brother, slightly put out that Tim isn't waving back.

As Tim and Harriet walk back to their places amongst their friends, Ms Treadwell continues to talk.

'Now, as you know, boys and girls, we have a very special event coming up shortly, which is the fashion show. Not only are our mums and one of our dads being models for the day, we also have the opportunity to model some of the clothes ourselves. And one of you will design our new mufti-day outfit, so please be creative and think of things you know you and your friends would like to wear and keep your ideas coming. The announcement will be made before the half term. We will also be looking for volunteers to model these outfits. Tim and Harriet, as Boy and Girl of the Year, will be on the catwalk, and the design winner will model his or her own creation. To make things fair, there will be a lottery for the rest of those who want to take part, and the winners will be picked by myself in a month's time.'

So she's found a way to circumvent the parents' onslaught. Very good.

'Today we are going to be talking about Africa and the children who live there,' she continues, as I gradually edge out of the hall, closely followed by Mike, who has to leave for work.

'Why do we have to go?' Henry whines, tugging my hand. 'I want to know about the children in Africa.'

'Because Daddy has to go to work, you have to go to nursery and Mummy has to meet someone about the fashion show,' I explain, heading towards the nursery.

'I think I got some really good footage, Lily,' says Mike, kissing me on the cheek, 'something for us to watch when we're old and grey and have grandchildren,' he adds, squeezing Henry's cheek. 'I've got to go. Good luck with the golf club,' he says, waving to me as he quickly walks towards the car.

I drop off Henry, after spending the walk to the nursery talking about children in Africa, then head back to sort out some last bits and pieces before our meeting later this morning. When I arrive at the café, it is buzzing with other lunch-time mums. Navigating around high chairs and pushchairs, I find Paul and Julie already on the large brown leather sofa, with three large coffees and some cakes in place. No Karen, but I guess that shouldn't be a surprise any more. When we've all greeted and hugged each other, I announce proudly:

'Tim had his presentation for Boy of the Year today in assembly!'

'Wow! Well done, girl,' says Julie, clapping her hands.

'Nothing to do with me, Julie,' I say, sitting down next to Paul on the sofa. 'Entirely Tim's achievement.'

'It's great. Congratulations, Lily,' says Paul, grinning at me.

'Well, shall we get down to business,' I say, looking at my notes. 'It's not long now. May isn't that far away.' I take a sip of my coffee and swallow half my piece of carrot cake. 'I'm sure Dr Totham is going through the applications as we speak. Have you been interviewed yet?'

'Yes, a couple of weeks ago. Jessica and I thought he was a bit stiff, but we like the school. What do you think of him?' Paul says as he turns to Julie, who is mid-bite into a croissant.

'He's OK,' she says through a mouthful of crumbs. 'Eddie did his bit and came with me. He thought Totham was a little slimy, but as you said, the school is good and Dom will love all the sports stuff, so Eddie and I did our best. But really good news, guys. He mentioned the fashion show before we did, so it's obviously filtered through that we're organising this for the Somerset library and he was very impressed that we were part of it. That's a big tick for us already, Lily.'

I suppress a twinge of irritation that she has had the chance to actually flaunt the show in front of Totham. It's really my baby. I hope my name – and Tim's – fell as well somewhere in there. I pretend to pick up my cup while throwing her a furtive sideways glance. Would she have mentioned my name?

'Now we're just waiting for the letter,' she continues, oblivious to my inner battle.

'It's a bit like waiting for exam results, isn't it?' I say quickly, remembering that sick feeling I had just before I opened my A-level results and found I'd got Ds instead of Bs.

'Yes,' Julie sighs. 'I was in France on a French exchange

when my exam results came through and my mum had to read my grades to me down the phone. The line was so bad I was never quite sure how I'd done until I arrived home.'

'I just thought there were loads of typos on my results,' Paul says, taking a chunk out of a pain au chocolat. 'I thought the Es were meant to be Bs, but unfortunately it was wishful thinking. Never mind.'

'Well, let's get down to work, then,' I say bracily, opening my fashion-show folder. Paul goes first and takes out a black book with copious notes and action points.

'Right, the good news is that I've sourced a free marquee for the event from someone I used to work with who owes me a favour, but the bad news is – we don't have a venue yet.'

'Ms Treadwell has offered the school field,' I interject, 'but it's not big enough and it *definitely* isn't glamorous enough.'

'Well,' Paul continues cheerfully, 'I think there's a field that's part of the golf club that would be perfect – a friend of ours rented it out for a joint birthday and it was a huge bash – so I thought maybe we could ask Masterton today if he wouldn't mind us using it for a good cause.'

Paul takes a slurp of coffee and continues.

'Now. I've checked out the sound system your friend Angela Flexor recommended, Lily. Unfortunately, it's way too expensive, and I've been having trouble finding anything cheaper.' He puts down his list and looks round the table, sighing. 'It's been such a pain to research, especially now that Jessica is away and I have to juggle Mia's ballet exams and extra tuition, Cara's horse riding and everything else,' he says plaintively, sounding more like a harassed mother by the minute.

Julie and I can't help but giggle as Paul heaves another sigh. He gives us a playful punch, mouthing, 'Piss off,' to Julie who's been rolling her eyes.

'But I'm on to it, so hopefully more next week.'

Julie's news is all good – she's got a catwalk from one of her PR friends who now works in fashion and the model mums are all on track to visit the designers' studios next week for a fitting, which they're all very excited about.

Speaking of catwalk – 'How about the music?' I ask, looking around the group. 'Let's sit down next week sometime to choose the songs. I personally think stuff like Grace Jones, "Slave to the Rhythm", and Roy Orbison's "Pretty Woman", would work well.'

'Bit old-fashioned,' comments Paul dismissively. 'How about more recent stuff like Black Eyed Peas, Faithless, Snow Patrol or Morrissey?'

'I don't think Morrissey does catwalk rhythm,' I say drily, 'but I could be wrong. Perhaps we should get Andrea to help? She'll know what works best for models, plus we can't have anything that has too many swear words.'

We all giggle, thinking about Jane Anderson strutting her stuff to Eminem and P Diddy.

'Oh, I forgot,' Julie says suddenly. 'I've also lined up some extra clothes for the children to model, on loan from some local clothes shops that need the extra publicity. And that's it from me,' she closes her notebook and ticks off the last point with a satisfied look on her face.

We talk a bit about advertising, flyers and what the PTA has done, and I fill the others in on threats to boycott the event by various mums led by Linda Black. Ms Treadwell pulled me aside on our way to assembly this morning to assure me that they have this in hand. The invitation has finally been approved by the PTA and Ms Treadwell: black type on a white background with two cartoon characters of mothers holding hands with their children, all looking very chic.

'The idea came from Fifi,' I say. 'She sent it free of charge, which is very sweet of her,' I add.

Julie is perusing the text, smiling at the cartoon figures.

'Ten pounds is a bit steep, don't you think?' she then says, frowning. 'Some mums won't be able to afford it.'

'Well, to make enough money for the library, we need to charge enough and, if you think about it, it's quite good value for what they're getting. They'll be fed, watered and have unparalleled entertainment. Plus, both Ms Treadwell and Jane were going to ask fifteen pounds!'

We shake our heads. So the price stands.

'I've organised a hundred chairs to be delivered,

dishes will be done by Giorgiano's, the PTA mums will be bringing loads of cakes and Tony is producing all the canapés, I believe,' I say, looking at Julie who gives me a knowing smile. 'I hope you haven't been distracting him from his work,' I say, familiar with that cheeky look.

'No, no,' she replies, grinning from ear to ear. 'He's been helping me find my rhythm and I've been helping him fill in the vol-au-vents.'

Sadly, I have no such distractions. Mike and I are just too busy for a night of passion these days. Before we completely lose Julie to her fantasies, Paul mentions that he's trying to get more sponsorship to pay for drinks and will contact the local off-licence for their support later on today.

'We definitely need to secure the golf-club sponsorship today, Lily,' he adds urgently, making another note in his book. 'It could potentially cover the bulk of the costs and as we've got a big "no" from the local boutiques – except your friend Tatiana, Lily, who seems to be the only one who doesn't mind the mums not wearing her clothes in the show – the costs seem to be escalating. The local grocers, cab company and dry-cleaners have kindly offered to display advertising in their shops and have given money towards catering and drinks, but we've really got to see how much we can get from Masterton today,' he says, a worried look on his face.

'I know.' Rather a lot seems to depend on this meeting now. 'We'll be fine. Everything seems to be on track so far, and people are very positive about it, so I think we should be proud of ourselves. So far, so good,' I say, raising my coffee cup to both of them, only realising when I go to drink it that it's empty.

Chapter 12
Can We Play Ball Now?

Paul and I leave the café and head for Paul's blue Beamer, which will hopefully be in keeping with golf-club standards. As we're both dressed rather more smartly than usual, we're getting several looks from the other mums, who are obviously putting two and two together and getting five.

When I stumble and Paul grabs a hold of my arm, I push myself away quickly, laughing and nodding at some mothers passing by. The last thing I need is an undeserved reputation round here.

Paul's car smells reassuringly of children, mess, sports clothes and riding gear. 'Sorry about the tip,' he says as I move some books and PE tops off the front seat and throw them in the back, which is already full with stuff.

The drive to the golf club only takes about five minutes, despite the morning traffic, and we arrive early at the gates of the club, which are large wrought-iron monstrosities with the words 'Letchbury Park' emblazoned across the middle.

'Bit over the top with the security gates, don't you think, Lily?' Paul says after we have had to shout our names three times into the intercom and the gates finally open slowly. 'What do they have here, gold-plated balls?'

Paul zooms through quickly, as though they're likely to close the gate at any moment and we've got to make a dash for it. We drive along a tree-lined gravel path, perfectly symmetrical and immaculately groomed on either side. There's even a huge lake with swans and ducks to our left, and what looks like a small orchard to our right. It's about three minutes before we catch our first glimpse of the clubhouse building, which we soon discover is only the gatehouse that leads to the course itself. There's another gate, but this time a distinguished-looking man asks who we are and allows us in. We feel as though we're entering Fort Knox.

After another five-minute drive we finally see people playing golf. To our left and right and in the far-off distance, figures are walking with caddies and hitting balls, looking at where they've hit them, calling out and banging the ground. It all looks so incredibly dull and pompous, but then I know nothing about the game, so I remind myself to keep an open mind. I was probably a tennis bore when I used to play and a jogging bore when I jogged around Letchbury Park. Perhaps I'm a kick-boxing bore now, but I hope not – I never talk about my upper cuts and my jab kicks the way I hear some golfers talk, in painful detail, about what they did with their balls on the eighteenth hole.

We follow the sign which says 'Guest Car Park' (instead of 'Members' Car Park', 'Special Members' Car Park' or even 'Board Members' Car Park') and park the Beamer amongst the other Beamers.

'I wonder what makes of car are allowed in the Board Members' Car Park?' whispers Paul with an envious glint in his eyes as we get out.

'Shall we take a peek?' I say, feeling like a naughty child.

'No time, Lily,' says Paul in his best parent's voice. 'Now behave, this meeting with Masterton is important and we've got to impress him, even if we have to seriously brown-nose the guy,' he says sternly.

Just as we're walking towards the entrance a man emerges, clearly coming out to greet us. When he is only a couple of feet away from us, I freeze.

I know this man. I recognise him. I know that hideous pink-and-blue blazer. He walks towards us, gait high, back straight, big smile that doesn't quite reach his wide-set clear-blue eyes. He's Karen's mystery man!

Masterton introduces himself, shaking me warmly by the hand.

'Hello, you must be Lily Dearl, very nice to meet

you,' he says, showing a full set of perfectly even (probably capped) white teeth. I know a smile is supposed to be welcoming, but he reminds me a little of *The Jungle Book*'s Shere Khan as he is just about to take a bite out of Mowgli.

'And you must be Paul Wilton,' he says, turning to Paul and shaking hands though this time a bit more vigorously. 'I know your wife vaguely through work. A very busy, very successful lady, Jessica Wilton Routledge,' he says. Obviously Jessica includes her maiden name for business as well, although it sounds like an unnecessary mouthful to me.

'Yes,' Paul nods politely. 'That she is.'

'If you'd like to follow me through here, I thought we could talk while walking through the grounds. It's so much more civilised, don't you think?' he says. He seems to be smiling at me with all his teeth showing. We follow him through an anteroom full of golf relics and noticeboards containing the names of members. It reminds me of the waiting room at The Oaks, with all the gold-leafed names. A lot of the same ones, too, I notice. Inevitable, perhaps, in a small town like ours. There's Fisher Bolden, the property tycoon, Tyler Villier, the mobile-phone maverick and Lynda Dunworthy, the famous ballet dancer. Even our MP Wallace T. Heavie is up there. Apparently everyone who is anyone in the area meets here on a Saturday morning. I must get Mike to apply for that membership.

As I follow Paul and Masterton through the anteroom and out through the other door, I wonder how

Karen could fall for this sleazy louche charm. Maybe he's got a hidden side? He'd have to hide it well, though, I just can't picture them together.

As if I've conjured her up with my thoughts, I see a woman who looks just like Karen walking towards one of the other buildings. I'm sure it's her, well, she's a member after all, but she just said last night that she was busy with yet another project. No, I must be wrong. I've just got her on the brain and am getting paranoid.

As we start to walk the grounds, stunning in the spring light, people keep coming up to Masterton to say hello. I start to realise why so much business is done while playing the game. There is a staggering amount of time to talk and think while walking. Masterton weaves his way around the various holes, grandly waving to Colonel this and Jeremy that, like Moses parting the seas. Paul and I trail behind him like two stray dogs and listen to his running commentary.

'And that was Charles Manders, ex-banker who now has his own hedge fund and mountaineers in his spare time,' Masterton nods at an odd, skinny-looking man in a bright red sweater and cream jodhpurs. 'He climbed the Eiger this year, not the north face, of course, the south side. But he did it for a local charity, and it's the thought that counts, don't you think?' he says, making our fashion-show efforts look more pathetic by the minute. 'Charles supported our own golf-club charity too, which helps a variety of good works in the community,' he adds. Is Masterton heavily hinting that some of the monies we raise from the fashion show should go to the golf-club charity? I'm just about to tell him, very kindly, of course, that this would be near impossible when another woman comes up to him. Somehow, she looks familiar as well. Maybe I'm just having some kind of clairvoyant day?

Masterton asks us to excuse him for a few minutes. The woman seems to have a lot to say. And I don't know why, but they seem familiar with each other. Old friends maybe? Intimate almost. She's attractive in a hard sort of way. More glamorous than beautiful and, like Masterton, she has a wide open face, but her eyes are cold. She pats his arm in a farewell gesture and sashays off. As Masterton walks back towards us, I whisper to Paul under my breath, 'What do you think of him?'

'Slimy, but we need the money and the connections. Like the bird, though,' he says, winking at me.

'I'm so sorry about that, one of our board members – we just had to catch up on something,' Masterton explains, slightly out of breath, ushering us over to a row of buggies.

'I thought you might like to travel in style and have a look at the course. The easy way to do it,' he says. 'Would you like to drive?' He magnanimously offers me the wheel. 'I don't believe what they say about women drivers.' He laughs. Paul and I smile politely, but I like him even less.

I take the wheel while Masterton explains how to operate the buggy: 'Turn that knob and push that pedal. That one is the brake,' he explains as though I'm Jenny's age. I want to punch him, but I try to focus on the money and on Tim. The Oaks.

As I start the engine and we move off (at first admittedly fairly jerkily), I explain, rather more loudly than necessary to cover my nervousness, what we need and when we need it. 'As I think Paul explained on the phone, we're organising a fashion show to help build a new library at Somerset School. The clothes will be designed by top fashion designers,' well, almost, 'and we're hoping to generate a lot of good publicity not only for the school but for our children. We've had little time to devote to the local community and want to give something back. This is our way of doing it. But we need your help, Mr Masterton.'

He smiles blandly, so I blurt out, 'To put it bluntly, we'd like to ask you for your back field on the twenty-fourth of May, and we're also looking for sponsorship to help with catering and paying for the sound system.' Maybe it's a bit too much to take in all at once, so I try to sound reasonably needy without coming across as pathetic. From his comments about women drivers and his gracious but ever so slightly old-fashioned good manners I'd guess he doesn't like his woman assertive. He's the sort of person I should imagine keeps his wife in the kitchen. But I could be wrong; for all we know, the woman we just saw him talking to could be his wife.

Masterton smiles at me as though he's actually about to take a bite, which I find a little startling. 'I like the idea of sponsoring local projects, Lily,' he then intones, rattling it off like a well-rehearsed speech. 'I'm keen to involve the golf club with local schools as education is our future, and I already donate quite a bit to Somerset and The Oaks where a lot of our members have children.'

I seize upon the opportunity like a hawk.

'Yes, I know, I recognised a few names on your membership board from The Oaks waiting-room notice-board. We're actually both very much hoping to get our children into The Oaks.' He must like that.

Masterton looks us both up and down appraisingly, then gives us a beaming smile.

'I think if your children are anything like you, they'll fit in very well at The Oaks, very well indeed. And it's important that you realise how much your support, especially your financial support, is to them at this stage,' he says. Huh? I sneak a look at Paul and am relieved to see that he's got no clue either. I make a noncommittal sound. Sure as hell, this guy isn't getting a penny of my fashion-show money.

'I would like to offer £5,000 towards the event and you have my permission to use our land,' Masterton says grandly. My head jerks upwards, and just like that the smug git is forgiven.

'Thank you, Mr Masterton,' Paul says gratefully, obviously genuinely touched by this level of generosity. He takes Masterton's hand and shakes it hard, much to the man's surprise. I eagerly grab hold of his other hand. He may be a sleaze ball, but he's a generous sleaze ball.

After suffering a lengthy tour of the grounds and much more mindless chit-chat, Paul and I wave goodbye to Masterton and head back to the school in silence, our minds buzzing. Despite spending over an hour at the golf club, we get back to the Somerset almost an hour too early for pick-up and wait around parked in a side street. I don't really want to go back into the café – once was enough to fuel speculation about Paul and me. Although if any of them saw us in the car, rumours would be just as rife. I call Julie from my mobile, shouting excitedly into the phone until she interrupts to say that she's coming over right now to meet us. After fifteen minutes of listening to Paul's Morrissey tapes, which I can only take so much of, we get out of the car and head towards the gates. Julie is already there, waving to us, and I give her the thumbs-up from afar, laughing, making wild big-pile-of-money gestures. She skips towards us, but just as Paul and I are about to launch into an excited recap of the meeting, another woman approaches, walking straight towards us. For the third time that bloody day, I have a déjà vu moment. I definitely know this woman from somewhere.

Yes, of course, it's the woman who was with Masterton this morning. How bizarre. She's trying to appear serene, but she looks unnerved and slightly alarmed by the noise of parents and young children milling about. She does stick out like a sore thumb amongst this crowd, in a long, elegantly cut cream coat with brown high-heeled velvet boots and a jaunty brown hat. She's with another lady, who's dark, squat and much smaller than her. They look an unlikely pair but they're clearly headed for us, so I smile at the taller woman, trying to ignore the snarl of the smaller.

'Hello,' the tall woman says, 'I'm Henrietta Diet, local councillor and author.' Brief expectant pause. 'And this is my assistant Allyson Dyer,' she turns abruptly and nods to Allyson, who looks as though she's about to spit blood, but as her mouth has been set that way for the past minute I'm beginning to think that's just her normal expression.

'Matthew Masterton has told me about your wonderful idea for the fashion show,' Henrietta Diet launches straight in, 'which I think is very worthy, rather splendid and desperately needed. I'm here to say I'd like to help in any way I can.' She takes both my hands and clasps them in hers, in the way I do with Henry sometimes when I want his full attention and he's refusing to give it to me.

'Why thank you, but I think we have it all under control,' I say, pulling my hands from hers as gently but firmly as I can. Who the hell is this woman?

'Well, perhaps we can have a little chat, because you don't know what I can offer now, do you, Lily. May I call you Lily?'

No, you can't, I think but out loud I graciously say, 'Of course, Hettie.'

She winces a little, but nods and suggests reconnoitering to the café across the road. Not really knowing how to get out of this, Paul, Julie and I follow in her wake, her cream coat faintly billowing in the wind.

'I've got to collect my son from nursery in ten

minutes, Hettie,' I explain, belatedly hitting upon a get-out-of-jail-free card.

When we arrive at the café, Henrietta hesitates and Allyson runs forward to open the door for everyone, clearly knowing what's expected of her, even if she doesn't seem to enjoy doing it.

Allyson then proceeds to commandeer chairs from other tables and place them by the window so we're all in a small circle, facing each other. It's very efficient but slightly intimidating, though admittedly I could do with an Allyson Dyer around the house to make my life easier.

As we sit down, Allyson quickly and quietly takes orders for tea and coffee – Paul, PG; Julie, latte; me, green tea; and Henrietta, warm water, 'because it's good for the digestion and skin'. As Hettie drones on about the fashion show, outlining all her various ideas, it suddenly dawns on me. That's how I know her. Not only from the golf course. She is none other than the woman I saw on TV talking about parenting skills and shamelessly plugging her own book.

As if on cue, she pulls out a book, hers of course, and starts talking about organisation. Why on earth is this woman foisting herself upon us? I feel the same irritation that I felt when I watched her all those weeks ago and I'm dumbstruck when she admits to not being a mother herself, having never married. I can't believe she's written a book claiming to know how a mother should manage and prioritise her time.

'Mothers so rarely get "me" time, Lily, don't they? Time to themselves?' she says.

'This is "me" time,' I say, trying hard not to bristle at her patronising tone. I want to know how she can help us and get the hell out of here. 'And the time I spend with my children is the time I want to spend with my children, not time I am forced to spend with them,' I say. I know I sound defensive about being a full-time mother, which I'm not, but this woman pisses me off with her sanctimonious pie-chart-to-solve-everything attitude.

She quickly changes tack.

'You may have seen me at the golf club, I'm a member there, and Mr Masterton – a good friend, you know –' Allyson coughs slightly at this comment, earning her a look of contempt from Hettie, '– was very impressed with your efforts and told me about the show, so I thought I'd be able to help.'

'We have enough models,' Julie says quickly, bless her, before I can even speak.

Hettie laughs. 'Oh no, no. I'm not one to take centre stage,' she insists, toying with her teacup. I notice that even Allyson winces at the hypocrisy. 'I thought I'd be able to help generate some local coverage, maybe? The editor of the *Letchbury Times* is a close friend of mine, you know. And perhaps I could MC on the day? It would help your efforts, I'm sure,' she says, taking a sip of her water.

'We couldn't pay you,' says Paul, ever conscious of the budget.

'Oh, I don't want paying, it's the taking part that matters, and this is all for a good cause,' she says, patting

Paul on the hand like some sort of daft lapdog. 'I'll try to get Wallace T. Heavie to attend as well to add gravitas to the event, if you like, and there are so many well-heeled parents who belong to the golf club; I'm sure I can get them to come along too.'

It is definitely worth considering – the more public the event, the higher Totham will rate this on his personal scale of community-mindedness.

'Do you really think they would come to something like this, Henrietta?' Allyson says, looking us up and down as though we and our plans are not worth the time of day.

'Leave the decision-making to me, please, Allyson dear,' says Henrietta, grimacing. A brief but awkward silence ensues.

Thinking on my feet, I explain quickly, 'Thank you for your very kind offer, Hettie, but we'll have to run this by the PTA and the headmistress, so if you could give us a few days, we'll be in touch. Is that all right?' I try to sound as reasonable as possible and Henrietta buys the bullshit, while Allyson eyes me cautiously. I like her even less than her boss.

We walk briskly back to the school, now almost a little late for pick-up time, and I leave Henrietta and Allyson standing by the gates, grandly surveying the scene. Poncho, Jane Anderson's dog, is tied to the gate and as he goes to lick Allyson's hand (why he would be tempted, I don't know), she brushes him off, kicking him in the process. Poncho lets out a little whimper and skulks away in the other direction. She looks round quickly to see if anyone is watching and, noticing that I am, looks straight back at me as if to say, And what are you going to do about it then, huh? I don't like Henrietta's patronising ways, but at least she's not a bitch. The same cannot be said for Allyson.

Our children are waiting forlornly by the playground benches like abandoned waifs.

'We thought you'd forgotten us,' says Dominic, looking at Julie accusingly.

'I've got to collect Henry,' I say, quickly heading for the nursery. 'Can you look after Tim and Jenny for a second, while I go?' I call back to Paul and Julie, vaguely aware that Henrietta and Allyson are still hovering by the gates, probably wondering if we could organise a piss-up in a brewery, let alone a fashion show.

When I get back to the playground, Julie and Paul are deep in conversation, and Hettie and Allyson are gone.

'Sorry,' I say. 'So what do you think of Miss Diet and her sidekick?'

'I don't like her, or her bitchy-titchy assistant,' says Julie. 'I'm sure Karen will help generate some media coverage, if she can find the time, and you'd make a good MC, so I don't see why we need her,' she says, impatiently beckoning to Dominic and Alexander.

'Well, she's in a good position to help with media coverage and attract further attention, and if she is close to Masterton, who seems to know everyone including a lot of Oaks parents, then that's probably not a bad thing,' Paul says, and then adds, as if in sudden inspiration, 'Then you can model, too, Lily!'

Hmm. Tempting, tempting. I see Julie briefly weighing up Hettie's pros and cons, and she finally grins at me. 'Yes, that would be fab, Lily.'

'Oh good,' Paul nods enthusiastically, 'and then *I* don't have to do the stupid catwalk thing.' Julie shoots me a look and we each take Paul's arm and drag him over to the school gates, our waifs following us, pummelling each other and pulling Henry along, and explain yet again just why he needs to masquerade as a metrosexual and strut down the runway.

Julie and Paul continue heatedly debating whether or not male models are sissies, when Henry stops me to tie his laces. Crouching down on the ground, partially hidden by the throng of my and Julie's children, I overhear Suzanne Morrison telling Linda Black about Andrea Jeremiah, who apparently has been cautioned by the local police for stalking the headmaster of The Pulpit outside his home in an attempt to persuade him to let her child in that year. I strain to catch the last bit in which Ms Treadwell had to act as a character witness. Lord. Linda, unaware that I'm right next to her, whispers back that her husband has decided, to her great relief, not to sell his kidney after all. Instead they're looking to rent a flat near the school that falls into the catchment area. I'm starting to worry that half our model mums will be held in custody and the others won't have the strength to walk on the day.

The word 'catchment area' apparently prompts

Suzanne to deliver a hearsay version of our encounter with the wheelie-stick man (which has Charlotte running down the street screaming obscenities and hurling flowerpots) but just as I grab my children and try to slink off, Linda suddenly spies me mid-manoeuvre.

'Oh, hello there, Lily! Well done on Tim becoming Boy of the Year, you must be very proud?' she smiles and grits her teeth at the same time.

'Thank you,' I reply serenely. 'It was a lovely ceremony and we're very proud of him.'

She sighs, her tight blonde permed curls glistening in the late afternoon sunlight. 'It's such a pity that it wasn't announced before he went for his Oaks interview. You could have talked about his new role in the school and the fact that you're organising this little fashion show of yours. He probably would have stood a better chance. Would have given you something to talk about in any case,' she says, distinctly spitefully.

'I'm sure word will spread, Linda,' I say, smiling back as genuinely and warmly as I can. 'Perhaps you can help with the publicity?' I add, winking at Julie who's just joined in. Linda doesn't get the joke and turns her back on us to walk towards a small group of women waiting for her to lead them out of the playground. Well, frankly, I don't give a damn.

Julie mumbles, 'Jealous cow,' just loud enough for me to hear but hopefully bypassing the children, who are now engaged in talking excitedly about the competition to design the mufti-day outfit, when I'm almost knocked over by a figure barrelling by. It's Karen, looking more than a little flustered, arriving late to collect Claire and Simon.

'It's good to see I'm not the only one who's late today,' she cries as she flies past.

When she's gathered her two, the last in the playground, she joins us.

'How is everything?' she asks, slightly out of breath.

'Fine, fine,' I say. 'How are you?'

'Very busy,' she says, looking genuinely stressed and regretful to have to rush off to Claire's dance class. 'Gotta run, Lily, but I'll speak to you later, OK?'

What a full-on, weird day it's been, but a productive one. We now have five grand and a location for the marquee, which we didn't have this morning.

'So what do you think?' Paul is unlocking his car.

'About what? Hettie, Allyson, Karen?'

'About Hettie. Shall we agree to her being MC and help with exposure?' he asks, keeping one eye on the girls.

My instinct is to say no, but I do think we can use the help, so I nod.

'I'll call her in the morning and say we'd be delighted for any pointers she can give us. She's ambitious, so she'll want to look good, and if she gets good exposure, so do we, I guess,' I say.

'Bye, Lily,' Julie shouts as she heads towards her Beetle. 'Chill this evening, you've worked hard today.'

I walk home with the children who are pestering me to take them to the cinema. I'll take Mike along this weekend, he'll enjoy it and we all need a break, a chill, as Julie suggested.

For the first time in a long while, the children are all at home for tea. There are no clubs, and we sit and chat about our day, Tim talking about how well the school rugby team is expected to do in the county matches and how excited and nervous he is about being Boy of the Year. Jenny talks about what clothes she'll design, which sounds strangely like a combat outfit to me, and Henry just watches everyone else.

'So how did it go today at the golf club?' Mike asks, when the children have been bathed, read to and put to bed, where they're pretending to be asleep.

'Brilliant! Can you believe it – we got five thousand pounds from Matthew Masterton! He's the MD of the place and apparently keen to strengthen his links with Somerset. A lot of the members seem to have kids at The Oaks in any case, so don't forget to apply for that membership – it may help Tim's chances more than we think,' I say.

'God, can't we leave it, Lily? What with all the fashion-show stuff and our boy now Boy of the Year, me joining the golf club isn't really necessary any more. We seem to have it pretty much covered.'

'What do you mean *we* seem to have it covered? Excuse me, Michael Dearl, but you haven't done anything towards getting Tim into The Oaks, so a little thing like joining a golf club doesn't seem too big a request,' I say crossly.

'It's a stupid game,' he says, obviously not prepared to concede the point. 'The working classes play football, the middle classes play tennis and the upper classes play golf – the higher up the social scale people are, the smaller their balls.'

That makes me giggle and I lean over to him, stroking his cheek and kissing him on the lips slowly and gently, keeping my eyes open, watching him watching me. He kisses me back, and it's tender and lovely and sensual. But I can sense he's tired and I've had a long day too. I know that as soon as our heads hit the pillows we'll fall asleep. But at least I'll fall asleep feeling as though I've achieved something for my family today. I've even managed a furtive snog with my husband, which is something I hadn't expected. At this rate we might even get to have sex one day.

Chapter 13
Coming, Ready or Not

'Post,' shouts Tim, who's the first down the stairs this morning. It's Thursday, the rain is pounding on the roof and Henry woke up earlier than his normal 6 a.m. start, all of which puts me, not at my best in the mornings anyway, over the top so when Mike lets Henry bounce energetically on our bed, I'm too tired to even summon up the energy to react, despite feeling as if we're in the middle of a very stormy sea on a huge inflatable raft.

'It's the letter, Mum and Dad. I think it's the letter from The Oaks,' I can hear Tim's voice wafting up from downstairs like the ghost I've been expecting to appear. Suddenly awake, I sit bolt upright, so quickly that I nearly send our water baby flying off the bed into the wardrobe.

'Argh, Mummy,' Henry cries after a moment of silent shock, deciding in a split second whether or not to milk this for all it's worth. He milks, but I ignore him.

Grabbing my dressing gown, I sprint down the stairs, catching a glance at the hall clock. It's still only just after half past six but it's light outside. Tim is waiting at the door in his pyjamas, with the post in his hand.

'I think this is the letter,' he says, still in his pyjamas, looking suddenly ridiculously young and vulnerable. Too young for all this. 'I was just getting the paper to check the rugby score when I saw it. It says "Oaks School" on the envelope.' He hands it to me with a resigned shrug.

I have a sudden overwhelming urge to rush upstairs, lock myself in the bathroom, sit on the toilet and clap my hands over my ears, but I desist.

'Do you want to open it yourself, Tim?' I ask, buying myself some time.

'You do it, Mummy,' he says quickly. I look at the envelope for a few moments before unpeeling and opening the gold-embossed, crested letter, with the names of the headmaster, deputy, and The Oaks motto '*Validus quod honestus quod pia*', something to do with being strong and noble if my admittedly rusty Latin serves me well.

The letter is quite long, but I try to focus on the all-important sentence that says whether Tim's in or not. Then I notice the crucial word in the second line of the second paragraph: '*Unfortunately . . .*'

'*Unfortunately, Tim has not been accepted into The Oaks School on this occasion . . .*'

And I know what this means. I hate the word 'unfortunately'. It's a softener that gives hope where there is none. It's redundant, vague, offering no comfort. Slightly patronising even. 'He could have survived the accident, but unfortunately he didn't.' 'She could have passed her exam, but unfortunately she didn't.' I read on: '*However, we were so impressed with his performance and interview that we are placing him on the waiting list. We will be in touch should circumstances change and a place become available.*'

But no one says no to The Oaks. Every child who's accepted at The Oaks says yes. I don't know of one instance, short of a family moving away, in which the child hasn't gone when they've been offered a place. This badly phrased sentence gives us false hope and that makes me angry. I want to cry.

But Tim is peering intently at my face, trying to detect an expression – of happiness, misery, relief, any display of emotion that will tell him whether or not he's got in – so I pull myself together with a huge effort. Too late.

'I didn't get in, did I, Mummy?' he says so quietly that I step forward to hug him.

He seems so calm, standing there in his pyjamas. He pulls away after a few seconds, sits down on the bottom step and takes the letter from my sweaty hands, reading slowly, as though the words on the page might change and somehow I'll have misread it. I want him to cry, because then I can hold him and squeeze him and kiss him better, just like I do with Henry, but he doesn't.

'It's not the end of the world, Mummy,' he says philosophically. I remember his face when he walked round The Oaks for the first time, his shining eyes when he saw the playing fields. He was like a Duracell bunny bouncing around. I know how much he wanted to get in. Perhaps we're the ones who let *him* down. Maybe it was that bloody interview. Yes, I can see that now. We aren't pillars of industry, we're not gold-embossed names, we're just ordinary people who have an extraordinary little boy.

'I wonder if the others got in,' he says, looking up at me again. 'Mia, Dominic or Claire?' I shrug wordlessly. We sit on the stairs for some time, occasionally patting each other's knee and sighing. My disappointment is so huge I can feel it like a big lump in my throat.

'Well, I'd better get ready for school, Mummy,' he finally says, handing me the letter and slowly disappearing up the stairs.

I read the letter again, and as I read it I feel myself getting angry. I'm furious with a bloody system that doesn't allow the cream to rise to the top. And Tim's response has made me even angrier. If he'd been upset I could have at least confronted him, but now I'm bottling it up inside. I crumple up the letter, suddenly feeling sick because the full implication of him not getting into The Oaks is beginning to hit me like a ton of bricks. If he doesn't get in, where else is there to go? He'll have to go to Readmere, start learning how to vandalise bus stops. God, Lily, stop being so middle class, they can't all be like that; just the ones you see, just the ones you notice. Just the ones that make the most noise and take up all of the teacher's time so the good ones in class can't concentrate, get bullied, get disheartened. Stop it, I finally tell myself firmly. Readmere is not an option. Put it out of your head – it's too depressing.

I walk into the kitchen, starting aimlessly pulling out plates, toast, forks. Should I follow Suzanne Morrison and sell up and move to get into a good school? The timing is awkward, though, and other areas probably have the same difficulties. And I won't know the community or have any contacts, so it might be an even greater problem. God, is the fashion show all a waste of time now? Is it even worth doing? I've got so many people involved now that I can't suddenly cancel, and anyway, it's for a good cause. But still.

When Mike comes downstairs I can see from his face that Tim's told him the news, and he can see from my face how bad I'm feeling. He hugs me.

'Tim will be fine, there is still hope,' he says. Tears suddenly well up in my eyes, all the anger, resentment and memories ringing in my head. This one fucking letter that's probably been sent out to hundreds of other kids, being read at this very moment by mums, dads and children who are just as upset as we are. Well, except the ones who got the 'well done' letters, they'll all be jumping for joy. Visualise us jumping for joy, Lily.

Visualise us jumping for joy, it might make you feel better.

Mike strokes my hair and pulls me back slightly, brushing away my tears.

'Lily, Tim will be fine. He'll be OK, I know it. I'll join the golf club and schmooze with the locals and everything will be all right,' he says, trying to make me laugh which half-works because I smile.

'Can you knock out Dr Totham with one of your shots while you're at it?' I say aggressively. Maybe I do know where my daughter gets her vengeful streak from.

'I can try, if that makes you feel better,' he says. 'But Tim's a great candidate. If he is on the waiting list, as the letter says, then he's bound to be at the top. We have to keep this in perspective, because if we show Tim how worried and upset we are, he'll become worried and very upset himself. We've got to keep calm and focused. You continue with the fashion show, and I'll – Lily, have you toasted buttered and jammed bread?' He pulls the burned mess out of the toaster just in time.

'Mmm,' he then says more gently, taking a big bite and giving me a kiss of crumbs. 'It will be fine, Lily.'

'What happens if he has to go to Readmere?' I say, dreading to even say it out loud.

'We'll move,' replies Mike reassuringly quickly.

'But where to? And we'd be uprooting the others from Somerset,' I say.

'Then we'll look elsewhere,' he says. 'Lily, he'll be all right. You're always telling me, everything happens for a reason. This should only make us more determined.

You've got to be strong, OK?' He pats my back as if I was Henry's age.

I nod grimly. I fill up the kettle and then start to pace again, Mike silently munching on his toast and watching me closely until Henry clatters down the stairs, looking for his breakfast.

'Hi, Mummy. Can I have some Shreddies?' he asks, looking around for the bowls.

'Yes, darling, just warming up the milk and they'll be on the table. Why don't we get dressed first, sweetheart?' I say, tugging him back towards the staircase, briefly looking back at Mike, who's staring into space as though he's trying to figure out what to say next.

At the breakfast table, Jenny is totally oblivious to the news, Henry noisily munches his way through two bowls of cereal, and Tim still seems calm albeit a little dazed.

'Do you want a lift to the dentist?' I ask Mike a little later as I get the children into the car, Jenny having to rush up to her bedroom because she's forgotten her book bag.

'No, I'm fine,' he says, 'it will make you late.'

He walks over, kisses all the children on the forehead and then gives me a hug, whispering in my ear, 'Call your mum, Lily, she'll be good with this. I know you're worried. We will sort something for Tim, darling. We will,' he says, giving me a squeeze. 'And it's still worth doing the show to raise money for the library, so don't give up hope.'

*

At the school gates I see Paul, Julie and Karen with their broods. As the children run to tell each other their news, I realise they must have received their letters too. Do I ask or wait for them to tell me? I don't need to – their faces tell the story.

'Mia didn't get in,' says Paul glumly, coming over and giving me a hug.

'Neither did Tim,' I reply, trying to be composed. Paul looks genuinely shocked.

'Bloody hell, girl, what's going on. I was absolutely sure that if anyone it would be Tim. What on earth are they looking for, for God's sake?' he says. My thoughts exactly.

'Dominic didn't get in either,' says Julie, coming towards us and overhearing the news. 'Is it even worth doing the fashion show now?' She gives me a quick hug and a peck on the cheek.

'Yes, it is. Don't forget it's for the library, and, of course, the waiting list. Are you on it?'

They both nod.

'In which case,' I say firmly, 'we've got to try even harder. It might still make a difference.' The other two nod mutely. 'I spoke to Henrietta last week and confirmed that she'll MC the event – I think she'll be good, despite her annoying attitude. The more high-profile people she can get to attend it, the better,' I say, trying to bring us back to the positive side of our project.

I wave at Tim and Jenny as they head towards the playground, Tim chatting to Mia and Dominic, Claire trailing a bit behind with Jenny, when Karen joins us. She gives me a quick hug.

'Hello, guys,' she says. 'Letter time, huh?'

'Oh, so you heard,' I say, smiling at her. She's always a good one to have in a crisis. 'None of us got in. Did you get a no as well?' I ask, sympathetically.

'Actually, no,' she replies, hesitating a fraction of a moment and seeming almost a little embarrassed. 'Claire got accepted.'

There's a pause that lengthens and lengthens.

'Oh, well done,' I finally say. Just because Tim didn't get in doesn't mean we all have to suffer. At the same time, well, it *is* gutting that Karen, with her slapdash, careless attitude is reaping rewards while we slog away racked with nerves and get nowhere. But she's my friend and I'm trying my hardest to be genuinely happy for her.

'Tim's on the waiting list, so there's still hope,' I smile, covering up the icy silence from Paul and Julie. We all fidget around by the gates for a moment and I can hear the other people talking about their acceptance letters, the ones who got their children into their school of choice being just as vocal as those who didn't. I notice Linda Black talking to some of the other mums and try to avoid eye contact, just in case she learns that Tim didn't get in and comes over to gloat. Sally Day and Christine Hawes are smiling, Ella Fritz and Daniella Frost are looking quite tearful. Jane Anderson is talking animatedly to Tanya Reed, Andrea Jeremiah and Suzanne Morrison, and I'm not quite sure if it's good or bad news or something totally different altogether. It could even be about the fashion show for all I know. I'm so tired now and I don't really want to speak to anyone else this morning, miserable or happy – either way they'll be insufferable. The children play pat ball and football and I'm vaguely aware of the girls pretending to be catwalk models and parading up and down the hopscotch part of the playground, practising their poses, turns and walks.

I'm just about to walk on ahead when Karen suddenly says, her words rushed and anxious, 'I'm so sorry about Tim, Lily. I know how much you wanted to get him into the school. And I'm sorry I haven't been around much lately. If you want any help with photography at the fashion show maybe?' she says, sounding both apologetic and conciliatory.

'I think it's a bit late now,' Julie says frostily before I can speak. 'We've got that one covered, haven't we?' She turns to Paul, who's giving Karen an equally reproachful look.

He hates confrontation, though. 'Thanks for offering, anyway,' he says, peering down at his feet, avoiding looking her in the eye.

'Well, the offer is there, and sorry again for not being part of it. It really isn't my fault that Claire got in and yours didn't,' she then adds, starting to sound defensive.

I snap. This is too much. 'Well, I suppose playing golf all day *can* tire you out, can't it, Karen?' I say icily. 'Going to the golf club and networking with all the right people?' I'm suddenly beyond annoyed that she spent her time working and playing golf when she could have been helping us. It's probably what got her in, that she and Jamie were members. So why didn't she call me and insist I do the same? Julie and Paul were probably right; she didn't want to be involved. Blood is thicker than water and all that and I'm stupid to think otherwise. I'm as angry with myself as I am with her. I should have organised that golf membership myself or been more firm with Mike, but, to be honest, it's not really us, The Oaks or not, I just couldn't see us on the green. Jessica was right though, mixing strategically does matter. And Henrietta was right as well, I do need to manage my time more effectively.

Karen doesn't pick up on the golf-course reference; on the contrary, she looks faintly confused. 'Well, I've got to go now,' she finally says, after another awkward pause. 'Everything will work out, I just know it.' She hugs me, pretending not to notice my stiffening, and briskly takes off.

'Do you have time for a coffee?' asks Paul, looking at me as though he's in need of a hug too.

'No, I've got to sort out some of the runway schedules after dropping Henry off,' I say, impatiently waving him over. 'And lots of other errands. My house is sadly neglected with all this fashion stuff,' I say, shrugging my shoulders and sighing.

On the way to Henry's nursery I see Harriet Jones, one of the mothers who didn't quite make the final catwalk line-up for the fashion show. She is sitting on a bench just outside the school gates with a boy who must be her son, Marcus. She is one of the Mrs Pepperpots we declined and since the fashion-show audition I've nodded to her in the playground at drop-off and pick-up when I've seen her, but I don't know much else about her. Tim tells me that Marcus is in his rugby team and a pretty good player.

'What is Daddy going to say?' I can hear Marcus saying as we walk past, desperately appealing to his mum, who keeps patting his back and making soothing noises. I don't want to interfere and, anyway, it's none of my business, but when her mobile rings I can't help overhearing her conversation. She starts to speak quietly at first, then more loudly.

'Oh hi, Gerald, yes, the letter arrived after you left. No, I'm so sorry. Marcus didn't get in. He's quite upset about it.' She looks at her son and ruffles his hair while she listens to the person at the other end, who I presume must be Marcus's father. Her face changes and her whole posture stiffens. She gives Marcus a last pat, then gets up and walks a few paces, hissing something into the phone. Another pause, then she replies, her voice dripping with disdain. 'You know, you are a pompous arsehole sometimes. It is not a case of Marcus not having the right tutor. He couldn't have done any more tests if he tried. He was tired and exhausted and absolutely burned out by the amount of material he was given by the tutors. It got ridiculous and I put a stop to it.' Another long, icy pause, her face getting redder by the minute, then she erupts, 'You cannot compare those children who go to private pre-prep and prep schools with the state system. Your office friends are completely up their own butts.' She listens for a second, then more shouting. I can see Marcus cowering on the bench, clearly either immensely embarrassed or utterly terrified of 'Gerald'.

'Oh, don't be so ridiculous. No, he shouldn't go to a boarding school just because all your friends send their children to boarding school.' She lowers her voice and is back to the hissing. 'He is not –' a furtive glance over her shoulder and more hissing, '– a failure, so don't you *dare* use that word in front of him.'

Harriet turns off her phone and is just about to throw it against the wall of the school building when she notices me standing there. I'm torn between wanting to hug Marcus or Harriet or both. Her husband sounds like a bully, and listening to her makes me realise I've got to be careful that I don't make Tim feel as though he has failed us – or himself.

'Hi,' I say carefully. 'I'm sorry, but I couldn't stop overhearing. Is it The Oaks? You know my son didn't get in either, I think very few people did this year.'

'I know, I know,' she says, trying half a smile. 'It's not The Oaks but Merton, over in Burley.' One of the most expensive private schools in the county (and beyond, I bet). 'They are silly, aren't they? Not realising how wonderful our children are? Those stupid tests tell them nothing about the child really. You see, my husband went to private school, then his parents piled him off to boarding school so that's all he knows.

He was always against sending Marcus to a state school, even in infants, but the private school we initially sent him to asked him to leave in Year Three. He didn't fit in, they said. He was diagnosed with dyspraxia, but a very, very mild case, and I think if he'd got slightly more support he would have been fine. The private school simply couldn't cope with their grades being lowered by our son. Somerset is a nice school, with a nice headmistress, and they've managed to help him brilliantly. I think he's even slightly above average here, in terms of grades.'

'That's great,' I say kindly, smiling over at Marcus. 'Don't worry, something will sort itself out, I think.'

'Aren't you Tim Dearl's mummy?' Marcus has walked over hesitantly, now grabbing hold of his mum's hand.

'Yes, I am,' I say. 'You're not in Tim's class, are you?'

'No, Miss Piper's. Did he get into wherever he wanted?'

'No. He tried for The Oaks and didn't get in,' I say, shrugging my shoulders.

'We tried for that one too, didn't we, Mummy? Well, Tim Dearl is Boy of the Year and *he* didn't even get in,' he says, looking relieved. Harriet is smiling at her son and nods.

'But we're on the waiting list and where there's a waiting list, there's hope.' She gives him a tight squeeze, which makes me want to get up and rush into the school and give Tim a tight squeeze too. 'Now, off you go, Marcus, and have a good day. Don't worry about anything, it will be fine,' she says, waving him off.

I realise that I've got to go this minute, or Henry will once again be late for nursery, so I flash Harriet a smile and rush off. After Henry's safely deposited, I need to go and pick up some bits and pieces from the place we're renting the tables from for the show. I'm quite grateful for the drive – the silence feels nice after that chatter at the school gates and the annoying exchange with Karen – and on a whim I call my mother as Mike suggested, hoping I can reach her wherever she is at the moment. I put the phone on hands-free.

'Hello, darling. How are you?' Her voice is so clear it sounds as though she's in the seat behind me.

'Fine, well . . . Not fine, actually. Tim wasn't accepted into The Oaks and the alternatives are appalling, and I'm worried about him,' I say, trying to be calm.

'Really?' Mum sounds startled, which I'm pleased about. 'Stupid people. Don't they know what they're turning down?' she asks. A rhetorical question if ever I heard one.

'But he's on the waiting list,' I add, quickly reassuring myself more than anything else.

'Well, that's it, then. He'll get in. I know it. That boy is a credit wherever he goes. Don't worry, Lily. And be careful putting too much pressure on him, I know what you can be like sometimes. You're a real worrier, and if he thinks you feel he's a failure he'll start to doubt himself and you don't want that. He's a confident, balanced boy and you want him to stay that way, don't you? Focus on the good stuff,' she says, almost scolding me. 'And talking of the good stuff, how's the fashion show going?'

'Fine,' I say, more cheerfully. 'We've almost got everything in place, just the rehearsals in the next week and the event itself on the twenty-fourth.'

'I'll be there, Lily. I'm so proud of you and what you're doing with the fashion show. It will all turn out right in the end. Don't you worry yourself.'

This makes me smile because she's the fourth person today who's said that to me and it's not even eleven o'clock.

Just as I've hung up, the phone rings again.

'Hello, it's Allyson Dyer, Henrietta's assistant?' a tinny voice booms out of the speakers. 'I'm just calling to say that Henrietta is working on her speech and we have contacted the local newspapers; and they'll be there on the day. Actually, it turns out that one of your acquaintances, Karen Field, will be covering the event, so that's all sorted. Henrietta has also asked Tyler Villier, a good friend of hers, to help sponsor the catering. I trust that is in order? And, lastly, Henrietta has invited Mr Masterton and Dr Totham, headmaster of The Oaks, which I believe you want your son to attend?' She pauses meaningfully, expecting me to say something, but I don't so she continues. 'That's all.'

'Thank you,' I say. 'We've already contacted the press, but the more the merrier.' I try my hardest not to be ungracious, realising that Villier's money might come in handy for Tony.

'They now know Henrietta will be there, so there will be more interest. This is also why Mr Masterton and Dr Totham will be at the show, and we have invited several other local celebrities to add some style to the event. Thank you.' And she clicks off.

Arrogant cow, I think to myself. That is one miserable lady. But at least she's managed to get Masterton and Totham along to the event, so everything is now at stake. It's got to be good.

As I drive, I'm thinking about the fashion show, about Karen covering the show, which is interesting news, and about Henrietta and her spiteful sidekick. Quietly determined but unexceptional, innocuous, beige, the sort of person you wouldn't notice but exactly the sort of person you've got to watch out for. I even get the feeling she'd stab Henrietta in the back given half the chance.

Chapter 14
Fancy Dress

It's Friday morning, and I'm on my way to the dress rehearsal. It's bright and dry, and still a bit cold, but it hasn't rained for a few days, so I'm hoping the field won't be too muddy. Either way, Paul's managed to hire some plastic mats, which will form pathways on the grass. And the show is on Sunday, so we still have a couple of days to smooth out any problems. I'm tired and a bit weary, with The Oaks letter and things being so busy lately. On Wednesday I stayed up half the night to write a test column for Angela, which was huge fun but exhausting. Then Mike and I had a massive row last night.

I know we've all been busy, but I've been getting so fed up about our dwindling sex life, that I had vowed to force the issue. I'd just put the children to bed and found Mike in the dining room, working late. I didn't care if he was exhausted, I wanted to make this work. So I slipped on a black slinky number I hadn't worn for ages, opened a bottle of wine and had a glass, then two, and put on 'You're Not Alone' by Olive and started to dance around Mike sitting at the table. Admittedly the dance was a little peculiar, a sort of Indian belly-dancing with a touch of kick-boxing and some flamenco thrown in for good measure, plus a little bit of Uma Thurman in *Pulp Fiction.*

He wasn't really reacting and I finally pulled his chair out from under the table so I could sit on his lap, and that forced him to stop working.

'What are you doing, Lily?' he said tiredly, putting down his pen and scowling at me.

'I'm trying to seduce my husband,' I replied as I slid myself onto his lap and tried to kiss him. He pulled back.

'God, Lily, there's so much work on and I'm beyond tired,' he said, pushing me off his lap and picking up his pen again. I shudder at the memory now.

I tried to keep the momentum going by getting back up to dance: 'We've really taken each other for granted recently, Mike. Do you remember when we had sex everywhere, remember all the weekends away, and how wonderfully spontaneous it always was?' I was trying to ruffle his hair playfully, but he wasn't having any of it.

'Lily, don't be ridiculous, we have three children. We lead busy lives and now this worry about Tim's schooling. On the train today there was some guy in the carriage talking about how dreadful Readmere is, and for a moment I seriously thought about moving, or even pay to go private, in which case I've got to bring in more money. Darling, if this is about you feeling insecure about yourself or us or anything, let me just say this,' he leaned over and took my hands, which by then had stopped writhing in the air and hung down limply by my sides, 'I love you, I'm in love with you, I don't fancy anyone else, I don't want to sleep with anyone else, and when this is all over we can have some time together again. But right now I'm not feeling in the mood, darling. Is that OK?' He looked at me as though I was about twelve.

'You're never in the mood,' I finally said. 'This is pathetic. My best friend is having sex with a younger man, my other best friend may be having an affair with an older man, albeit one with lousy fashion sense, and I can't even have an affair with my own husband? You're being selfish and unfair. I feel like a lump of lard the way you treat me, Mike Dearl, and you don't get it, do you?' And I stormed back upstairs.

I still feel slightly sick thinking about it. Mike only gave me a cold peck on the cheek this morning – so much for relighting the passion in our marriage – and the kids were particularly restless too. Jenny wouldn't stop talking about her combat-style entry for the mufti-day outfit competition and Henry was trying to practise his catwalk moves but kept falling over when he turned. Tim was a little quieter, perhaps having a delayed reaction to the schools news.

My phone rings and I turn on the speaker. Tamara from my photography class.

'Darling Lily, how are you?' she says, sounding as though she is on hands-free herself.

'OK, Tamara, just on the way to the dress rehearsal now and hoping that everything and everyone is ready. I'd rather have things go wrong now than on Sunday,' I reply.

'Well, I'm calling to say that Leon and Gilbert are coming and we all want to bring our other halves, is that OK? And –' She stops mid-sentence, shouting to the driver in front of her, 'If you drive any slower you'll go backwards, arsehole,' which makes me smile. I need something to smile about this morning.

'Sorry about that, darling, it's some prat in a four-wheel drive who's driving like a learner. Anyway, what was I saying? Oh yes. We'd love to take some pictures at the show, and Gilbert said it would be wonderful practice for all of us, but you may already have a photographer? In which case we wouldn't bring all our gear,' she says without pausing for breath.

Karen has offered to take photos, but she's already doing a piece, so surely can't be taking photos as well, plus, we haven't really spoken since the letter day. So I say quickly, 'Yes, Tamara, that would be lovely. You've got the invites, so you know what time it starts and everything, don't you?'

'Yes, yes, we've got all that.' I can hear her beeping at someone else and calling them a number of unspeakable things. 'Well, bye for now, Lily, good luck with the rehearsal and see you on Sunday, darling,' she then says, blowing a kiss down the phone and clicking off.

I pull up at the field – thank God there's a back road and we don't all have to truck through the golf course – and walk over to the marquee. It looks rather splendid, a bit like a huge canvas castle, although it's fairly bare inside at the moment despite teeming with mothers. I'm taking heed of the pep talk my mum gave me, and am thinking positive. It will all work out in the end, I know it will.

'Do you want us to wear knickers?' Andrea Jeremiah shouts up to me as I'm ten foot up a ladder, balancing precariously, trying to make absolutely sure the marquee won't fall down mid-show. The last thing I want is for mums and children to be injured by falling tarpaulin: that would generate the wrong sort of publicity altogether.

'Er, yes please,' I shout back.

'But the panty line,' she shouts, looking anxious.

'It won't matter, honest,' I say. All the other model mums look relieved that they can keep their knickers on.

Paul and Julie wait at the bottom of the ladder. 'How are you feeling this morning?' asks Julie, looking fairly subdued herself.

'Still a bit disappointed about The Oaks letter,' I admit, stepping off to give her a hug, 'but never mind. This will be great though, don't you think?' I add optimistically.

'Come on, let's go over to the clubhouse and go through everything one last time.' Paul's got a pile of papers in his hand. 'We can probably find some coffee there too.'

As we walk over to the golf clubhouse, Julie mentions that she's had a look at some other schools for Dominic. God, already? I can't give up on The Oaks yet. And yet – I need to be prepared. I feel as though I'm paralysed.

'I had a look at Readmere, Lily,' Julie is still talking next to me. 'And it's every bit as awful as everyone says. I'm going to visit St Thomas's, but I hear they're very strict and old-fashioned.'

'And we've put the house up for sale, guys,' Paul chimes in. 'Jessica is determined to move into another catchment area. We haven't been getting on too well recently, to be honest, apparently I haven't been taking things seriously enough. She went on about me joining the golf club after your lunch, Lily. But I bloody hate golf. I just don't see the point of it,' he says, looking down at his shoes as we're walking.

So much for optimism: I'm obviously not the only one who's feeling the pressure of school selection on their marriage.

'Eddie is just leaving me to it,' Julie says, sighing, 'which is good. The last thing I need at the moment is for him to not compromise over schools. I know Christine is having real problems. The counselling isn't really working and her husband wants their children to go to a different school altogether, which Christine thinks is just to spite her.'

'Oh, that's awful,' I say, feeling for Christine. 'No

wonder she's lost so much weight recently, and she doesn't even need to. Why can't they just leave the children out of it,' I say, thinking myself lucky that Mike and I largely agree on most things, despite our rows. 'We've also got to remember that there will be parents who'll put their kids' names down for more than one school and leave it till the last minute to choose which one they want,' I say, trying to sound positive. At this rate the fashion show will be a roaring success, everyone grimly cheering on the droopy models, for God's sake.

We walk into the clubhouse. There are a few grey-haired blue-blazered men sitting at the bar, looking bemused by our presence.

Paul goes to get the coffees while I sit down with Julie and start going through my action list, checking off all the things we need to sort out today.

'How did Mike take the letter?' asks Julie.

'Well, let's just say we're not planning to move. But Mike is feeling the stress of it all as well and I'm trying to be really casual about it because I don't want it to affect the children. We're all in the same boat, I think.'

'Apart from Karen,' she says quietly.

Yes, Karen. I half-expected to see her at the club actually but when I look round I can't see her anywhere. I say nothing and just nod. It's all getting too complicated.

'Things are going really well with Tony, though,' Julie says more cheerfully. 'He keeps feeding me which is making me pile on the pounds. I'll have to be careful or I really won't fit into the outfits Pooky has chosen for me,' she says, patting her tummy.

I smile for a moment, genuinely happy that something is working out amongst all of this. Though I can't help feeling slightly wishful for some similar romance in my own life. It doesn't last long though, as Paul quickly returns with the coffees and we get down to business.

'The marquee is great,' I say. 'Thanks for arranging that, Paul.'

'The boys seem to have done a very good job putting it up,' he says, 'and they've already installed the pathways so no one gets muddy. The DJ is here and has the playlist we requested and a few ideas of his own. I've got a sound system coming too. Not the pricey one, but I think it'll be fine.'

'We can always get the school orchestra to play something if it's not working out,' Julie jokes.

'All the model mums are here,' I say, ticking things off. I saw Pooky, Smokey and Fifi waiting around as well, all wearing head-to-toe black, chain-smoking furiously and looking edgy but excited. I suppose they know there are going to be some people in the audience, who could be of use to them. 'Tiffany is here to try out hair ideas and make-up with the mums. Oh, and Fifi told me she's a bit concerned that some of her mums have lost weight, which might be a problem – her designs are really for the fuller figure. But I think they'll work it out.'

'What about photos?' asks Paul, taking such a loud slurp of his coffee that it stirs the seventy-somethings in the corner from their sleep.

'I think the paper is bringing someone, but my friends

from the photography course will all be coming with their cameras as well for a course assignment, so we've got a good back-up plan. As far as I know from Jane Anderson, all the tickets have now been sold. Full house, guys! Over 250 people in the audience.' I'm suddenly beginning to get excited now – it's all working out brilliantly and I'm sure everything else will too. Didn't Allyson say she'd invited Totham and Co.?

'Tony's on track to produce hundreds of profiteroles and cakes for the day. Do we have the drinks all sorted?' Julie asks Paul.

'Yes, the local off-licence has helped us price-wise, so we've got wine, water and fruit juices, which I think is fine. I thought champagne was a bit over the top, but it's a good wine. Recommended by the *Sunday Times* wine guide, if anyone should ask.'

'What about our catwalk?' I say, suddenly seeing an un-ticked action point.

But Paul's got it covered.

'We're expecting it any minute; at about the same time as the sound system, Lily. God, I'm hoping it's the right size,' he says, half-smiling.

'Great,' I say, looking down at my checklist, 'we're not in bad shape. We'd better finish up and go back over to wait for the deliveries.' We get up and leave the clubhouse, much to the relief of the grey-haired mob in the corner. 'The advertisements have obviously generated a lot of interest,' I said as we are walking back. 'Allyson called to say that Hettie has her speech all ready and has contacted the local press.'

'We've done that already,' says Paul.

'I think she meant that they contacted the local press to tell them Henrietta was going to be there,' I say meaningfully.

'I very much hope she's not trying to take all the credit herself,' says Julie. 'We should never have used her.'

'She'll be good,' I say, sounding more convinced than I am, 'and anyway, we can't un-ask her now, can we?'

I see Jane Anderson rushing towards us. 'Hello there. Just to let you know the lorries have arrived with the sound system and the catwalk. They want to know where to put it?'

'How are you feeling?' Jane asks as we walk the last bit across to the lorries where the drivers are lounging against the huge tires, watching the activities in the marquee.

'Nervous and excited,' I say, trying to sound positive.

'I must admit, Lily, this is an excellent idea. I wish you'd been more involved with school events. We can do with someone like you, you know,' she says, smiling at me warmly, which I thought threatening before and now actually find quite touching.

'Do you know if Ms Treadwell is pleased?' I ask, looking at the men, who are now starting to lower what looks like enormous crates of stuff to the ground.

'She's delighted, Lily. She announced the winner of the mufti-outfit competition today in assembly, but Fifi already knew earlier, so she could start working on the winning entry; she's really excited too. The PTA have made lots of cakes, so I don't think the audience will be going hungry. And we're all on track to make enough funds for a whole new library. Wonderful,' she says, squeezing my shoulder, and adding apologetically as Poncho bounds up, 'I hope you don't mind that I brought him today, I'm sure he'll behave well.'

'Where do you want us to put this, guvnor?' says the driver, ignoring us and looking at Paul.

'What is it?' asks Paul, peering at the boxes.

'Haven't got a clue, we just deliver things,' he says unhelpfully.

'In that case you'd better bring them in here,' I say, pointing to the marquee. It will either be sound, lights or catwalk.

'Can anyone help?' he says, looking around for some more men, but finding only mums, designers and Poncho.

'I think the guys who put the marquee up are still here,' says Paul. 'I'll go and find them.'

Five minutes later the boxes are still in the lorry and the driver refuses to start unloading unless he has help. 'You've got to understand, it will take me all day if I do it by myself,' he says. 'Any chance of a cuppa?'

Julie scowls at him and says, 'No, not at the moment, but I'll help you, I'm strong and I'm sure some of the mums can help, too.' And with that she rolls up her sleeves and she, Andrea, Christine and Daniella climb on board the lorry and start to unload, coordinated by Jane and myself. Paul returns with the marquee men and a few volunteers from the golf club, all of whom are dressed smartly but seem willing and able to help.

A long procession of men and women are now walking into the marquee, placing boxes by the main entrance. I open one of them marked 'BOOM' and see what looks like a large speaker so hopefully everything marked 'BOOM' is something to do with sound. Other boxes seem to contain parts of the catwalk, which looks as though you need to be an engineering expert to assemble it, but Paul seems confident.

Half an hour later, the lorry is emptied and the driver, having had his cup of tea, waves us goodbye and wishes us luck. Perhaps he wasn't so bad after all.

Paul coordinates the unpacking while I head towards the mums and designers, who are all traipsing over to the clubhouse to get cleaned up.

The golf club has kindly allowed us to use its changing rooms, although on the day, between outfit changes, they will only have a small section behind the stage for their designers.

'I design for the fuller figure,' Fifi approaches me importantly, cigarette in hand, drawing me to the side so the other designers can't hear what we're saying. Speaking quickly between puffs, she explains, 'I've put a lot of effort into this, and now Jane and Tina have put themselves on diets which is simply not on,' she says, looking crossly at the two women who are just coming out of the loo, happily comparing their new slimline figures and flat tummies.

'I think they wanted to look good on the day,' I say, trying to calm Fifi down. 'You must understand it's the first time they've modelled.'

'They *will* look good on the day, Lily. They're wearing *my* designs.' She draws herself up to full height and, against my better judgement, I shrink back a little. 'I only hope the mufti-day winner doesn't turn out to be anorexic: it won't do my reputation any good at all,' she says with a dramatic sigh and heads back to the mums, who are standing eagerly by the clothes rails waiting to be dressed.

I walk over to Pooky with Julie and Sally, suddenly just as eager as everyone else. Pooky has agreed to provide a series of outfits for me at the last minute, and I can't wait to see what she's got.

'Can we try on our clothes now, Pooky?' I appear next to her so suddenly that she jumps. 'Sorry! I've got a brief half-hour before I need to go and check if the catwalk is OK and the lighting and sound systems work, and then we can get the mothers onto the catwalk.' Sounds of arguing are getting louder behind me and I hear Christine's voice saying, 'I can't wear that, it will make me look fat,' to which Smokey unhelpfully replies, 'Good.'

For me, Pooky has chosen a green-and-orange mini-dress with long brown-and-burgundy canvas-and-leather over-the-knee boots which I immediately fall in love with but am not quite sure I can pull off. Pooky reads my mind. 'I've chosen each outfit for the woman, and I know what your personalities are like. You *can* wear this, Lily,' she says, brooking no argument and handing me the outfit, along with a brown trouser suit.

I start to try on the outfits when I suddenly see Paul

coming in, covering his eyes for the sake of the half-undressed ladies milling around. 'Slight problem. Lily, can you come over to the marquee? I've got something you need to see,' he shouts into the room at large, a worried look on his face.

It's the start of a long list of problems. The catwalk is too long by twelve inches, but Paul says we can shorten it if we remove one of the sections. But then the other two sections may not join up properly, so there might be a chance the models will trip up. 'So should we put down some sort of rug or will that look silly?' He looks at me for an on-the-spot decision.

'How are the lights and sound system?' I ask, looking at all the wiring I've stepped over. 'Are these wires still going to be here on the day?'

'Well, we can't get the lights or sound system to work, but I called Angela and she put me in touch with this specialist guy, who's coming down to have a look at it. He should be here in about an hour.' Angela is really going beyond the call of duty. I owe her massively.

'Anything else?' I say, looking hopeful that he's going to tell me something good.

'The weather forecast for Sunday is warm and sunny,' he says, smiling.

'Great,' I say, 'there's always a silver lining. I think we'll be OK without a carpet. Let me pop back to the ladies and make sure they're all OK with their outfits, then we can try a dress rehearsal with the models, music or no music.'

*

For the next hour Andrea tries to show the others how to walk and turn, and stop and turn and walk. As there's no music it's difficult, but someone has had the genius idea to bring in a mini CD player. With Beyoncé, Faithless and Grace Jones in the background, we proceed.

Christine, Ella and Sally all have excellent rhythm but Jane, Tina and Julie can't quite grasp where they should turn, when they should pose and when they should walk, so there are a few collisions. But after an hour of Andrea talking and eventually shouting, 'Walk, walk, walk. Turn, stop, pose, pose, turn. Walk, walk, walk, stop. Turn, pose, pose, turn. Turn and walk. Listen to the beat, Julie. Listen to the music, Jane. Watch your timing, Tina. Slow down, slow down, speed up, speed up, and smile. Smile, God damn it!' they sort of, almost, get it. Thankfully, my teenage years at dance school and recent kick-boxing have kept my sense of rhythm reasonably strong, so I'm not finding it as difficult as some of the others. Perhaps I should have asked Daisy to coordinate the catwalk – she'd have come in handy with the lorry drivers too.

The designers have collectively agreed that none of the models should wear heels after Ella and Jane fell quite badly in the first half-hour of practice. So everyone is wearing flat shoes and boots or going barefoot, which is fine as many of the clothes wouldn't look out of place on a hippy, albeit a designer one.

Just when I think we've got it all sorted, an argument about music and lyrics erupts. Julie thinks Pink Floyd's

'Another Brick in the Wall' would be good for the children to walk to, but Jane thinks the anti-education lyrics are totally inappropriate, considering what the show is about. On this occasion I side with Jane. Groove Armada's 'I See You Baby (Shakin' that Ass)' is considered borderline because of the lyrics, and Faithless's 'Insomnia' only gets in because we agree that the rhythm is strong and good for walking. The line about ripping tights off with your teeth gets a few raised eyebrows from Jane and Tina, though. Everyone wants to walk to Roy Orbison's 'Pretty Woman', Annie Lennox singing 'Who's That Girl?' and Beyoncé's 'Crazy in Love'. We practise till noon and although the designers are concerned that only a few of the mothers will be able to undress and dress quickly enough for the outfit change – they've timed everyone and by the designated time most of the mums are still in their knickers – we decide to have a twenty-minute break.

I walk over to Paul who has managed to get the lighting and sound systems working just as Henrietta Diet turns up, with Allyson Dyer, to rehearse her speech. Unfortunately, the microphone keeps letting out a high-pitched squeal, and in the end she has to shout the speech, a lot of which is about her and only a little about the show. I can't quite give it my full attention, though, as our DJ, one of the dads, has just rung to say he's got salmonella. Paul, bless him, having managed to get the lights and sound to work by himself, thinks he can DJ on the day too, but when he tries to turn up the music and nearly blows the system, he smiles at me sheepishly.

'I'll find someone by Sunday.'

'Ring Angela,' I suggest, trying to keep a note of desperation out of my voice. 'She'll give you a contact. I know she has loads,' I say, hoping that this won't be the final straw. I wouldn't blame Angela if she simply put down the receiver and cried.

Slumped over fish and chips that evening, Mike asks me how my day went. 'We hope that everything that could go wrong, has gone wrong *today*,' I say, spreading ketchup over the chips. 'The models don't fit the clothes, the designers are having a strop, the marquee wasn't put up correctly and no one bothered to check if we're breaking any health-and-safety laws, although Ms Treadwell and Mr Masterton said they would see to that. Paul can't handle the music, lighting and sound altogether. Well, we can't agree on the music anyway. But the catering is fine,' I say, popping a chip in my mouth. 'Oh yes, and Henrietta Diet has done her speech, the press will be there and she's managed to get Dr Totham and Mr Masterton to come which is great. And my photography class are turning up too.'

'That sounds brilliant, Lily,' Mike says, giving me a hug. I'm still annoyed about the non-romance our relationship has become, but I'm glad our argument has blown over.

Henry pops up next to me and copies his dad, trying to reach his little arm around me and saying, 'Brilliant,' but only managing to squeeze my arm.

'The winner of the competition was announced in

school today,' says Jenny, looking a big dejected. 'I didn't win.' Not entirely surprising – her mufti outfit was an urchin-looking combination of combats and layered T-shirts. 'Ben Saunders in Year Five came second and Claire won with her design. We can come and watch, can't we?' she asks eagerly.

Claire? If that's not absolutely the last straw. Once again, Karen seems to have managed to get something good out of this without putting any effort in herself.

I'm making a huge effort to compose myself and reply calmly, 'I think the whole school can come and watch if they like.'

'I'm looking forward to seeing my mummy on the catwalk,' Tim looks at me bracingly, as though he knows how tired I feel. They all seem to think I need some support because they go up to bathe by themselves, without me even having to harass them, while Mike clears the table. When I go upstairs and kiss them all goodnight a little later, Henry doesn't ask for another glass of water, Jenny doesn't sulk about going to bed early and Tim, well, Tim just hugs me, and tells me everything will be OK. By the time I get downstairs, Mike has cleared the table and put on *Like A Star*, a Corinne Bailey Rae CD, which he knows I love, and offers me his hand.

'You're right. I will make more of an effort. I was just really, really tired yesterday.' He smiles, the same smile I fell in love with years back.

'I know,' I say, taking his hand in mine and starting to massage the palm gently, then one by one pulling his fingers and intertwining them with mine. 'I just don't want to be a sexless mummy all the time, I want to be a sexy lover as well,' I say, raising his hand to my lips and kissing it.

He looks at me, cupping my face in his hands, and kisses me very gently on the lips. 'You're amazing, Lily,' he says as I kiss him back, and then more intensely as Corinne warbles in the background. It's lovely and I want to cry, but I don't. I don't have the diamantés or the fishnets, the suspender belt or the right lingerie, and I'm not bathed in scented oils, but it doesn't seem to matter to either of us. This evening it's just the two of us.

Chapter 15
Show and Tell

I open my eyes at five and feel good. It's Sunday morning, the sun is shining and we've just made love for two consecutive evenings. Friday night was special, but Saturday was unexpected, spontaneous and all Mike's doing and, of all places, it happened in the kitchen. The children were all well and truly in bed, but I was still terrified that Henry would pop down for a glass of milk mid-orgasm.

I'm happy and it's almost as though the weather senses my happiness and is glowing back, radiating a smile at me. I lean over to Mike and kiss him on the forehead, which he responds to with a light snore and turns over. Well, it was great while it lasted anyway.

It's 24 May, T Day as Julie, Paul and I have come to call it – the day Totham sits in the front row and admires our community spirit.

Mike has agreed to look after the children and bring them to the show, so I can go on ahead and coordinate the event. I take a bit of time to cover myself in Dermalogica products from top to toe, to make me smell, feel and look glowing. I want to look my best today.

Then I look at my roots. Shit, I should have got them done, but in the rush I haven't had time to go to the hairdressers. I hope nobody notices the grey and hopefully Tiffany will work her magic with the hair and make-up. I dose myself up with two Berocca and a few Emergen-C super-energy boosters, but my stomach obviously can't take that much Vitamin C in the morning as I spend the next five minutes on the toilet.

After the short drive, I pay and thank the driver, who, on closer inspection, looks as tired I do, and head toward the marquee, hoping it's somehow been transformed in twenty-four hours from a spaghetti-wire mess into a polished fashion hall. As I walk in I notice the lights in place, and the hanging baskets – Julie must have arranged this because I know I didn't put it on my list. It's a nice touch. I peer at one of the nearest baskets, which is full of red and yellow primroses. There's a note saying, 'Good luck from Tatiana's,' and as I look closely, each basket has been sponsored by somewhere local – Giorgiano's has a basket of purple and white hyacinths, and there's another from St Michael's College photography group, bless them, and another from Tony's Restaurant. I feel quite tearful, but perhaps it's just the caffeine in the Coke.

The chairs have all arrived and are lined up neatly around a catwalk that looks the perfect length, without gaps or an uneven surface. The sound system has somehow managed to hide all its wiring and the floors are clear of anything that could be a hazard. The marquee looks stable and the tables have been laid out ready for the food and drinks to be displayed. There are signs pointing to where the golf-club toilets are. Thankfully we didn't have to get a Portaloo, which would have pushed us over budget; I hadn't realised it was so expensive to pee in a field.

I'm the only one in the marquee for now, although I hear voices outside so I'm not the first to arrive. It's like the calm before the storm and I savour the moment, realising it's make-or-break time and that Tim's chances of a place at The Oaks hang in the balance. When all this is over, tomorrow, I have to start thinking of alternatives, but right now I've got to concentrate on what lies immediately ahead.

'Hello, darling,' shouts a recognisable voice and I turn round and see Fifi, smoking furiously and in top-to-toe black as usual, grinning at me, accompanied by two short, overloaded and harassed girls, each struggling with a rack of clothes.

'So, the day is here,' she says, giving me a hug and turning to the girls. 'Can you put the clothes over there, at the back behind the catwalk, and be careful with them, please.'

The girls quickly pull the rails past us and head off towards the little changing room.

'I hope that room is big enough for the mums to change in,' I say, looking after them. There might be a few elbows and knees in faces.

'There are going to be assistants to help them, Lily, it'll be fine, I think. You know from your fashion days that it's always chaos behind the scenes, but it always works out in the end, and even if it doesn't, the idea is to have fun. I've also got the winning design for the mufti-day outfit all made up, which I think you'll like.'

'I know, Jenny said it's lovely,' I sigh. 'I just hope both her parents are here to see her.'

'Don't worry,' Fifi says, patting me on the shoulder as Pooky and Smokey, looking highly stressed, rush through the entrance.

'Hello, darling,' says Smokey, looking like a rainbow in an outfit that would put Joseph to shame. She gives me a kiss on the cheek.

'Hiya, Lily,' Pooky chimes in, dressed in tight orange leggings and a bright orange baggy jumper that's almost fluorescent. 'Let me know when you want to put on your first outfit, sweetie,' then she suddenly turns round and booms in the flattest vowels, 'Will you girls 'urry up,' and two more unfortunate girls promptly appear, dragging clothes rails behind them as well as bags of shoes, boots, scarves and gloves.

Fifi sidles up to me. 'I hope my models haven't lost any more weight. You did tell them, didn't you, Lily? I just can't do skinny. My dressmakers were up all night trying to take some of the clothes in. At this rate they'll look better on the kids.' She laughs, but I'm not sure she's joking.

An hour later, Tony arrives, with a large silver-foil-covered tray. 'I've got another thirty of these, Lily,' he says, walking towards the tables that have been designated for catering.

'Can I help?' I ask, falling in step and giving him a peck on the cheek.

'No, no, I've got help,' he says, nodding towards the door where Julie is standing, grinning at me, another silver-foil tray in hand.

'We were up all last night making them,' she says, looking mischievous.

'Well, I was,' Tony corrects. 'Julie was trying to distract me, but I've still managed to make enough to feed an army.'

Then Paul arrives, looking as anxious as I feel. He's with a young man with a pony-tail whom he introduces as Judd, the DJ. He'll be coordinating the lights, sound system and music. He doesn't look a day older than twenty, but I'm sure Paul knows what he's doing. As if he's read my mind, Paul whispers in my ear, 'He's very good. He's done shows in Paris, and Angela recommended him and, most importantly, he comes cheap,' he says, giving me a wink.

Next a line of PTA members arrive with cake tins and trays of sweets and savouries. They greet us enthusiastically, then get busy helping arrange the canapés and PTA offerings. The model mums appear, all looking beautifully coiffeured and made up, thanks to Tiffany who follows behind them like a mother hen, looking very proud of her work. I touch my own hair self-consciously, hoping Tiffany will be able to do the same magic for me. At the very end, there's a woman I don't recognise, looking very slick with highlighted blonde hair in a tight bob, low-slung jeans, shirt and jacket. I don't know who she is – perhaps one of the mums has sent her in their place? She comes up to me and gives me a hug, 'Thank you so much for this,' she says with shining eyes.

'My pleasure, but I'm sorry, I don't know...' and then it hits me: it's Sally Day. Mousy Sally Day beaming at me, looking so much like a new woman that I didn't recognise her. I can't help staring at her, just to make sure she hasn't had any cosmetic surgery. Her hair is short, bobbed and highlighted blonde, her skin is clear and Tiffany's done an amazing job with her eyes – I'd never noticed she had such high cheekbones before. She looks years younger.

'Sally, I hardly recognise you,' I say, stepping back to take another look. 'You look wonderful.'

'It's all Tiffany's and Pooky's doing. When we were having our fittings and went to meet the designers she gave me a few hair and make-up tips and, well, transformed me into this,' she says, opening her arms and doing a twirl.

It's ten o'clock now. The show starts at twelve and we need to make sure everything is perfect before the first guest arrives.

Parents have been told not to bring their families until half past eleven and to take the middle rows, and Ms Treadwell has told all the children to behave impeccably or they will be asked in front of everyone to leave immediately. The children's fashion show has proven very popular (and highly political). Tim seems fairly laid back about being asked. His main concern is that he has to walk on with Harriet Scott and his friends may think they're going out, which he quite categorically tells me they are not.

As I listen to the mums meet and greet the designers in the changing room, the lights and music start – Judd is obviously testing out the system. Pooky walks along the catwalk with Paul to make sure it's even and not slippery, and men start to come in with boxes of bottled water, juices and cases of wine.

I can see everything taking shape around me. 'Well, that's the food out and drinks out,' says Julie, businesslike, giving me a kiss.

'Great, and the PTA ladies said they would man the food and drink during the whole thing, yes?' I say, hoping I haven't missed anything.

'Yes, we have five of them. They're very officious-looking so no one will get away with having two of anything,' she smiles, looking over at the trestle tables.

As Paul approaches me from the front, I hear my name called and turn to find a broadly smiling Henrietta Diet, wearing a power suit, with Allyson Dyer at her side, unsmiling as usual.

'Hello, Lily,' she says, pecking me on the cheek. 'This

is it then. All your hard work is about to pay off – very well done. Most of the people I called will be here, Matt and some other local movers and shakers, so it will be a great chance to impress,' she says.

'Who's Matt?' Julie asks before I can.

'Oh,' Henrietta blushes a little. 'I mean Matthew, Matthew Masterton.'

It's now eleven thirty and the guests start to arrive. I see lots of children and a few familiar faces from the playground, then Tamara with someone who looks old enough to be her father, but who, I presume, is the long-suffering Terence. White-haired and handsome, he dresses as though he belongs on a horse, a little like a handsome, mellow-looking John Wayne. Tamara waves at me enthusiastically and blows me a kiss, gesturing to the Nikon she's got dangling round her neck. 'Can we go backstage and take some photos there as well, darling?' she shouts across the marquee.

I point firmly to the area Paul has designated as the 'photo area', thinking that none of the mums will appreciate pictures of themselves half-dressed floating around later. Gilbert arrives with Leon, who looks as though he has come with his mother, although in this case I think it *is* his mother.

Finally, Mike arrives with the children. Tim rushes backstage to change into his outfit, and Jenny and Henry stay with Mike, who keeps hold of Henry by putting him on his shoulders. As Henry now has the best view in the house, he's happy, looking down at everyone and everything.

I give Mike a kiss. 'Don't forget to introduce yourself to Masterton,' I whisper before rushing off backstage. 'He's the golf-club MD and he'll probably be wearing a disgusting blazer. And say hello to Dr Totham as well, but don't be too sycophantic.' I look round for the last time in the hope that I'll be able to say hello and welcome him in person, but it's twenty minutes to start time, Henrietta Diet is ready, the microphone's working (minus the squeals), and the seats are almost filled. It's time for me to change. I wave goodbye to Mike, who mouths, 'Good luck.'

Before I go, I feel a tap on my shoulder.

'Hello, darling,' my mum beams at me, looking every inch a model herself in a bright lime-green cropped jacket, simple deep-purple shift dress, and black boots. I'm so pleased to see her and to be able to hug her that I want to cry.

'I know you're very busy, darling, but I just wanted to say how proud I am of you and that I'm going to be sitting next to Mike, Henry and Jenny. Is The Oaks's headmaster here?' she asks, peering around. I look behind her and suddenly see Totham in Conservative blue, talking to Masterton, who's still wearing that ghastly blazer. Henrietta is hovering on the sidelines, ready to step up to the mike, looking like Alexis in *Dynasty*, all shoulder pads, shocking bright-yellow shift and tailored black trouser suit. She is shadowed, as always, by Allyson, who is scowling a few paces behind and obviously doesn't want to stand out at all in her drab grey skirt suit.

'He's over there,' I nod. 'The one with the blue blazer talking to the one in the pinstripes.'

Mum turns and looks casually at the group. 'Hmm, they all look as though they could do with some fashion advice. Perhaps they'll learn something today,' she says, kissing me on the cheek and giving me a hug, before walking back to Henry, who is now straining to get out of his dad's arms and into his grandmother's. Henry throws himself at her with such force she almost topples over backward. I wave at Mike for the last time, and head backstage just as I hear Judd turn up ELO's 'Mr Blue Sky' to silence the audience, then fade out to Henrietta Diet saying, 'Hello and welcome, mums and dads, boys and girls, and everyone who is anyone in Letchbury.'

I'm in the changing room, listening to her speech, only half-aware of what I'm taking off and what I'm putting on. Tiffany did my hair and make-up earlier, so I just have to touch it up now. Pooky is talking to me and Jane is beside me saying, 'How do I look in this dress, Christine?' The children are in a separate area and wearing their outfits; in fact, they're behaving in a more mature and less self-conscious way than the adults. Ella is asking Sally if she looks fat in her outfit. Smokey loses patience and says, 'Absolutely fucking massive, now get the top on,' at which everyone hushes and listens to the speech.

'It is my great pleasure to introduce the Somerset School fashion show in aid of the school library. In my book *How to Keep the Yummy in Mummy . . .*'

Julie, who's listening over my shoulder, tuts loudly. 'Of course, she would bring this in on the second sentence. I haven't read her lousy book, and I wouldn't if you paid me,' she says, putting on the bright-orange-and-black crêpe dress with knitted wool panels Pooky has chosen for her.

'. . . They have managed to combine motherhood with an ability to show that they are still people in their own right, who can dress with style and polish.'

'God, she's making us sound so superficial.' Jane is listening over my other shoulder, caught up in a bright-purple cashmere jumper she's trying to get over her head.

I peek through a crack in the curtain to see Henrietta looking down at some notes when I suddenly notice Karen in the audience, manically clicking away, taking loads of photos. Her photographer must have deserted her. I'd almost forgotten she was coming at all.

'I would like to thank Mr Masterton for allowing us to use the golf-club grounds and for all those sponsors who have helped make this day a success. The designers have offered their time and fashion advice, and had to work with real women as models,' she pauses to wait for polite laughter in the audience. 'The children will be modelling some wonderful clothes by designer Fifi Lord, who is already famous for her children's range but now wants to make mums as well-dressed as their offspring. Jane Anderson, Andrea Jeremiah and Tina Gerard will be wearing her clothes. Then we have Smokey Popham, whose range has a distinctive bohemian style, and will be modelled by Christine Hawes, Daniella Frost, Suzanne Morrison and Ella Fritz. And finally Pooky Hasdammami, whose clothes are as exotic as her name. Lily Dearl, Julie Rose, Paul Wilton and Sally Day will be models. We'd also like to give a big thank-you to Mr Wallace T. Heavie for gracing us with his presence at this occasion.' She nods to the fat, ruddy-cheeked, bulbous-nosed man sitting next to Masterton.

'*She's* done all the thank-yous,' says Andrea, who came to the curtain when her name fell. 'Aren't *you* supposed to thank everyone?' she asks me now. 'She's making it sound as though she's organised it all,' she says, frowning and patting me on the shoulder.

'Those who are important will know who's put all the hard work in,' says Jane reassuringly. 'Henrietta is a politician, it's in her blood to take all the credit for other people's work. But if she's brought in more publicity and helped with the golf club, then she has been some use,' says Jane philosophically.

Outside, Henrietta continues: 'A huge thank-you to Tony Herald for the catering, and the PTA for all their wonderful cakes – what would we do without you. And, finally, a last big thank-you to Lily Dearl, Julie Rose and Paul Wilton, the organisers behind the show.'

Hmmph. Finally. At the very end, but I hope Totham is paying attention. But if she's done her job properly, then it'll all be written up in the papers tomorrow. I can see a couple of other people taking notes, one or two tape recorders.

'Now there's nothing more to say other than welcome

and I hope you enjoy this very special event,' Henrietta says, as everyone applauds and she bows and waves.

'She's a bit like the Queen,' Christine says drily, peering over Jane's shoulders.

'Right,' I say, clapping my hands, 'no time for cattiness, we've got a show to put on. Let's go, ladies. What's the line in *Pretty Woman*? "Work it, work it." That's what we've got to do.'

Ms Treadwell, who has just poked her head through the curtains, catches the last of that. 'I completely agree. I just wanted to say good luck, ladies, and well done for all your hard work.' She winks at me and goes back to her seat in the front row.

There are quite a few famous local faces in the audience. Perhaps they're here to support us, or perhaps it's just because they know the press are going to be here, but all of the names on Totham's and Masterton's wall plaques seem to sit here in the flesh. Dennis Resnaur and Francesca Frederic, Randy Hasbro (who is probably pissed off he's not doing the catering), Fisher Bolden, Tyler Villier and Lynda Dunworthy.

I can see Mike and Henry, Tony, Tamara, Terence and Gilbert who's snapping away from his seat. There's Leon and his mother, Giorgiano and Tatiana, and my mum. I can see Jessica with Cara – Mia is one of the models in the children's section – and I wonder how Jessica will feel when she sees Paul as a male model? Next to Jessica is Jamie, who also has his camera, and Simon, who's tapping his feet in time to 'Mr Blue Sky'. I'm on parade in front of everyone today, please don't let me mess up. Finally I see Dr Totham a few rows away from where we are behind the curtain, sitting with Mr Masterton, Wallace T. Heavie and Henrietta, who has just squeezed her way through and now seems to be having an argument with Allyson. I can't hear what they're saying but both women look daggers at each other for a few moments, as though they're on the verge of coming to blows, then Masterton whispers something into Henrietta's ear and she looks around, suddenly aware that people are starting to watch. She smiles graciously as though nothing has happened, while Allyson sits stiff with rage, looking as though she's about to explode.

Paul rushes into the changing rooms, looking very smart in a grey-and-purple pinstripe number designed by Pookey.

'Can the DJ start up now?' he asks, slightly breathless.

'Yes,' I say, my heartbeat getting faster and louder.

'Are you ready?' he asks, looking down at my orange mini-dress and over-the-knee boots – from his smile I can see he approves.

'As ready as we'll ever be,' I say. 'Tell Judd to start up the music.'

Just as he leaves, Angela rushes in, nearly knocking Christine over in the process, and trips over to me. 'Darling, darling, sorry I'm late, I just wanted to see how gorgeous you all are,' she says, looking me up and down critically. 'You clean up nice,' she says. 'By the way, huge surprise, we decided to give two pages to the show in the next issue, not entirely because of you mums, I'm afraid, but more because we want to show-case the designers – but it'll be a brilliant spread for you, so I thought it'd be perfect. I've got my photo-grapher out there covering it all. And I loved the column you emailed over last week. Very *us*, darling. Well done, well done. OK, darling, good luck.' Before I can even get a word in edgewise, she air-kisses me, shouts at everyone to break a leg (which I don't think Daniella and Ella fully appreciate) and disappears again.

Chapter 16
Show Off

Andrea Jeremiah is the first model to appear, to the sound of the Scissor Sisters. Looking professional and gorgeous, she starts to strut.

She gets a rapturous reception of wolf whistles, claps and cheers as she gracefully walks along the catwalk, moving her hips and grinning from ear to ear. She starts the show off with a bang. I can see Karen clicking away hectically. Tamara is getting up, annoying the people behind her, while Gilbert moves so he can get clearer shots. Henry's little face is staring at Andrea, totally bemused and fascinated by the whole experience. Harvey Jeremiah stands and cheers, with Daniel and his sister. Andrea's wearing an embellished belted tunic over skinny cropped trousers, and looks luxuriously chic. To add to the outfit, she's wearing a silk headscarf around her head, giving her the appearance of a funky Indian girl, especially as she's gone out barefoot. Thank goodness I don't have to do that – I can't remember the last time I painted my toenails.

I look over at Judd, looking scruffy and cool and decidedly unfazed by all the noise and excitement. Headphones on, he nods in time to the rhythm and isn't even looking at what or who is on the catwalk.

As Andrea does her second turn and pose at the top of the catwalk, Jane Anderson walks on and the room erupts once more.

Fifi's dressed Jane in a feather-light tulle dress with bold herringbone-inspired print, tailored with a dark red gilet, but because she's barefoot, she looks quite designer boho and very good. She's finally got the rhythm and I can see from her face that she's loving every minute of it as she walks past Andrea, who offers her hand for a high-five. Jane obliges. As she comes to the end of the platform she stops, poses, turns, poses again and twirls. She looks as though she'd love to stay there all day. The PTA members, sitting near Henrietta, Allyson (who still refuses to smile), Masterton and Totham, are all cheering her, and Ms Treadwell, who usually maintains her composure even on sports days, is actually standing up and clapping, perhaps half-regretful that she didn't offer to model herself.

As Andrea comes off for her outfit change, Paul is the next one to go on.

'I feel sick,' he says, looking for me to cue him on.

'You look gorgeous,' I say, impatiently watching Jane do her second turn. I can't wait for him to go out there.

'I never knew you had such a cute bum,' adds Julie, as I gently shove Paul forward.

The audience explodes with whistles when he appears, and I can see Jessica looking surprised and delighted. Paul cheekily blows her and Cara a kiss in passing. Karen waves at him and clicks away.

After Paul come some of the children. Judd makes a smooth transition from Grace Jones to Queen, and Emma Walters, one of the Third years, comes out holding hands with a Fourth year girl I don't know to the sound of 'We Will Rock You', looking fabulous in jewel-encrusted dresses in bright turquoise, again with headscarves and no shoes. They're walking in perfect time to the music. Andrea's done a lot of work with them, too, although she confided in me that the children had much better rhythm than their parents.

As the girls turn and pose at the top of the catwalk, Tim comes out with Harriet Scott. Unsmiling, mostly because of nerves I should imagine, but consequently looking dead cool. Tim's in tailored pinstripe trousers and a loose pink shirt, while Harriet wears a brocade dress with pearl-studded flat shoes.

'God, they're young men and women now, aren't they,' says Julie, dewy-eyed as she looks at the couple over my shoulder. 'Where's your little boy gone?'

'I know,' I say, looking proudly on at Tim as he turns and poses like a professional. It seems like only yesterday that I was cradling him in my arms, and watching *Teletubbies* with him.

After Tim and Harriet make their grand exit (Harriet trying to hold Tim's hand, Tim desperately avoiding it) and one of the Third year boys comes on to do his turn in a bright blue tailored suit, which causes lots of cameras to flash, Judd exchanges Queen's rock beat for the more sophisticated Eurythmics's 'Who's That Girl?' Christine and Ella, looking every inch the super-models, walk on, their skinny frames stunning in clothes that, admittedly, aren't really meant for the real world or the real woman. Then Julie's up, to a huge round of clapping and cheering.

Sally Day makes her entrance as Annie Lennox mixes into the Bodyrockers's 'I like the Way You Move' and suddenly the room quietens. Dowdy Sally Day, the mum we almost didn't choose in the auditions, has been trans-formed. Her neat bob has been slicked back, her eye make-up darkened, her cheekbones are now high, her lips full, so she looks like a slightly softer version of Angelina Jolie. Pooky has put her in an outfit Lara Croft wouldn't say boo to – tight brown trousers and a skinny-rib jumper with a large, low-waisted belt and thigh-length black leather boots. After the initial shock from those parents who know her, the applause rises to a crescendo.

'Your turn.' Pooky taps me on the shoulder as I take in the crowd, most of whom are now standing up. There's a break for food coming up soon, and a second round before the winner of the children's competition is announced, but everything seems to be going brilliantly so far. Taking a brief look in the mirror as Sally does her second twirl and pose, I walk on to Roy Orbison's 'Pretty Woman'. I feel quite sick, but am vaguely aware of loud applause and shouts. Somewhere someone's saying, 'There's Mummy. Mummy, hello!' There's clapping and more flashes, and I remember Andrea's advice about keeping my head up. They make it look so easy.

I can hear Angela's voice shouting to her photographer, 'Get lots of her, get lots of this one!' while Mike whoops. I can vaguely see my mum looking up, clapping away and jumping up and down, and Henry pointing at me and telling everyone who can hear him above the noise, 'She's my mummy. She's my mummy!' I see Tamara clicking away, and Karen stopping to clap at me, mouthing, 'Well done, girl.'

Suddenly I want to cry. I stop and turn, pose and turn, twirl and pose, and know exactly why Jane didn't want to leave the stage. I feel an overwhelming sense of relief and exhilaration, finally allowing myself to accept that it's all come together brilliantly. I don't even think about looking at Dr Totham, Masterton or Henrietta, I just know if they're not smiling and clapping, they're the only ones in the marquee who aren't.

I turn and pose and walk down the catwalk again, all the models now joining me to walk along the catwalk and show off their clothes again before the break.

The children stand at the front, the parents behind. I can see Jessica jumping up and down and looking unusually mischievous as she blows kisses at her husband. After a minute, Judd starts up the music again with Grace Jones (whom I succeeded in getting in twice despite some protest) and we all turn and walk off.

Pooky and Smokey clap as we enter the changing rooms. Fifi is in with the children. The second half is shorter, but this is when the mufti-day-outfit winner is announced.

'I don't think any of the models should go out now,' says Pooky firmly. 'You'll get the clothes messy and there's already a queue for the food. So if everyone can stay here I'll take your orders.'

'Actually, Tony's got some food for us and the children,' says Julie. 'We thought of that last night, Pooky. He should be coming in soon.' As if on cue, Tony pops his head round the corner with a huge tray.

All the mums sit down around the rails of clothes in dressing gowns, so as not to get their outfits messy. 'Are we even allowed to eat?' says Christine, obviously expecting to grow a size if she eats a grape.

'Yes,' replies Smokey, rolling her eyes to heaven and offering her the tray.

'Well, I think it's gone very well so far,' says Jane, grinning with the afterglow of the applause she received when she went on the catwalk. 'So much nicer than the usual school fête or wine evening. We should make this a regular event.'

I'm not sure my nerves will take it.

'Can you see any of the local papers?' asks Julie, stuffing half a tuna sandwich in her mouth.

'Loads of photographers out there,' I say, famished myself.

'Everyone seems to be enjoying themselves,' Andrea says, taking a quick peek out through the curtains. 'The catering is going down well, too. People are devouring your hors d'oeuvres, Tony.' She sits back down, cheekily pinching a spring roll from Ella's napkin.

'I've really enjoyed this, Lily. Thank you for organising it,' says Sally, looking almost a bit tearful.

'It wasn't only me, Sally,' I say modestly, seeing Jane's look. 'Everyone helped.'

For a few moments we sit silently, eating, thinking and listening to the noise outside the changing room, which is buzzing with laughter and chatter. I feel on such a high, as if I've had too many Red Bulls.

'Does anyone need touching up?' shouts Tiffany, coming in with cheek blush and brush just as Judd pops his head round the curtain. 'You ladies ready to party again?' he says cheekily, grinning at us in our dressing gowns and giving Tiffany a wink.

'Yes,' and 'Ready,' we all shout, getting up and bustling over to our outfits.

'Great,' Judd says. 'But let's up the pace a bit, OK?' He's gone again and I can hear 50 Cent starting.

Our second outfits are evening wear. Andrea leads the way in a chiffon number, more glitzy than the previous one, then Jane follows in a diaphanous creation, and Paul in a dinner jacket-look, but in a fabric that resembles a William Morris design – somehow it works on him. Next come Christine and

Ella in slinky black numbers that make them look like sexy Morticia Adamses. Daniella and Sally look amazing again in shades of pink and purple.

Tim and the other boy walk on, casual in pinstripe trousers and T-shirt, then comes Emma and the other girl, then Tina and Julie, and then me again.

As suddenly as it started, it's over. After I do my final turn, I lead the other models down the catwalk to Groove Armada's 'I See You Baby', this time pulling along Pooky, Smokey and Fifi. I savour the moment and the applause and I look around the audience. I can see all the familiar smiling faces, some still stuffing themselves with PTA cakes. Only Karen is suddenly missing. I can't see her anywhere. Of course, odd, though, because the winner of the children's competition is going to be announced next and it would be a pity if she isn't there to see her daughter collect the prize.

As the applause subsides, Fifi steps out with Pooky and Smokey slightly behind her. Holding the microphone, she bows and starts to speak. The marquee gradually comes to a hush.

'Thank you all very much for coming today. I can't tell you how much fun it's been to be a part of such an event. Pooky, Smokey and myself all deal with models and have fashion shows on a regular basis, but these are the loveliest ladies we have ever worked with,' Fifi says, looking back at us and smiling amidst another round of applause. I hear Jenny shout, 'And one of them's my mummy,' to which everyone laughs.

'The amount of work that's been put in for today has been amazing. There's one more thing to introduce, though, and that's the winner of the mufti-day-outfit competition. Would everyone please give a warm round of applause to Ms Treadwell, headmistress of Somerset School, who will reveal the winner.'

Ms Treadwell walks onto the catwalk, thanking Fifi and taking the microphone from her. 'Thank you so much, everyone, for all your efforts. The sun has shone for us and the mums have shone for us and the children have shone for us. This has been a real team effort but I want to give special thanks to the three people who instigated the project. Lily Dearl, Julie Rose and Paul Wilton should receive most of the praise,' we step forward and bow to earth-shattering applause, 'as well as Jane Anderson and her wonderful PTA. That sounds a bit like a rock band, doesn't it,' she says, giggling like a girl, which makes everyone else laugh too. 'Anyway,' Ms Treadwell says, more serious now, 'they have raised over £3,000 in aid of the Somerset library fund – a brilliant achievement.'

The applause crescendos, then gradually dies down as Ms Treadwell goes into headmistress mode and does her 'quieten down now, children' hand movement, even though it's the parents who are making all the noise. 'We asked children from our school to come up with an idea for a non-uniform outfit. We received hundreds of entries, some of them very unusual – the designers behind me say they've never worked with papier mâché before, but there's always a first time. Fifi, Pooky and

Smokey looked through all the designs and chose the overall winner according to style and attention to detail, the practicality as well as the overall originality of the idea. The winner is Claire Field of 6C.'

Pooky and Smokey part as Claire emerges in a startling brown-and-blue layered creation. She's wearing a brown shirt over what looks like a sky-blue string vest, over a light-brown T-shirt. Her knee-length skirt is also layered, has a brown petticoat and sky-blue overskirt. It looks amazing – I wouldn't mind wearing a grown-up version of it myself. Everyone stands and applauds. Karen is still missing but Jamie, the proud dad, looks on with both thumbs up, seemingly oblivious to the fact that his wife isn't there to share the moment.

Claire turns, bows, poses, turns and bows again along with the designers, and Judd turns up the music to 'We Will Rock You' as Andrea leads everyone off the stage, waving, smiling and clapping.

In a trance, almost trembling with relief and the thrill of everyone's applause, I change and step outside where husbands and PTA members are waiting. Suddenly, I feel hands grip my waist.

'You are very sexy on the catwalk, Mrs Dearl,' Mike says mischievously. I allow myself a triumphant grin.

'It reminds me of the time we went to see *The Rocky Horror Picture Show*, do you remember that?'

'Yes, I do.' I turn around to smile back at him.

'And do you remember what happened in the hallway?' he whispers, surreptitiously kissing my neck.

'Yes,' I say, laughter bubbling in my throat.

'Well, there just so happens to be another production of *The Rocky Horror Picture Show* on next week and I've got two tickets. Don't suppose you fancy dressing up again?'

I turn round and push my body up against his, our lips almost touching. 'Only if you promise to wear stockings, suspenders and high heels,' I say, laughing out loud now. Mike suddenly pulls away and I realise that we've got an audience – Ms Treadwell and Jane are waiting with my mum, Henry, Tim, all the other mums, Tony, Julie and Claire. Tamara, bless her, who is also in the crowd, takes her last picture for the evening, shaking with laughter.

Chapter 17
Food Fight!

'What the . . . shit.' I'm still in my dressing gown, walking into the sitting room, ripping open one of the local papers. It's the *Letchbury Times*, the paper where Karen works, and I'd picked it up eagerly, expecting it to be full of photographs of the fashion show, as well as details of the money we raised. If anything could sway Totham, this would be it.

I'm dumbstruck as I read the headline:

GOLF-CLUB SCHOOL SCAM – HOW LOCAL PARENTS GET THEIR HOLE IN ONE WITH LOCAL SCHOOL and immediately underneath it in large, neat, black print:

Exclusive by Karen Field.

I stand in the middle of the sitting room, my hands becoming clammy as I read on, half-wanting to skip every other line, half-wanting to avoid what I read altogether. I start to feel dizzy, as though my brain is working overtime; I've overdosed on caffeine and my head's about to explode.

Dr Henderson Totham, headmaster of The Oaks School, is currently being questioned by police over his involvement with fixing entrance places at the well-established grammar school in Letchbury. Notoriously difficult to get into, the school, which has several famous former pupils, including Oscar-winning actor Terence Darby and England cricket captain Thomas Harding, gives all children an interview and various written tests which last a day. Parents are also interviewed by Dr Totham (pictured left) who has been quoted as saying, 'We only select the best of the best at this school.'

Totham is pictured here sitting next to Mr Matthew Masterton, MD of the Letchbury Golf Club (left) and local MP Wallace T. Heavie, at a recent event. Following an undercover investigation, Totham and Masterton have both been arrested for their suspected involvement in a scam that allows parents to pay for places at The Oaks. Parents who wanted their children to go to The

Oaks were told to join the local golf club where they would be approached by Masterton who explained that their child would be guaranteed entry if they paid towards a certain fund. The scam was revealed when someone in the accounts department started asking questions about the 'special membership' fund and was dismissed without pay. The woman, who does not wish to be named at present for legal reasons, contacted this newspaper, setting in motion the undercover investigation.

Well, I'll be damned.

Our source claims, 'The parents would pay anything between £2,000 and £3,000 up front. This money was laundered into the accounts of Totham and Masterton, and then moved into an offshore account.' Local councillor and author, Henrietta Diet (pictured right), who has been having a long-time affair with Masterton, is also believed to be involved in the scam, according to Allyson Dyer, her PA.

There's a picture of Allyson Dyer to the right and, yes, she's actually smiling.

Ms Dyer talked exclusively to the Letchbury Times. *'I think it's dreadful how Henrietta Diet puts herself forward as a family-orientated person, standing up for family values and education, when she's having an affair with a married man, isn't married herself and doesn't even have children of her own. She wouldn't recognise family values if they whacked her on the head,' says Ms Dyer, 32, from Briarton, who has been Ms Diet's assistant for several years. Totham, 55, who is divorced with two grown-up children, and Masterton, 49, who is married with two children, are now being questioned by police. Staff at The Oaks are in a state of shock and Totham has been suspended until further notice.*

My mouth is hanging open and I can't quite get my head around what's been happening. Here I was, desperate to please Totham, putting my entire life on hold for the fashion show. And all this time . . .

Parents at The Oaks and the golf club will all be questioned by police over the next few days, and all parents will be notified by post how to reapply to the school. Totham, Diet and Masterton were not available for comment yesterday. Local MP Wallace T. Heavie has said that he is outraged at the scandal: 'This puts the integrity of the entire state-school selection system into question, a system which is confused and complicated enough without this sort of criminality. I will be speaking to the House about this in the coming months.'

I finally sit down to re-read the article, then make myself a strong coffee and read it again. There are so many terrible implications: Totham is a fraud, Masterton is a cheat and the money the golf club offered now won't be able to go to the school library by the time they cover the costs of the show. The fashion show hasn't received *any* coverage, so all our work has been for nothing. I can only hope that Henrietta's other media contacts will have yielded something. Even worse, though, *her* involvement with the fashion show and the golf-club sponsorship almost implicates us in the whole mess. And I just can't believe that Karen has used me to get an exclusive, and used the fashion show to get her name in print, even though her own daughter was up on stage. She couldn't wait a week; she had to do it the day after, without even mentioning the fashion show. There's nothing – not even a photograph. What a bitch. Of everything that almost hurts me most. What a friend.

I sit down with my fourth cup of coffee and a slice of cold toast and take a bite, but I'm too upset and angry to really focus. I'm still in a state of fury and shock when Mike comes down, expecting a sea of smiles.

'So, are you on the front page, darling, or page three?' he asks, almost skipping into the room. 'The children all want to see as well.'

'They can't,' I say, handing him the paper. I watch his face as he starts to read, a look of shock replacing the smile that was there a minute ago.

'Bloody hell, Lily. Bloody hell,' he keeps saying.

When he's done he puts the paper down on the kitchen table and comes over to hug me. 'Well, I guess the one good thing that will come out of it, Lily, is that the selection process will have to start all over again. So Tim will have another chance and now you've done the show it should hopefully really count. And another good thing is that we don't have to join the golf club,' he says, clearly desperately trying to look on the bright side.

'But all that effort, Mike? All that effort for nothing. We won't get the money for the library now, as the golf-club accounts will probably be frozen, and I don't know if I can go through the whole process all over again. And the interviews, the entrance exams. Tim will have to take them all over again, and we might be implicated because we asked for sponsorship from the golf club, have you thought of that?' I'm getting myself more wound up just thinking about it.

'We won't, Lily. We're not members of the golf club for one, and Tim didn't get a place, nor did Dominic or Mia. The only one of our friends who did is Karen, so if anyone, she should be under suspicion,' he says pragmatically, picking up the article again.

'But why couldn't she wait a week and give the fashion show some exposure first, Mike? Why now? She knew how much it meant to us. There'd have been no harm in that.' I open and slam the fridge door violently, as if Karen's head was in it. 'I'd expect some cow like Allyson Dyer to double-cross a friend, but not *my* best friend, Mike,' I say, getting the Shreddies out and plonking them on the table.

'Yes, I'm a bit surprised too,' says Mike thoughtfully. 'But perhaps the editor overruled her or published before she knew about it, Lily? She's not mean like that. She may be ambitious, but not mean.'

'She's ruthless and single-minded when she wants to

be, Mike, you know she is,' I say, putting the milk into the microwave and turning the knob to ten minutes.

'I don't think you need it that hot,' says Mike gently, turning it down to fifty seconds.

'I can't face the playground this morning, Mike. I just can't. Can you take them to school, please? I couldn't bear the look of disappointment on everyone's faces.'

'Why, Mummy?' I turn round to see Tim and Jenny dressed in school uniform, holding hands with Henry in the middle, all looking at me expectantly.

'Oh, nothing, darlings, nothing. Daddy will take you in to school today, OK.' I can't even bear trying to explain all this to the children so I usher them to the breakfast table and pick up Henry. What a bloody great day this is turning out to be.

'I've decided I don't want to be a rock climber when I grow up any more, Daddy,' Jenny says importantly as she's sitting down. 'I want to be a supermodel rock climber. Are there any supermodel rock climbers?' she says, munching on a spoonful of Shreddies.

'I'm sure there are,' says Mike, 'although I don't think you'd have much of an audience.' He takes Henry from me and sits down with him while I have another cup of coffee. At this rate, I'll have a heart attack by eleven a.m.

'People could watch you in helicopters and planes,' says Tim, 'or you could suspend the audience from a long rope,' he suggests. 'It could be a bit windy, though, so it might be dangerous.' I get up to get him some toast and kiss him on his head.

The children look at Tim as though he's given them the secret to eternal life or, in Henry's case, transformed him into a Red Power Ranger.

'Wow! Do people really want to do that? I'd only do that with a parachute,' says Jenny, finishing her toast.

'But what happens if the audience doesn't like heights?' says Jenny. 'They could get vertical, couldn't they, Daddy?'

'Vertigo,' Mike corrects her absent-mindedly.

'What's vertical?' asks Henry, through a mouthful of Shreddies.

'A fear of heights,' says Tim, 'and it's vertigo.'

The conversation calms me down. I gather up Henry and take him upstairs, waving goodbye to Jenny, Tim and Mike at the door. I get myself ready, my mind still buzzing, angry and full of questions. My mobile goes, and I recognise by the ring tone that it's Karen, but I don't want to speak to her at the moment, I'm still too angry. I feel as though I have two voices in my head – the reasonable one that says Mike is right and everything will be OK, and the other one that's spitting blood, telling me to answer the phone and shout at her very loudly. I do a little punch, punch, kick as I'm getting dressed, and turn my phone off. I've got to be reasonable about this, I've got to calm down. I'll take Henry to nursery, then pop into Waitrose. There's nothing like food shopping to bring me back down to earth.

Mike drops the car back and asks if I want him to take Henry to nursery.

'No, that's fine, I'm OK now. I'll give you a lift to the station, drop Henry off and then I've got to do some shopping, so I'll need the car,' I say, smiling at him reassuringly.

I half-expect Ms Gold to be cross because Henry is twenty minutes late *again*, but she's smiling as I walk through the door.

'I thought the fashion show was wonderful,' she enthuses. 'It made me think we should do that instead of a school fête every year. Those things are so boring,' she says, taking Henry by the hand and bending down to his level. 'Isn't your mummy clever?'

I wave goodbye to Ms Gold, feeling slightly better. Oh, to hell with it. Angela's doing a large spread on the show in *De Rigueur* and some of Henrietta's stuff will have come through. And the notoriety might even make the publicity last a little longer. It was brilliant fun and I enjoyed it. I wouldn't mind organising something like that every year, if my nerves can stand it. It's actually really nice, what with the column Angela was talking about and now this as well; things are really starting to fall into place for me. I'd realised I was missing something, but I hadn't realised just how much.

Ms Gold obviously hasn't read the local paper, though; perhaps when she does she won't think Henry's mummy is quite as clever.

But why couldn't Karen let me into her confidence? I can feel myself getting wound up again, and I mustn't do that or I know I'll spend too much in Waitrose, and that will make me even more cross.

As I park the car, collect my trolley and enter the brightly coloured shop, I feel myself relaxing again. I've remembered to take a list, thank goodness, so I've still got some wits about me. Now, first things first: bread.

Two baguettes, some Scotch pancakes (Henry likes those), a malt loaf (Jenny) and some rice cakes (everyone but me thinks they taste of cardboard, but that's fine). Later I walk over to the fresh fruit and vegetables. There, looking furtive by the mixed-salad counter, is Karen. The cheek of it. The cow.

'Why didn't you tell me what you were up to?' I hear my voice hissing and realise I've marched straight up to her.

Karen looks startled and a bit shamefaced as well.

'Didn't you trust me?' I say, realising that for some reason I've picked up the baguette and am poking her with it. 'Why didn't you tell me, huh? Your best friend? And you weren't even there to see your own daughter win the competition. Your work comes before your friends and your family, Karen. Always. You've got your priorities seriously screwed up, you know that?'

'I tried to call you but you . . .' she starts to explain, backing into the salad mix. Suddenly she lets out a cry, her hand deep in the potato salad. For some reason, fury and all, this makes me burst into laughter. Karen doesn't find it quite as funny, however, and when I try to reach over to help her, she obviously thinks I'm going to prod her again with the baguette and throws some of the salad in my face. How dare she retaliate when it's all her fault? I whack her with the baguette and grab a handful of marinated olives which I throw at her, hitting her with the baguette at the same time.

Then she throws pasta mix and wild-rice salad, but I come back with the sweetcorn salad and chick-pea mix, getting her straight between the eyes. We're now throwing huge handfuls of salad mix over each other, hardly pausing to draw breath, and just as I'm about to pick up a whole tub of beetroot and red cabbage to up the ante – a particularly clever manoeuvre on my part as I know she'll never be able to get it out of her cream coat – I slip, arse over tit, and the beetroot goes up in the air, landing on one of the Waitrose attendants who's been called to see what all the fuss is about. As I fall I pull Karen down with me, onto the floor awash with salad. There we lie, eye to eye, with olives, pasta pieces and sweetcorn kernels in our hair and all over our clothes. Karen starts to giggle, then I join in.

'Now ladies,' the attendant says, looking down at us, trying to look cross, 'we don't expect this sort of behaviour in Waitrose.' We must look a very marinated pair.

'I'm so sorry,' I say, getting up carefully and helping Karen up at the same time. 'There was a misunderstanding and, well, I apologise. We'll pay for the damage,' I promise, looking at the salad mix all over the floor and the group of shoppers who have gathered to gape. At least we've given them something to talk about for the rest of the week.

'I apologise too,' says Karen, regaining her footing.

'Some misunderstanding,' the attendant says, looking us up and down. 'Were you arguing over who had what?

We usually only get fights at Christmas. I've had a few women battling it out over the smoked salmon but nothing remotely like this. At least there are no bruises this time. If you'd like to follow me, ladies,' he says, brushing some marinated mushrooms off my collar. We walk after him, watched by the other shoppers, both feeling utterly ridiculous.

As we're waiting in the manager's office to be told how much we've got to pay, Karen turns to me.

'I'm so sorry, Lily, I couldn't tell *anyone*,' she says desperately, trying to brush the salad cream off her cuff. 'I've been working on the scam story for months, ever since we were approached by someone who worked in the golf-club accounts department and we realised there was something strange going on. As soon as I found out it was something to do with fixing school selection at The Oaks, I knew I couldn't let you in on it. Secrecy was of the essence if we were to get everyone talking, plus I didn't want to implicate any of you. I really didn't want you to join the golf club. When Jamie got us our membership it helped me get the inside story and infiltrate the accounts department,' she says, finding an olive lodged in her coat pocket. 'I befriended Masterton, who finally offered me the chance to enter the scam. He seemed to like me, so we went out a couple of times and I tried to get as much info as possible. I wanted to cover the fashion show, but I wouldn't have used it for the scam story if it hadn't been the only time I could get Masterton, Totham and Diet all together, and having Heavie there was an added bonus. Allyson Dyer gave me the inside track, as one of the parents who paid the money but didn't get a place last year.' She looks at me urgently. 'I promise, I was going to run their story in a week's time so as not to hog the fashion show's coverage, Lily, and I was almost fired this morning because I let rip at my editor. He just went to press immediately without even consulting me. Corruption on such a grand scale has the potential to make the nationals. Pounds for places, local celebrity outted as a fake, sex, corruption, infidelity – it has everything and he wanted to go with it. I'm so sorry, Lily, it was dreadful for me, having to hang back and not be involved, but I was so busy and I just couldn't quite be in with it all, potentially blowing my cover. And I couldn't tell *you*, because I knew you'd have been so angry and certainly blown my cover. I know how much The Oaks meant to you, but you'd never have got a place for Tim and nor would Paul or Julie, even if you'd got the Queen to walk down the catwalk. It was a complete fix. It wasn't even just a case of playing golf or paying the money, it was a huge nasty network of who knows who and if your face fits, that's great. The whole community-spirit thing is bullshit, utter bullshit; they didn't give a damn. The only thing they were interested in is money and keeping their friends in high places. Some people slipped past their net and got in their kids – ironically I was one of them – but I figure Totham had to keep a slight random element up in order not to be too obvious about it. But it wasn't really the tutoring, the entrance exams, moving house, moving in with your mother, moving away, pretending to someone you're not, taking up golf or having a child like Tim who is genuinely worthy of a place at The Oaks that was going to make a difference. We play fair and the system isn't and wasn't fair.' She sighs, looking down at her hands, which are still covered in herb marinade. 'The whole thing has left me completely jaded and cynical. God knows what goes on in other areas, but I wanted to do something about Letchbury, and I needed to do it, not just for Claire's sake, but for everyone's, Lily. For everyone's.'

As we're waiting outside the manager's office, a beaming face I know but can't put a name to suddenly pops out and says 'Lily Dearl.'

'Er, hello,' I say, confused and not wanting to offer him my marinated hands.

'My name is Gary Hawes, I think you know my wife?' he says, looking us up and down.

'Er, yes, I do, Christine,' I say, feeling sheepish. What on earth must he be thinking.

'I really enjoyed the fashion show yesterday, it really was quite splendid and I know Christine loved it. It's made a completely new woman out of her,' he says, offering his hand to shake.

'I'm so sorry about the food fight,' I say, trying to explain.

'Yes,' he says, suddenly looking stern, although there's a twinkle in his eye.

We both shake our heads feeling as though we're in the headmaster's office being told off.

'Right,' I say quickly, glancing at Karen. 'What do we

owe you? I think we've wasted quite a bit of salad,' I say. Talk about overspending at Waitrose.

'Oh, don't worry about that, Lily, don't worry. We'll put it down as spillage. Happens all the time. Admittedly not on as grand a scale as this,' he says, eyeing our coats, 'but that's OK. Try to stick to dry goods next time: it'll save on the dry-cleaning,' and he smiles.

'Great event, Lily. You should do another one next year and ask us to help with catering. Please do ask, we'd be delighted to provide anything,' he says, waving us goodbye.

Karen and I leave Waitrose, our heads held high, passing the salad stand, which has been efficiently cleared by a few attendants before any other shoppers go flying.

My mobile buzzes; a text from Mike. *Hi hun, can you go to see Ms Treadwell immediately. She wants to speak to you urgently.* I feel suddenly sick again. She's obviously read the paper and I'm being told off for bringing Somerset into disrepute. Jenny and Henry may be asked to leave the school. My mobile suddenly rings. Mrs Grant's grating voice blares out loud enough for Karen to hear. 'Mrs Dearl? Just wondering if you could make an appointment in half an hour? Great, see you then.' She clicks off and Karen and I look at each other, wondering what the hell is going on.

'I'll come with you, Lily. Maybe I can help explain?' Karen says. 'I'm so sorry I haven't been there for you these past months,' she goes on, looking suspiciously dewy-eyed.

'You had good reason, and it was a very brave thing you did. I was worried I'd lost a friend, and even worse, I worried I'd lost the plot and put that worry over and above my friendships. Wherever Tim goes, or any of our kids go, for that matter, they'll be OK.'

The playground, usually teeming with children and parents, is empty when we arrive. I can't even hear anything coming from the classrooms.

I'm aware that we still stink of oily marinade and it adds to the slightly surreal feeling. As we walk towards reception, I resist the urge to hold hands with my friend, feeling a bit sick again, just as I did when we got Tim's rejection letter. We open the large double doors to the reception, on any morning buzzing with pupils and teachers, now a bit like a ghost school. We walk down the corridor toward Ms Grant's office to find her sitting at her desk.

'Hello,' I say, trying not to sound pathetic, although I feel my voice breaking a little under the pressure. My stomach is going nuts, too, churning the slice of toast I barely managed to digest and the copious amounts of coffee I couldn't get enough of this morning.

She looks up at both of us and smiles, which scares me a little as I've never seen her smile. This must be really bad.

'Ah, you're here. Come with me, ladies,' she says, getting up as we walk in. I expect to be led into Ms Treadwell's office, but she creeps past us, beckoning us to follow. What the hell – are we going to be ridiculed in front of everyone in assembly this morning?

Ms Grant is walking quite quickly and we have to hurry to keep pace. Karen and I look at each other anxiously but I don't think it's the time to make conversation.

Ms Grant opens the doors to the assembly hall. It's packed, not just with children and teachers, but everyone; all the mums I recognise from Tim's year. I can see Christine and Ella, Daniella and Sally, still stunning; there's Suzanne, Jane, Tina, Tanya, Linda and all the other members of the PTA, and in the middle of them all Ms Treadwell, looking quite straight-faced. Faces turn when we come in, then everyone gets up. Christ, this is going to be the Spanish Inquisition.

Then suddenly, and most wonderfully, they start to clap, slowly at first, then louder, until people are smiling and cheering all around the room. I spot Tim with Claire and Dominic, and Jenny sitting slightly further away. And, good God, there's Mike. What's he doing here? I dropped him off at the station. And there's Ms Gold with Henry and the rest of the nursery class. And there's Jamie, grinning at Karen, with Simon by his side. I can see Julie and Paul as well with Mia, Cara and Alexander.

After what seems like an endless round of cheering and applause, Ms Treadwell gets everyone to quieten down and the noise gradually fades.

'Our guests of honour have now arrived.' She beckons us forward, through the crowds of seated children who are now parting like a great sea, and onto the stage.

'Lily Dearl, thank you and your team for organising

such a brilliant event. We've got everything and more for the library, and the fashion show was a great success, so much so that we – and I'm talking on behalf of parents, teachers and children – would like to turn it into a regular event. Rumour has even spread to other schools and I've had a call wanting to know who the inspiration behind the idea was and could they possibly borrow them. But the members of the PTA tell me you're irreplaceable, so unless you are able to set up some sort of fashion-show franchise you will just have to stay with us in Letchbury. For all your hard work and initiative and determination to make this a success, thank you!'

There is a round of applause, Jenny whooping the loudest as usual. The teachers shush the assembly again as Ms Treadwell continues.

'Thanks to the effort of Karen Field and her investigation, the headmaster of The Oaks is no longer the head, so Mr Elliott, his deputy, will be running the school. The application procedures will come direct from The Oaks itself, but I have great faith in Mr Elliott. I think the selection process will be fair this time. There were a lot of pupils who didn't make the grade this time round, so thank you, Karen, not only from us at Somerset, but from every child in the area, for exposing a deceit that affects us all.'

There is another round of applause and Jamie comes up to hug his wife, stopping short when he notices her messy appearance, then grinning broadly, holding his nose.

'As for the Somerset School library, Mr Terence Hershaw, a local entrepreneur, has kindly donated a replacement for the five thousand promised by the golf club. And it seems *De Rigueur* magazine will be covering the event in full, giving it eight pages which I am reliably informed is a lot of "ad spend".' She turns to Mike and Paul, who nod and smile back at her.

With that, everyone claps again and Karen and I just stand on the stage, in all our smelly glory, and savour the moment.

Epilogue
Four Weeks Later . . .

One Saturday afternoon, about a month after the fashion show, I get a call from Julie.

'Tony is moving in with me, Lily.'

'Wow! That's sudden,' I say delightedly. Who would have thought my matchmaking would have been so successful?

'I feel it's right. Life is too short to wait. We're having a party next Saturday if you can make it,' she says, sounding excited.

'I'd love to, Julie, but Mike's taking me away for the weekend. Mum is treating the kids to EuroDisney, and we're going with Paul, Jessica and the girls. They've booked a suite at the Disney Hotel.'

'Aha, so things are going well?' she says, obviously fishing.

'Yes. We went to *The Rocky Horror Picture Show* last week, both of us dressed to kill, and let's just say it brought back a few memories and created a few new ones. And we're heading to Cornwall soon to bring back some more,' I say, smiling at Mike, who's just come downstairs. 'Anyway, must go. Great news, Julie. Speak soon.'

That evening, we've just sat down for supper when I hear a familiar voice on the television. I walk into the sitting room. Henrietta doesn't look as confident as she did the last time I saw her on TV, or as well-groomed as in any of the newspaper articles she's appeared in since the school-selection scandal was released.

She has been cleared of any involvement with the scam, but her affair with Masterton has vilified her as a marriage wrecker and, let's face it, a hypocrite. Masterton's wife is divorcing him, citing adultery. 'I have no comment,' Henrietta now keeps repeating to the reporter doorstepping her home in Letchbury, burying her head behind a copy of the *Telegraph*.

'She doesn't seem to want the publicity now,' Mike grins behind me.

'Now there is a lady who would *definitely* like to be invisible,' I agree. 'I'm sure she'll write another book and want to promote it at some point, then we'll hear from her again. Perhaps about nurturing family values,' I add spitefully.

According to Karen, who is still working on the school-selection story, the scam has been going on for years and a lot of famous parents have put money into the special golf fund to get their kids into The Oaks. And it's not just The Oaks – other schools are involved as well. Local celebrities Dennis Resnaur, Fisher Bolden and Tyler Villier have been implicated and are currently being questioned. There's even been discussion about it in the Houses of Parliament, and Karen suggests there may be some politicians who've been implicated as well. That sounds a bit far-fetched to me, but who knows. Sometimes it's the smallest domestic crises that spiral out of control.

Letchbury hasn't changed much since the scandal. The national media buzzed about for a few weeks after the *Daily News* got hold of the scam and hooked onto Henrietta as a marriage wrecker – nothing sells better than a good sex scandal.

Jamie tells me membership at the golf club has dropped dramatically and Karen claims Wallace T. Heavie is unlikely to survive the next local election, his reputation tarnished by the association with Totham and Masterton and their regular games of golf. And the last thing I heard about titchy bitch Allyson Dyer was that she was working as a publishing assistant for Randy Hasbro, whom she met at the fashion show. Tony tells me he's come across the guy a few times and he's a slimy sleaze bag.

I've agreed to write a regular monthly column for

Angela called 'Suburban Sluts', having pinched the idea from my meeting with the designers O. I didn't like their attitude, but their concept was so outrageous I thought it would appeal to Angela's wicked sense of humour, and it has. She had a few problems getting 'slut' past the publisher but she managed in the end. I'm writing under a pseudonym, Poppy Go Lightly – a name thought up by Henry. I manage to squeeze writing the column in between the school runs, club runs and photography classes, which I'm still enjoying immensely, having taken the basic three-month course and started on a slightly more advanced one. I have made firm friends of Tamara and her husband Terence.

From this day, I am officially the annual fashion-show coordinator for Somerset School. I don't belong to the PTA and I still try to keep out of the numerous other events they organise during the year, but we're on good terms. I've even managed to get a smile out of Linda Black in the playground, so perhaps global warming has even had an impact on the ice queen. Of course, Jane Anderson is convinced that Linda wants to be on the catwalk herself next year and that's why she's bending over backwards to be civil.

All the designers were delighted with the commissions and coverage they got from the exposure at the fashion show. I try to keep in touch with them, but they're fairly busy themselves now. Fifi children's range has broken out in a big way and is selling in department stores around the country, and Tatiana is selling a label launched by Pooky and Smokey called PS – for stylish women who just happen to be mothers. I know that's the strap line because Mike was the one who thought of it.

Angela wants me to write more features, but I don't have time, what with the column, my photography, the fashion-show and my friends. I've even been asked to appear on the breakfast show where I first saw Henrietta Diet all those months ago, talking about how I came up with the fashion show idea. They wanted me to try out for a regular slot, but I sent Karen instead, as she enjoys the limelight more than me and gave the presenter some really good sound bites. It wouldn't surprise me if I see Karen move into TV presenting one day soon.

I still go to kick-boxing with Karen when I can, and Tamara now comes along too, as does Leon when his mum lets him. Daisy is still kicking ass and making everyone crawl out of the studio cursing her, although I don't have as much frustration and aggression to burn off these days – any passion I do have goes into my writing, my photography, my children and my man. Mike and I have organised a weekend break in Prague in a few months' time and last week we took a break to Tuscany and stayed at the hotel L'Andana, a former residence of the Duke of Tuscany. Surrounded by clear blue skies, olive groves and vineyards, we cycled to the beach. Siena was only an hour's drive away, where we held hands, walked quietly round the Duomo, and sat at a café, eating traditional bean soup in the Piazza del

Campo, just happy to *be*. We watched sunsets, made love and drank lots of the wonderful Italian coffee with tiny *biscotti*.

I know the kids will have fun while Mike and I are away on our occasional weekends – they always come back from my mum's with wonderful stories of ghosts, ogres and dragons. Although I must talk to her about the head-eating demons because Henry has started having nightmares. I've even managed a full lunch with Mum, just the two of us, and we went to a photography exhibition in Hoxton at the White Cube; Gilbert recommended it and we talked about Dad and tennis, her travels and my dreams. She'll be a great source of material for my columns in *De Rigueur*.

I told Paul about seeing *The Rocky Horror Picture Show* with Mike and he took Jessica the following week – and I think their sex life has got a new lease of life. Paul certainly walks with a spring in his step now when I see him on the school run, while Jessica has a sparkle she didn't have before. Paul's also started to work with Tony on marketing his restaurant, which he enjoys.

As for the children, Henry remains edible and still wants to be a Power Ranger, although it's now the green one, and Jenny continues to challenge Mike, myself and her brothers on absolutely everything. She's become much more feminine since the fashion show, though, especially since Angela has introduced a junior fashion page to the magazine, and has asked Jenny to model for her, which I've allowed as long as it doesn't interfere with her school work.

And Tim, I know, will change quickly when he goes to big school. The letter hasn't arrived yet, but whatever happens, I know he will be fine. He's starting to be more moody these days and I can sense the hormones waiting to bubble.

But at least this time the selection at The Oaks will be fair. We've been contacted by the school, and we've been to see Mr Elliott, Totham's deputy, who seems wonderful and much warmer than Dr Totham. Mike liked him instantly and noted his favourite game, tennis, and we've been assured that there's no special fund at the tennis club. Tim has to take a test again, as the other papers mysteriously disappeared, but we have every hope for him, and if he doesn't get in – well, it's not the end of the world, I guess.

ALSO AVAILABLE IN ARROW

The Playground Mafia

Sarah Tucker

Meet Caroline Gray: divorcee and newly-single mother. Firmly closing the door on her acrimonious divorce, Caroline and son Ben have moved to the trendy town of Frencham where they join Caroline's long-time best friends, Heather and Eva. Settling into their new life is easy, but nothing has prepared Caroline for the demands of motherhood at The Sycamore, the school the trio's beloved offspring attend. Forget class-room bullies, forget trips to the head's office, this is full-scale adult playground politics. This is battle with the mothers who won't take no for an answer – the Playground Mafia.

Amidst the four-wheel drives, Ben's complicated afterschool play-date schedule and her friends' perilous extra-marital affairs, Caroline tries to keep a low and very single profile. But it's not long before she too finds herself under the mafia's scandal-radar, and her life takes an unexpected turn . . .

arrow books

ALSO AVAILABLE IN ARROW

The Accidental Mother

Rowan Coleman

Sophie Mills has worked her Manolo Blahniks off to reach the near-top of her profession. And she's very happy with her priorities in life – her job, her neurotic cat Artemis and her passion for shoes. After all, relationships only get in the way. And as for children? She hasn't even begun to think about them yet. Until one day an unexpected visitor brings news of a strange inheritance and Sophie is suddenly, out of the blue, in sole charge of two children under the age of six. But motherhood can't be all that hard, can it?

Within twenty-four hours, her make-up is smeared all over the bathroom, Artemis has taken up residence on top of her wardrobe, and Sophie is in despair. And all her unconventional mother can suggest is Dr Roberts' *Complete Dog Training and Care Manual*.

Determined to rise to the challenge, Sophie soon realises that she'll need more than a business plan to cope with all this . . .

Praise for Rowan Coleman

'A witty, wonderful, warm-hearted read' *Company*

'Touching and thought-provoking' *B*

arrow books

Diary of a Hapless Househusband

Sam Holden

When father-of-two Sam loses his job, he reluctantly agrees to stay at home while his wife returns to work. Secretly thinking this whole parenthood thing a breeze of leisurely jaunts to the park, reading the paper while the children play quietly and occasionally attending a civilised play date or two, Sam quickly realises just what exactly it means to be a stay-at-home parent.

Inevitably, domestic mayhem ensues. Just trying to get dressed in the morning and out of the house without going to A&E is a feat, as is managing the children's complicated play-date schedule while fending off the unwelcome advances of Jodhpur Mum at the playground. And Sam's foolproof 72-step Childcare Programme doesn't seem remotely up to the task.

Desperate to get his life back on track, Sam seizes upon a variety of mad schemes, but just as things look like they're beginning to fall into place, he makes a very surprising discovery . . .

'A very, very funny and often touching account of one man's struggle to try and run Planet Home.' Allison Pearson

arrow books